THE SHADOWS
AND OTHER TALES

* * *

Collected Tales of George MacDonald, Vol. II

Other books by GEORGE MACDONALD
available from CLUNY MEDIA

THE PRINCESS AND THE CURDIE

THE PRINCESS AND THE GOBLIN

LILITH: A ROMANCE

PHANTASTES: A FAERIE ROMANCE

THE COLLECTED TALES OF GEORGE MACDONALD
    VOLUME I: THE LOST PRINCESS AND OTHER TALES
    VOLUME II: THE SHADOWS AND OTHER TALES
    VOLUME III: THE GIFTS OF THE CHILD CHRIST AND OTHER TALES

THE SHADOWS
AND OTHER TALES

GEORGE MACDONALD

* * *

Collected Tales of George MacDonald, Vol. II

CLUNY
Providence, Rhode Island

CLUNY MEDIA EDITION, 2021

For information regarding this title
or any other Cluny Media publication,
please write to info@clunymedia.com, or to
Cluny Media, P.O. Box 1664, Providence, RI 02901

✳ VISIT US ONLINE AT WWW.CLUNYMEDIA.COM ✳

The stories in this collection first appeared in the following:
"The Shadows": reprinted from *Adela Cathcart* (1864).
"The Giant's Heart": reprinted from *Illustrated London News*, Christmas Number (1863) entitled "Tell Us a Story."
"The Cruel Painter": reprinted from *Adela Cathcart* (1864).
"Cross Purposes": reprinted from *Dealings with Fairies* (1867).
"The Golden Key": reprinted from *Dealings with Fairies* (1867).
"The Gray Wolf": reprinted from *Works of Fancy and Imagination* (1871).
The Carasoyn: first part appeared as "The Fairy Fleet" in *Argosy* (1866); the expanded form "The Carasoyn" appeared in *Works* (1871).
"Little Daylight": reprinted from *Works of Fancy and Imagination* (1871).

Cluny Media edition copyright © 2021 Cluny Media LLC

All rights reserved.

ISBN: 978-1685950040

Cover design by Clarke & Clarke
Cover image: Edward Burne-Jones, detail from *The Last Sleep
of Arthur in Avalon*, c. 1881–1898, painting
Courtesy of Wikimedia Commons

CONTENTS

Collected Tales of George MacDonald, Vol. II

* * *

THE SHADOWS	1
THE GIANT'S HEART	37
THE CRUEL PAINTER	61
CROSS PURPOSES	101
THE GOLDEN KEY	123
THE GRAY WOLF	155
THE CARASOYN	163
LITTLE DAYLIGHT	209

THE SHADOWS

* * *

Old Ralph Rinkelmann made his living by comic sketches, and all but lost it again by tragic poems. So he was just the man to be chosen king of the fairies, for in Fairyland the sovereignty is elective.

It is no doubt very strange that fairies should desire to have a mortal king; but the fact is, that with all their knowledge and power, they cannot get rid of the feeling that some men are greater than they are, though they can neither fly nor play tricks. So at such times as there happen to be twice the usual number of sensible electors, such a man as Ralph Rinkelmann gets to be chosen.

They did not mean to insist on his residence; for they needed his presence only on special occasions. But they must get hold of him somehow, first of all, in order to make him king. Once he was crowned, they could get him as often as they pleased; but before this ceremony, there was a difficulty. For it is only between life and death that the fairies have power over grown-up mortals, and can carry them off to their country. So they had to watch for an opportunity.

Nor had they to wait long. For old Ralph was taken dreadfully ill; and while hovering between life and death, they carried him off, and crowned him king of Fairyland. But after he was crowned, it was no wonder, considering the state of his health, that he should not be able to sit quite upright on the throne of Fairyland; or that, in

consequence, all the gnomes and goblins, and ugly, cruel things that
live in the holes and corners of the kingdom, should take advantage
of his condition, and run quite wild, playing him, king as he was, all
sorts of tricks; crowding about his throne, climbing up the steps,
and actually scrambling and quarrelling like mice about his ears and
eyes, so that he could see and think of nothing else. But I am not
going to tell anything more about this part of his adventures just at
present. By strong and sustained efforts, he succeeded, after much
trouble and suffering, in reducing his rebellious subjects to order.
They all vanished to their respective holes and corners; and King
Ralph, coming to himself, found himself in his bed, half propped up
with pillows.

But the room was full of dark creatures, which gambolled about
in the firelight in such a strange, huge, though noiseless fashion, that
he thought at first that some of his rebellious goblins had not been
subdued with the rest, but had followed him beyond the bounds of
Fairyland into his own private house in London. How else could
these mad, grotesque hippopotamus-calves make their ugly appearance in Ralph Rinkelmann's bedroom? But he soon found out that
although they were like the underground goblins, they were very
different as well, and would require quite different treatment. He
felt convinced that they were his subjects too, but that he must
have overlooked them somehow at his late coronation—if indeed
they had been present; for he could not recollect that he had seen
anything just like them before. He resolved, therefore, to pay particular attention to their habits, ways, and characters; else he saw
plainly that they would soon be too much for him; as indeed this
intrusion into his chamber, where Mrs. Rinkelmann, who must be
queen if he was king, sat taking some tea by the fireside, evidently
foreshadowed. But she, perceiving that he was looking about him
with a more composed expression than his face had worn for many

days, started up, and came quickly and quietly to his side, and her face was bright with gladness. Whereupon the fire burned up more cheerily; and the figures became more composed and respectful in their behaviour, retreating towards the wall like well-trained attendants. Then the king of Fairyland had some tea and dry toast, and leaning back on his pillows, nearly fell asleep; but not quite, for he still watched the intruders.

Presently the queen left the room to give some of the young princes and princesses their tea; and the fire burned lower, and behold, the figures grew as black and as mad in their gambols as ever! Their favourite games seemed to be *Hide and Seek*; *Touch and Go*; *Grin and Vanish*—and many other such; and all in the king's bedchamber, too; so that it was quite alarming. It was almost as bad as if the house had been haunted by certain creatures which shall be nameless in a fairy story, because with them Fairyland will not willingly have much to do.

"But it is a mercy that they have their slippers on!" said the king to himself; for his head ached.

As he lay back, with his eyes half shut and half open, too tired to pay longer attention to their games, but, on the whole, considerably more amused than offended with the liberties they took, for they seemed good-natured creatures, and more frolicsome than positively ill-mannered, he became suddenly aware that two of them had stepped forward from the walls, upon which, after the manner of great spiders, most of them preferred sprawling, and now stood in the middle of the floor at the foot of his majesty's bed, becking and bowing and ducking in the most grotesquely obsequious manner; while every now and then they turned solemnly round upon one heel, evidently considering that motion the highest token of homage they could show.

"What do you want?" said the king.

"That it may please your majesty to be better acquainted with us," answered they. "We are your majesty's subjects."

"I know you are. I shall be most happy," answered the king.

"We are not what your majesty takes us for, though. We are not so foolish as your majesty thinks us."

"It is impossible to take you for anything that I know of," rejoined the king, who wished to make them talk, and said whatever came uppermost; "for soldiers, sailors, or anything: you will not stand still long enough. I suppose you really belong to the fire brigade; at least, you keep putting its light out."

"Don't jest, please your majesty." And as they said the words—for they both spoke at once throughout the interview—they performed a grave somerset towards the king.

"Not jest!" retorted he; "and with you? Why, you do nothing but jest. What are you?"

"The Shadows, sire. And when we do jest sire, we always jest in earnest. But perhaps your majesty does not see us distinctly."

"I see you perfectly well," returned the king.

"Permit me, however," rejoined one of the Shadows; and as he spoke he approached the king; and lifting a dark forefinger, he drew it lightly but carefully across the ridge of his forehead, from temple to temple. The king felt the soft gliding touch go, like water, into every hollow, and over the top of every height of that mountain-chain of thought. He had involuntarily closed his eyes during the operation, and when he unclosed them again, as soon as the finger was withdrawn, he found that they were opened in more senses than one. The room appeared to have extended itself on all sides, till he could not exactly see where the walls were; and all about it stood the Shadows motionless. They were tall and solemn; rather awful, indeed, in their appearance, notwithstanding many remarkable traits of grotesqueness, for they looked just like the pictures of

Puritans drawn by Cavaliers, with long arms, and very long, thin legs, from which hung large loose feet, while in their countenances length of chin and nose predominated. The solemnity of their mien, however, overcame all the oddity of their form, so that they were very eerie indeed to look at, dressed as they all were in funereal black. But a single glance was all that the king was allowed to have; for the former operator waved his dusky palm across his vision, and once more the king saw only the fire-lighted walls, and dark shapes flickering about upon them. The two who had spoken for the rest seemed likewise to have vanished. But at last the king discovered them, standing one on each side of the fireplace. They kept close to the chimney-wall, and talked to each other across the length of the chimneypiece; thus avoiding the direct rays of the fire, which, though light is necessary to their appearing to human eyes, do not agree with them at all—much less give birth to them, as the king was soon to learn. After a few minutes they again approached the bed, and spoke thus:

"It is now getting dark, please your majesty. We mean, out of doors in the snow. Your majesty may see, from where he is lying, the cold light of its great winding-sheet—a famous carpet for the Shadows to dance upon, your majesty. All our brothers and sisters will be at church now, before going to their night's work."

"Do they always go to church before they go to work?"

"They always go to church first."

"Where is the church?"

"In Iceland. Would your majesty like to see it?"

"How can I go and see it when, as you know very well, I am ill in bed? Besides, I should be sure to take cold in a frosty night like this, even if I put on the blankets, and took the feather-bed for a muff."

A sort of quivering passed over their faces, which seemed to be their mode of laughing. The whole shape of the face shook and fluctuated as if it had been some dark fluid; till, by slow degrees of gathering calm, it settled into its former rest. Then one of them drew aside the curtains of the bed, and the window-curtains not having been yet drawn, the king beheld the white glimmering night outside, struggling with the heaps of darkness that tried to quench it; and the heavens fall of stars, flashing and sparkling like live jewels. The other Shadow went towards the fire and vanished in it.

Scores of Shadows immediately began an insane dance all about the room; disappearing, one after the other, through the uncovered window, and gliding darkly away over the face of the white snow; for the window looked at once on a field of snow. In a few moments the room was quite cleared of them; but instead of being relieved by their absence, the king felt immediately as if he were in a deadhouse, and could hardly breathe for the sense of emptiness and desolation that fell upon him. But as he lay looking out on the snow, which stretched blank and wide before him, he spied in the distance a long dark line which drew nearer and nearer, and showed itself at last to be all the Shadows, walking in a double row, and carrying in the midst of them something like a bier. They vanished under the window, but soon reappeared, having somehow climbed up the wall of the house; for they entered in perfect order by the window, as if melting through the transparency of the glass.

They still carried the bier or litter. It was covered with richest furs, and skins of gorgeous wild beasts, whose eyes were replaced by sapphires and emeralds, that glittered and gleamed in the fire and snow light. The outermost skin sparkled with frost but the inside ones were soft and warm and dry as the down under a swan's wing. The Shadows approached the bed, and set the litter upon it. Then a number of them brought a huge fur robe, and wrapping it round the king, laid him on the litter in the midst of the furs. Nothing could be more gentle and respectful than the way in which they moved him; and he never thought of refusing to go. Then they put something on his head, and, lifting the litter, carried him once round the room, to fall into order. As he passed the mirror he saw that he was covered with royal ermine, and that his head wore a wonderful crown of gold, set with none but red stones: rubies and carbuncles and garnets, and others whose names he could not tell, glowed gloriously around his head, like the salamandrine essence of all the Christmas fires over the world. A sceptre lay beside him—a rod of ebony, surmounted by a cone-shaped diamond, which, cut in a hundred facets, flashed all the hues of the rainbow, and threw coloured gleams on every side, that looked like Shadows too, but more ethereal than those that bore him. Then the Shadows rose gently to the window, passed through it, and sinking slowly upon the field of outstretched snow, commenced an orderly gliding rather than march along the frozen surface. They took it by turns to bear the king, as they sped with the swiftness of thought, in a straight line towards the north. The pole-star rose above their heads with visible rapidity; for indeed they moved quite as fast as sad thoughts, though not with all the speed of happy desires. England and Scotland slid past the litter of the king of the Shadows. Over rivers and lakes they skimmed and glided. They climbed the high mountains, and crossed the valleys with a fearless bound; till they came to John-o'-Groat's house and the Northern Sea. The sea was not frozen; for all the stars shone as clear out of the deeps below as they shone out of the deeps above; and as the bearers slid along the blue-gray surface, with never a furrow in their track, so pure was the water beneath, that the king saw neither surface, bottom, nor substance to it, and seemed to be gliding only through the blue sphere of heaven, with the stars above him, and the stars below him, and between the stars and him nothing but an emptiness, where, for the first time in his life, his soul felt that it had room enough.

At length they reached the rocky shores of Iceland. There they landed, still pursuing their journey. All this time the king felt no cold; for the red stones in his crown kept him warm, and the emerald and sapphire eyes of the wild beasts kept the frosts from settling upon his litter.

Oftentimes upon their way they had to pass through forests, caverns, and rock-shadowed paths, where it was so dark that at first the king feared he should lose his Shadows altogether. But as soon as they entered such places, the diamond in his sceptre began to shine, and glow, and flash, sending out streams of light of all the colours that painter's soul could dream of; in which light the Shadows grew livelier and stronger than ever, speeding through the dark ways with an all but blinding swiftness. In the light of the diamond, too, some of their forms became more simple and human, while others seemed only to break out into a yet more untamable absurdity. Once, as they passed through a cave, the king actually saw some of their eyes—strange shadow-eyes: he had never seen any of their eyes before. But at the same moment when he saw their eyes, he knew their faces too, for they turned them full upon him for an instant; and the other Shadows, catching sight of these, shrank and shivered, and nearly vanished. Lovely faces they were; but the king was very thoughtful after he saw them, and continued rather troubled all the rest of the journey. He could not account for those faces being there, and the faces of Shadows, too, with living eyes.

But he soon found that amongst the Shadows a man must learn never to be surprised at anything; for if he does not, he will soon grow quite stupid, in consequence of the endless recurrence of surprises.

At last they climbed up the bed of a little stream, and then, passing through a narrow rocky defile, came out suddenly upon the side of a mountain, overlooking a blue frozen lake in the very heart of mighty hills. Overhead, the *aurora borealis* was shivering and flashing like a battle of ten thousand spears. Underneath, its beams passed faintly over the blue ice and the sides of the snow-clad mountains, whose tops shot up like huge icicles all about, with here and there a star sparkling on the very tip of one. But as the northern lights in the sky above, so wavered and quivered, and shot hither and thither, the Shadows on the surface of the lake below; now gathering in groups, and now shivering asunder; now covering the whole surface of the lake, and anon condensed into one dark knot in the centre. Every here and there on the white mountains might be seen two or three shooting away towards the tops, to vanish beyond them, so that the number was gradually, though not visibly, diminishing.

"Please your majesty," said the Shadows, "this is our church—the Church of the Shadows."

And so saying, the king's bodyguard set down the litter upon a rock, and plunged into the multitudes below. They soon returned, however, and bore the king down into the middle of the lake. All the Shadows came crowding round him, respectfully but fearlessly; and sure never such a grotesque assembly revealed itself before to mortal eyes. The king had seen all kinds of gnomes, goblins, and kobolds at his coronation; but they were quite rectilinear figures compared with the insane lawlessness of form in which the Shadows rejoiced; and the wildest gambols of the former were orderly dances of ceremony beside the apparently aimless and wilful contortions of figure, and metamorphoses of shape, in which the latter indulged. They retained, however, all the time, to the surprise of the king, an identity, each of his own type, inexplicably perceptible through every change. Indeed, this preservation of the primary idea of each form was more wonderful than the bewildering and ridiculous alterations to which the form itself was every moment subjected.

"What are you?" said the king, leaning on his elbow, and looking around him.

"The Shadows, your majesty," answered several voices at once.

"What Shadows?"

"The human Shadows. The Shadows of men, and women, and their children."

"Are you not the shadows of chairs and tables, and pokers and tongs, just as well?"

At this question a strange jarring commotion went through the assembly with a shock. Several of the figures shot up as high as the aurora, but instantly settled down again to human size, as if over-mastering their feelings, out of respect to him who had roused them. One who had bounded to the highest visible icy peak, and as suddenly returned, now elbowed his way through the rest, and made himself spokesman for them during the remaining part of the dialogue.

"Excuse our agitation, your majesty," said he. "I see your majesty has not yet thought proper to make himself acquainted with our nature and habits."

"I wish to do so now," replied the king.

"We are the Shadows," repeated the Shadow, solemnly.

"Well?" said the king.

"We do not often appear to men."

"Ha!" said the king.

"We do not belong to the sunshine at all. We go through it unseen, and only by a passing chill do men recognize an unknown presence."

"Ha!" said the king again.

"It is only in the twilight of the fire, or when one man or woman is alone with a single candle, or when any number of people are all feeling the same thing at once, making them one, that we show ourselves, and the truth of things."

"Can that be true that loves the night?" said the king.

"The darkness is the nurse of light," answered the Shadow.

"Can that be true which mocks at forms?" said the king.

"Truth rides abroad in shapeless storms," answered the Shadow.

"Ha, ha!" thought Ralph Rinkelmann. "It rhymes. The Shadow caps my questions with his answers. Very strange!" And he grew thoughtful again.

The Shadow was the first to resume.

"Please your majesty, may we present our petition?"

"By all means," replied the king. "I am not well enough to receive it in proper state."

"Never mind, your majesty. We do not care for much ceremony; and indeed none of us are quite well at present. The subject of our petition weighs upon us."

"Go on," said the king.

"Sire," began the Shadow, "our very existence is in danger. The various sorts of artificial light, both in houses and in men, women, and children, threaten to end our being. The use and the disposition of gas-lights, especially high in the centres, blind the eyes by which alone we can be perceived. We are all but banished from towns. We are driven into villages and lonely houses, chiefly old farm-houses, out of which, even, our friends the fairies are fast disappearing. We therefore petition our king, by the power of his art, to restore us to our rights in the house itself, and in the hearts of its inhabitants."

"But," said the king, "you frighten the children."

"Very seldom, your majesty; and then only for their good. We seldom seek to frighten anybody. We mostly want to make people silent and thoughtful; to awe them a little, your majesty."

"You are much more likely to make them laugh," said the king.

"Are we?" said the Shadow.

And approaching the king one step, he stood quite still for a moment. The diamond of the king's sceptre shot out a vivid flame of violet light and the king stared at the Shadow in silence, and his lip quivered. He never told what he saw then; but he would say:

"Just fancy what it might be if *some* flitting thoughts were to persist in staying to be looked at."

"It is only," resumed the Shadow, "when our thoughts are not fixed upon any particular object that our bodies are subject to all the vagaries of elemental influences. Generally, amongst worldly men and frivolous women, we only attach ourselves to some article of furniture or of dress; and they never doubt that we are mere foolish and vague results of the dashing of the waves of the light against the solid forms of which their houses are full. We do not care to tell them the truth, for they would never see it. But let the worldly man—or the frivolous woman—and then—"

At each of the pauses indicated, the mass of Shadows throbbed and heaved with emotion; but they soon settled again into comparative stillness. Once more the Shadow addressed himself to speak. But suddenly they all looked up, and the king, following their gaze, saw that the aurora had begun to pale.

"The moon is rising," said the Shadow. "As soon as she looks over the mountains into the valley, we must be gone, for we have plenty to do by the moon: we are powerful in her light. But if your majesty will come here tomorrow night, your majesty may learn a great deal more about us, and judge for himself whether it be fit to accord our petition; for then will be our grand annual assembly, in which we report to our chiefs the things we have attempted, and the good or bad success we have had."

"If you send for me," returned the king, "I will come."

Ere the Shadow could reply, the tip of the moon's crescent horn peeped up from behind an icy pinnacle, and one slender ray fell on the lake. It shone upon no Shadows. Ere the eye of the king could again seek the earth after beholding the first brightness of the moon's resurrection, they had vanished; and the surface of the lake glittered cold and blue in the pale moonlight

There the king lay, alone in the midst of the frozen lake, with the moon staring at him. But at length he heard from somewhere a voice that he knew.

"Will you take another cup of tea, dear?" said Mrs. Rinkelmann.

And Ralph, coming slowly to himself, found that he was lying in his own bed.

"Yes, I will," he answered; "and rather a large piece of toast, if you please; for I have been a long journey since I saw you last."

"He has not come to himself quite," said Mrs. Rinkelmann, between her and herself.

"You would be rather surprised," continued Ralph, "if I told you where I have been."

"I dare say I should," responded his wife.

"Then I will tell you," rejoined Ralph.

But at that moment a great Shadow bounced out of the fire with a single huge leap, and covered the whole room. Then it settled in one corner, and Ralph saw it shaking its fist at him from the end of a preposterous arm. So he took the hint, and held his peace. And it was as well for him. For I happen to know something about the Shadows too; and I know that if he had told his wife all about it just then, they would not have sent for him the following evening.

But as the king, after finishing his tea and toast, lay and looked about him, the shadows dancing in his room seemed to him odder and more inexplicable than ever. The whole chamber was full of mystery. So it generally was, but now it was more mysterious than ever. After all that he had seen in the Shadow-church, his own room and its shadows were yet more wonderful and unintelligible than those.

This made it the more likely that he had seen a true vision; for instead of making common things look commonplace, as a false vision would have done, it had made common things disclose the wonderful that was in them.

"The same applies to all art as well," thought Ralph Rinkelmann.

The next afternoon, as the twilight was growing dusky, the king lay wondering whether or not the Shadows would fetch him again. He wanted very much to go, for he had enjoyed the journey exceedingly, and he longed, besides, to hear some of the Shadows tell their stories. But the darkness grew deeper and deeper, and the Shadows did not come. The cause was that Mrs. Rinkelmann sat by the fire in the gloaming; and they could not carry off the king while she was there. Some of them tried to frighten her away by playing the oddest pranks on the walls, the floor, and ceiling; but altogether without effect: the queen only smiled, for she had a good conscience. Suddenly, however, a dreadful scream was heard from the nursery, and Mrs. Rinkelmann rushed upstairs to see what was the matter. No sooner had she gone than the two warders of the chimney-corners stepped out into the middle of the room, and said, in a low voice, "Is your majesty ready?"

"Have you no hearts?" said the king; "Or are they as black as your faces? Did you not hear the child scream? I must know what is the matter with her before I go."

"Your majesty may keep his mind easy on that point," replied the warders. "We had tried everything we could think of to get rid of her majesty the queen, but without effect. So a young madcap Shadow, half against the will of the older ones of us, slipped upstairs into the nursery; and has no doubt succeeded in appalling the baby, for he is very lithe and long-legged. Now, your majesty."

"I will have no such tricks played in my nursery," said the king, rather angrily. "You might put the child beside itself."

"Then there would be twins, your majesty. And we rather like twins."

"None of your miserable jesting! You might put the child out of her wits."

"Impossible, sire; for she has not got into them yet."

"Go away," said the king.

"Forgive us, your majesty. Really, it will do the child good; for that Shadow will, all her life, be to her a symbol of what is ugly and bad. When she feels in danger of hating or envying anyone, that Shadow will come back to her mind and make her shudder."

"Very well," said the king. "I like that. Let us go."

The Shadows went through the same ceremonies and preparations as before; during which, the young Shadow before-mentioned contrived to make such grimaces as kept the baby in terror, and the queen in the nursery, till all was ready. Then with a bound that doubled him up against the ceiling, and a kick of his legs six feet out behind him, he vanished through the nursery door, and reached the king's bed-chamber just in time to take his place with the last who were melting through the window in the rear of the litter, and settling down upon the snow beneath. Away they went as before, a gliding blackness over the white carpet. And it was Christmas Eve.

When they came in sight of the mountain-lake, the king saw that it was crowded over its whole surface with a changeful intermingling of Shadows. They were all talking and listening alternately, in pairs, trios, and groups of every size. Here and there, large companies were absorbed in attention to one elevated above the rest not in a pulpit or on a platform, but on the stilts of his own legs, elongated for the nonce. The aurora, right overhead, lighted up the lake and the sides of the mountains, by sending down from the zenith, nearly to the surface of the lake, great folded vapours, luminous with all the colours of a faint rainbow.

Many, however, as the words were that passed on all sides, not a shadow of a sound reached the ears of the king: the shadow-speech could not enter his corporeal organs. One of his guides, however, seeing that the king wanted to hear and could not, went through a strange manipulation of his head and ears; after which he could hear perfectly, though still only the voice to which, for the time, he directed his attention. This, however, was a great advantage, and one which the king longed to carry back with him to the world of men.

The king now discovered that this was not merely the church of the Shadows, but their news-exchange at the same time. For, as the Shadows have no writing or printing, the only way in which they can make each other acquainted with their doings and thinkings, is to meet and talk at this word-mart and parliament of shades. And as, in the world, people read their favourite authors, and listen to their favourite speakers, so here the Shadows seek their favourite Shadows, listen to their adventures, and hear generally what they have to say.

Feeling quite strong, the king rose and walked about amongst them, wrapped in his ermine robe, with his red crown on his head, and his diamond sceptre in his hand. Every group of Shadows to which he drew near, ceased talking as soon as they saw him approach: but at a nod they went on again directly, conversing and relating and commenting, as if no one was there of other kind or of higher rank than themselves. So the king heard a good many stories. At some of them he laughed, and at some of them he cried. But if the stories that the Shadows told were printed, they would make a book that no publisher could produce fast enough to satisfy the buyers. I will record some of the things that the king heard, for he told them to me soon after. In fact, I was for some time his private secretary.

"I made him confess before a week was over," said a gloomy old Shadow.

"But what was the good of that?" rejoined a pert young one. "That could not undo what was done."

"Yes, it could."

"What! Bring the dead to life?"

"No; but comfort the murderer. I could not bear to see the pitiable misery he was in. He was far happier with the rope round his neck, than he was with the purse in his pocket. I saved him from killing himself too."

"How did you make him confess?"

"Only by wallowing on the wall a little."

"How could that make him tell?"

"He knows."

The Shadow was silent; and the king turned to another, who was preparing to speak.

"I made a fashionable mother repent."

"How?" broke from several voices, in whose sound was mingled a touch of incredulity.

"Only by making a little coffin on the wall," was the reply.

"Did the fashionable mother confess too?"

"She had nothing more to confess than everybody knew."

"What did everybody know then?"

"That she might have been kissing a living child, when she followed a dead one to the grave. The next will fare better."

"I put a stop to a wedding," said another.

"Horrid shade!" remarked a poetic imp.

"How?" said others. "Tell us how."

"Only by throwing a darkness, as if from the branch of a sconce, over the forehead of a fair girl. They are not married yet, and I do not think they will be. But I loved the youth who loved her. How he started! It was a revelation to him."

"But did it not deceive him?"

"Quite the contrary."

"But it was only a shadow from the outside, not a shadow coming through from the soul of the girl."

"Yes, you may say so. But it was all that was wanted to make the meaning of her forehead manifest—yes, of her whole face, which had now and then, in the pauses of his passion, perplexed the youth. All of it, curled nostrils, pouting lips, projecting chin, instantly fell into harmony with that darkness between her eyebrows. The youth understood it in a moment, and went home miserable. And they're not married yet."

"I caught a toper alone, over his magnum of port," said a very dark Shadow; "and didn't I give it him! I made *delirium tremens* first; and then I settled into a funeral, passing slowly along the length of the opposite wall. I gave him plenty of plumes and mourning coaches. And then I gave him a funeral service, but I could not manage to make the surplice white, which was all the better for such a sinner. The wretch stared till his face passed from purple to grey, and actually left his fifth glass only, unfinished, and took refuge with his wife and children in the drawing-room, much to their surprise. I believe he actually drank a cup of tea; and although I have often looked in since, I have never caught him again, drinking alone at least."

"But does he drink less? Have you done him any good?"

"I hope so; but I am sorry to say I can't feel sure about it."

"Humph! Humph! Humph!" grunted various shadow throats.

"I had such fun once!" cried another. "I made such game of a young clergyman!"

"You have no right to make game of anyone."

"Oh yes, I have—when it is for his good. He used to study his sermons—where do you think?"

"In his study, of course. Where else should it be?"

"Yes and no. Guess again."

"Out amongst the faces in the streets?"

"Guess again."

"In still green places in the country?"
"Guess again."
"In old books?"
"Guess again."
"No, no. Tell us."
"In the looking-glass. Ha! Ha! Ha!"
"He was fair game; fair shadow game."
"I thought so. And I made such fun of him one night on the wall! He had sense enough to see that it was himself, and very like an ape. So he got ashamed, turned the mirror with its face to the wall, and thought a little more about his people, and a little less about himself. I was very glad; for, please your majesty,"—and here the speaker turned towards the king—"we don't like the creatures that live in the mirrors. You call them ghosts, don't you?"

Before the king could reply, another had commenced. But the story about the clergyman had made the king wish to hear one of the shadow-sermons. So he turned him towards a long Shadow, who was preaching to a very quiet and listening crowd. He was just concluding his sermon.

"Therefore, dear Shadows, it is the more needful that we love one another as much as we can, because that is not much. We have no such excuse for not loving as mortals have, for we do not die like them. I suppose it is the thought of that death that makes them hate so much. Then again, we go to sleep all day, most of us, and not in the night, as men do. And you know that we forget everything that happened the night before; therefore, we ought to love well, for the love is short. Ah! Dear Shadow, whom I love now with all my shadowy soul, I shall not love thee tomorrow eve, I shall not know thee; I shall pass thee in the crowd and never dream that the Shadow whom I now love is near me then. Happy Shades! For we only remember our tales until we have told them here, and then they vanish in the shadow-churchyard, where we bury only our dead selves. Ah! Brethren, who would be a man and remember? Who would be a man and weep? We ought indeed to love one another, for we alone inherit oblivion; we alone are renewed with eternal birth; we alone have no gathered weight of years. I will tell you the awful fate of one Shadow who rebelled against his nature, and sought to remember the past. He said, 'I *will* remember this eve.' He fought with the genial influences of kindly sleep when the sun rose on the awful dead day of light; and although he could not keep quite awake, he dreamed of the foregone eve, and he never forgot his dream. Then he tried again the next night and the next, and the next; and he tempted another Shadow to try it with him. But at last their awful fate overtook them; for, instead of continuing to be Shadows, they began to cast shadows, as foolish men say; and so they thickened and thickened till they vanished out of our world. They are now condemned to walk the earth a man and a woman, with death behind them, and memories within them. Ah, brother Shades! Let us love one another, for we shall soon forget. We are not men, but Shadows."

The king turned away, and pitied the poor Shadows far more than they pitied men.

"Oh! How we played with a musician one night," exclaimed a Shadow in another group, to which the king had first directed a passing thought and then had stopped to listen. "Up and down we went like the hammers and dampers on his piano. But he took his revenge on us. For after he had watched us for half an hour in the twilight, he rose and went to his instrument and played a shadow-dance that fixed us all in sound forever. Each could tell the very notes meant for him; and as long as he played we could not stop, but went on dancing and dancing after the music, just as the magician—I mean the musician—pleased. And he punished us well; for he nearly danced us all off our legs and out of shape into tired heaps of collapsed and palpitating darkness. We won't go near him for some time again, if we can only remember it. He had been very miserable all day, he was so poor; and we could not think of any way of comforting him except making him laugh. We did not succeed, with our wildest efforts; but it turned out better than we had expected, after all; for his shadow-dance got him into notice, and he is quite popular now, and making money fast. If he does not take care, we shall have other work to do with him by-and-by, poor fellow!"

"I and some others did the same for a poor playwriter once. He had a Christmas piece to write, and being an original genius, it was not so easy for him to find a subject as it is for most of his class. I saw the trouble he was in, and collecting a few stray Shadows, we acted, in dumb show of course, the funniest bit of nonsense we could think of; and it was quite successful. The poor fellow watched every motion, roaring with laughter at us, and delight at the ideas we put into his head. He turned it all into words, and scenes, and actions; and the piece came off with a splendid success."

"But how long we have to look for a chance of doing anything worth doing!" said a long, thin, especially lugubrious Shadow. "I have only done one thing worth telling ever since we met last. But I am proud of that."

"What was it? What was it?" rose from twenty voices.

"I crept into a dining room, one twilight soon after Christmas day. I had been drawn thither by the glow of a bright fire shining through red window-curtains. At first I thought there was no one there, and was on the point of leaving the room and going out again into the snowy street when I suddenly caught the sparkle of eyes. I found that they belonged to a little boy who lay very still on a sofa. I crept into a dark corner by the sideboard, and watched him. He seemed very sad, and did nothing but stare into the fire. At last he sighed out, 'I wish mamma would come home.' 'Poor boy!' thought

I, 'there is no help for that but mamma.' Yet I would try to while away the time for him. So out of my corner I stretched a long shadow-arm, reaching all across the ceiling, and pretended to make a grab at him. He was rather frightened at first; but he was a brave boy, and soon saw that it was all a joke. So when I did it again, he made a clutch at me; and then we had such fun! For though he often sighed and wished mamma would come home, he always began again with me; and on we went with the wildest game. At last his mother's knock came to the door, and, starting up in delight, he rushed into the hall to meet her, and forgot all about poor black me. But I did not mind that in the least; for when I glided out after him into the hall, I was well repaid for my trouble by hearing his mother say to him, 'Why, Charlie, my dear, you look ever so much better since I left you!' At that moment I slipped through the closing door, and as I ran across the snow, I heard the mother say, 'What Shadow can that be passing so quickly?' And Charlie answered with a merry laugh, 'Oh, mamma! I suppose it must be the funny shadow that has been playing such games with me all the time you were out.' As soon as the door was shut, I crept along the wall and looked in at the dining-room window. And I heard his mamma say, as she led him into the room, 'What an imagination the boy has!' Ha! Ha! Ha! Then she looked at him, and the tears came in her eyes; and she stooped down over him, and I heard the sounds of a mingling kiss and sob."

"I always look for nurseries full of children," said another, "and this winter I have been very fortunate. I am sure children belong especially to us. One evening, looking about in a great city, I saw through the window into a large nursery, where the odious gas had not yet been lighted. Round the fire sat a company of the most delightful children I had ever seen. They were waiting patiently for their tea. It was too good an opportunity to be lost. I hurried away, and gathering together twenty of the best Shadows I could find, returned in a few moments; and entering the nursery, we danced on the walls one of our best dances. To be sure it was mostly extemporized; but I managed to keep it in harmony by singing this song, which I made as we went on. Of course the children could not hear it; they only saw the motions that answered to it; but with them they seemed to be very much delighted indeed, as I shall presently prove to you. This was the song:

> *Swing, swang, swingle, swuff!*
> *Flicker, flacker, fling, fluff!*
> *Thus we go,*
> *To and fro,*
> *Here and there,*
> *Everywhere,*
> *Born and bred,*
> *Never dead,*
> *Only gone.*
>
> *On! Come on,*
> *Looming, glooming,*
> *Spreading, fuming,*
> *Shattering, scattering,*
> *Parting, darting,*
> *Settling, starting,*
> *All our life*
> *Is a strife,*
> *And a wearying for rest*
> *On the darkness' friendly breast.*
>
> *Joining, splitting,*
> *Rising, sitting,*

Laughing, shaking,
Sides all aching,
Grumbling, grim, and gruff,
Swingle, swangle, swuff!

Now a knot of darkness,
Now dissolved gloom,
Now a pall of blackness
Hiding all the room.
Flicker, flacker, fluff!
Black, and black enough!

Dancing now like demon,
Lying like the dead,
Gladly would we stop it,
And go down to bed!
But our work we still must do,
Shadow men, as well as you.

Rooting, rising, shooting,
Heaving, sinking, creeping,
Hid in corners crooning,
Splitting, poking, leaping,
Gathering, towering, swooning,
When we're lurking,
Yet we're working,
For our labour we must do,
Shadow men, as well as you.
Flicker, flacker, fling, fluff!
Swing, swang, swingle, swuff!

"'How thick the Shadows are!' said one of the children—a thoughtful little girl.

"'I wonder where they come from,' said a dreamy little boy.

"'I think they grow out of the wall,' answered the little girl; 'for I have been watching them come; first one, and then another, and then a whole lot of them. I am sure they grow out of the walls.'

"'Perhaps they have papas and mammas,' said an older boy, with a smile.

"'Yes, yes; and the doctor brings them in his pocket,' said another, a consequential little maiden.

"'No; I'll tell you,' said the older boy: 'they're ghosts.'

"'But ghosts are white.'

"'Oh! But these have got black coming down the chimney.'

"'No,' said a curious-looking, white-faced boy of fourteen, who had been reading by the firelight, and had stopped to hear the little ones talk; 'they're body ghosts; they're not soul ghosts.'

"A silence followed, broken by the first, the dreamy-eyed boy, who said, '"I hope they didn't make me"'; at which they all burst out laughing.

"Just then the nurse brought in their tea, and when she proceeded to light the gas we vanished."

"I stopped a murder," cried another.

"How? How? How?"

"I will tell you. I had been lurking about a sick room for some time, where a miser lay, apparently dying. I did not like the place at all, but felt as if I should be wanted there. There were plenty of lurking-places about, for the room was full of all sorts of old furniture, especially cabinets, chests, and presses. I believe he had in that room every bit of the property he had spent a long life in gathering. I found that he had gold and gold in those places; for one night, when his nurse was away, he crept out of bed, mumbling and shaking, and managed to open one of the chests, though he nearly fell down with the effort. I was peeping over his shoulder, and such a gleam of gold fell upon me, that it nearly killed me. But hearing his nurse coming, he slammed the lid down, and I recovered.

"I tried very hard, but I could not do him any good. For although I made all sorts of shapes on the walls and ceiling, representing evil deeds that he had done, of which there were plenty to choose from, I could make no shapes on his brain or conscience. He had no eyes for anything but gold. And it so happened that his nurse had neither eyes nor heart for anything else either.

"One day, as she was seated beside his bed, but where he could not see her, stirring some gruel in a basin, to cool it for him, I saw her take a little phial from her bosom, and I knew by the expression of her face both what it was and what she was going to do with it. Fortunately the cork was a little hard to get out and this gave me one moment to think.

"The room was so crowded with all sorts of things, that although there were no curtains on the four-post bed to hide from the miser the sight of his precious treasures, there was yet but one small part of the ceiling suitable for casting myself upon in the shape I wished to assume. And this spot was hard to reach. But having discovered that upon this very place lay a dull gleam of firelight thrown from a strange old dusty mirror that stood away in some corner, I got in front of the fire, spied where the mirror was threw myself upon it, and bounded from its face upon the oval pool of dim light on the ceiling, assuming, as I passed, the shape of an old stooping hag, who poured something from a phial into a basin. I made the handle of the spoon with my own nose, ha! Ha!"

And the shadow-hand caressed the shadow-tip of the shadow-nose, before the shadow-tongue resumed.

"The old miser saw me: he would not taste the gruel that night, although his nurse coaxed and scolded till they were both weary. She pretended to taste it herself, and to think it very good; but at last retired into a corner, and after making as if she were eating it, took care to pour it all out into the ashes."

"But she must either succeed, or starve him, at last," interposed a Shadow.

"I will tell you."

"And," interposed another, "he was not worth saving."

"He might repent," suggested a third, who was more benevolent.

"No chance of that," returned the former. "Misers never do. The love of money has less in it to cure itself than any other wickedness into which wretched men can fall. What a mercy it is to be born a Shadow! Wickedness does not stick to us. What do we care for gold! Rubbish!"

"Amen! Amen! Amen!" came from a hundred shadow-voices.

"You should have let her murder him, and so you would have been quit of him."

"And besides, how was he to escape at last? He could never get rid of her, you know."

"I was going to tell you," resumed the narrator, "only you had so many shadow-remarks to make, that you would not let me."

"Go on; go on."

"There was a little grandchild who used to come and see him sometimes—the only creature the miser cared for. Her mother was his daughter; but the old man would never see her, because she had married against his will. Her husband was now dead, but he had not forgiven her yet. After the shadow he had seen, however, he said to himself, as he lay awake that night—I saw the words on his face—'How shall I get rid of that old devil? If I don't eat I shall die; and if I do eat I shall be poisoned. I wish little Mary would come. Ah! Her mother would never have served me so.' He lay awake, thinking such things over and over again, all night long, and I stood watching him from a dark corner, till the dayspring came and shook me out. When I came back next night, the room was tidy and clean. His own daughter, a sad-faced but beautiful woman, sat by his bedside; and little Mary was curled up on the floor by the fire, imitating us, by making queer shadows on the ceiling with her twisted hands. But she could not think however they got there. And no wonder, for I helped her to some very unaccountable ones."

"I have a story about a granddaughter, too," said another, the moment that speaker ceased.

"Tell it. Tell it."

"Last Christmas day," he began, "I and a troop of us set out in the twilight to find some house where we could all have something to do; for we had made up our minds to act together. We tried several, but found objections to them all. At last we espied a large lonely country-house, and hastening to it, we found great preparations making for the Christmas dinner. We rushed into it, scampered all over it, and made up our minds in a moment that it would do. We amused ourselves in the nursery first, where there were several children being dressed for dinner. We generally do go to the nursery first, your majesty. This time we were especially charmed with a little girl about five years old, who clapped her hands and danced about with delight at the antics we performed; and we said we would do something for her if we had a chance. The company began to arrive; and at every arrival, we rushed to the hall, and cut wonderful capers of welcome. Between times, we scudded away to see how the dressing went on. One girl about eighteen was delightful. She dressed herself as if she did not care much about it, but could not help doing it prettily. When she took her last look at the phantom in the glass, she half smiled to it. But *we* do not like those creatures that come into the mirrors at all, your majesty. We don't understand them. They are dreadful to us. She looked rather sad and pale, but very sweet and hopeful. So we wanted to know all about her, and soon found out that she was a distant relation and a great favourite of the gentleman of the house, an old man, in whose face benevolence was mingled with obstinacy and a deep shade of the tyrannical. We could not admire him much; but we would not make up our minds all at once: Shadows never do.

"The dinner-bell rang, and down we hurried. The children all looked happy, and we were merry. But there was one cross fellow among the servants, and didn't we plague him! And didn't we get fun out of him! When he was bringing up dishes, we lay in wait for him at every corner, and sprang upon him from the floor, and from over the banisters, and down from the cornices. He started and stumbled and blundered so in consequence, that his fellow-servants thought he was tipsy. Once he dropped a plate, and had to pick up the pieces, and hurry away with them; and didn't we pursue him as he went! It was lucky for him his master did not see how he went on; but we took care not to let him get into any real scrape, though he was quite dazed with the dodging of the unaccountable shadows. Sometimes he thought the walls were coming down upon him, sometimes that the floor was gaping to swallow him; sometimes that he would be knocked to pieces by the hurrying to and fro, or be smothered in the black crowd.

"When the blazing plum-pudding was carried in, we made a perfect shadow-carnival about it, dancing and mumming in the blue flames, like mad demons. And how the children screamed with delight!

"The old gentleman, who was very fond of children, was laughing his heartiest laugh, when a loud knock came to the hall door. The fair maiden started, turned paler, and then red as the Christmas fire. I saw it, and flung my hands across her face. She was very glad, and I know she said in her heart, 'You kind Shadow!' which paid me well. Then I followed the rest into the hall, and found there a jolly, handsome, brown-faced sailor, evidently a son of the house. The old man received him with tears in his eyes, and the children with shouts of joy. The maiden escaped in the confusion, just in time to save herself from fainting. We crowded about the lamp to hide her retreat, and nearly put it out; and the butler could not get it to burn up before she had glided into her place again, relieved to find the room so dark. The sailor only had seen her go, and now he sat down beside her, and, without a word, got hold of her hand in the gloom. When we all scattered to the walls and the corners, and the lamp blazed up again, he let her hand go.

"During the rest of the dinner the old man watched the two, and saw that there was something between them, and was very angry. For he was an important man in his own estimation, and they had never consulted him. The fact was, they had never known their own minds till the sailor had gone upon his last voyage, and had learned each other's only this moment. We found out all this by watching them, and then talking together about it afterwards. The old gentleman saw, too, that his favourite, who was under such obligation to him for loving her so much, loved his son better than him; and he grew by degrees so jealous that he overshadowed the whole table with his morose looks and short answers. That kind of shadowing is very different from ours; and the Christmas dessert grew so gloomy that we Shadows could not bear it, and were delighted when the ladies rose to go to the drawing-room. The gentlemen would not stay behind the ladies, even for the sake of the well-known wine. So the moody host, notwithstanding his hospitality, was left alone at the table in the great silent room. We followed the company upstairs to the drawing-room, and thence to the nursery for snap-dragon; but while they were busy with this most shadowy of games, nearly all the Shadows crept downstairs again to the dining-room, where the old man still sat, gnawing the bone of his own selfishness. They crowded into the room, and by using every kind of expansion—blowing themselves out like soap bubbles—they succeeded in heaping up the whole room with shade upon shade. They clustered thickest about the fire and the lamp, till at last they almost drowned them in hills of darkness.

"Before they had accomplished so much, the children, tired with fun and frolic, had been put to bed. But the little girl of five years old, with whom we had been so pleased when first we arrived, could not go to sleep. She had a little room of her own; and I had watched her to bed, and now kept her awake by gambolling in the rays of the night-light. When her eyes were fixed upon me, I took the shape of her grandfather, representing him on the wall as he sat in his chair, with his head bent down and his arms hanging listlessly by his sides. And the child remembered that that was just as she had seen him last; for she had happened to peep in at the dining-room door after all the rest had gone upstairs. 'What if he should be sitting there still,' thought she, 'all alone in the dark!' She scrambled out of bed and crept down.

"Meantime the others had made the room below so dark, that only the face and white hair of the old man could be dimly discerned in the shadowy crowd. For he had filled his own mind with shadows, which we Shadows wanted to draw out of him. Those shadows are very different from us, your majesty knows. He was thinking of all the disappointments he had had in life, and of all the ingratitude he had met with. And he thought far more of the good he had done, than the good others had got. 'After all I have done for them,' said he, with a sigh of bitterness, 'not one of them cares a straw for me. My own children will be glad when I am gone!' At that instant he lifted up his eyes and saw, standing close by the door, a tiny figure in a long nightgown. The door behind her was shut. It was my little friend, who had crept in noiselessly. A pang of icy fear shot to the old man's heart, but it melted away as fast for we made a lane through us for a single ray from the fire to fall on the face of the little sprite; and he thought it was a child of his own that had died when just the age of her child-niece, who now stood looking for her grandfather among the Shadows. He thought she had come out of her grave in the cold darkness to ask why her father was sitting alone on Christmas day. And he felt he had no answer to give his little ghost, but one he would be ashamed for her to hear. But his grandchild saw him now, and walked up to him with a childish stateliness, stumbling once or twice on what seemed her long shroud. Pushing through the crowded shadows, she reached him, climbed upon his knee, laid her little long-haired head on his shoulders, and said, 'Ganpa! You goomy? Isn't it your Kissy-Day too, ganpa?'

"A new fount of love seemed to burst from the clay of the old man's heart. He clasped the child to his bosom, and wept. Then, without a word, he rose with her in his arms, carried her up to her room, and laying her down in her bed, covered her up, kissed her sweet little mouth unconscious of reproof, and then went to the drawing-room.

"As soon as he entered, he saw the culprits in a quiet corner alone. He went up to them, took a hand of each, and joining them in both his, said, 'God bless you!' Then he turned to the rest of the company, and 'Now,' said he, 'let's have a Christmas carol.' And well he might; for though I have paid many visits to the house, I have never seen him cross since; and I am sure that must cost him a good deal of trouble."

"We have just come from a great palace," said another, "where we knew there were many children, and where we thought to hear glad voices, and see royally merry looks. But as soon as we entered, we became aware that one mighty Shadow shrouded the whole; and that Shadow deepened and deepened, till it gathered in darkness about the reposing form of a wise prince. When we saw him, we could move no more, but clung heavily to the walls, and by our stillness added to the sorrow of the hour. And when we saw the mother of her people weeping with bowed head for the loss of him in whom she had trusted, we were seized with such a longing to be Shadows no more, but winged angels, which are the white shadows cast in heaven from the Light of Light, so as to gather around her, and hover over her with comforting, that we vanished from the walls, and found ourselves floating high above the towers of the palace, where we met the angels on their way, and knew that our service was not needed."

By this time there was a glimmer of approaching moonlight, and the king began to see several of those stranger Shadows, with human faces and eyes, moving about amongst the crowd. He knew at once that they did not belong to his dominion. They looked at him, and came near him, and passed slowly, but they never made any obeisance, or gave sign of homage. And what their eyes said to him, the king only could tell. And he did not tell.

"What are those other Shadows that move through the crowd?" said he to one of his subjects near him.

The Shadow started, looked round, shivered slightly, and laid his finger on his lips. Then leading the king a little aside, and looking carefully about him once more, "I do not know," said he, in a low tone, "what they are. I have heard of them often, but only once did I ever see any of them before. That was when some of us one night paid a visit to a man who sat much alone, and was said to think a great deal. We saw two of those sitting in the room with him, and he was as pale as they were. We could not cross the threshold, but shivered and shook, and felt ready to melt away. Is not your majesty afraid of them too!"

But the king made no answer; and before he could speak again, the moon had climbed above the mighty pillars of the church of the Shadows, and looked in at the great window of the sky.

The shapes had all vanished; and the king, again lifting up his eyes, saw but the wall of his own chamber, on which flickered the Shadow of a Little Child. He looked down, and there, sitting on a stool by the fire, he saw one of his own little ones, waiting to say good night to his father, and go to bed early, that he might rise early too, and be very good and happy all Christmas day.

And Ralph Rinkelmann rejoiced that he was a man, and not a Shadow.

But as the Shadows vanished they left the sense of song in the king's brain. And the words of their song must have been something like these:

> "*Shadows, Shadows, Shadows all!*
> *Shadow birth and funeral!*
> *Shadow moons gleam overhead,*
> *Over shadow-graves we tread.*
> *Shadow-hope lives, grows, and dies.*
>
> "*Shadow-love from shadow-eyes*
> *Shadow-ward entices on*
> *To shadow-words on shadow-stone,*
> *Closing up the shadow-tale*
> *With a shadow-shadow-wail.*
>
> "*Shadow-man, thou art a gloom*
> *Cast upon a shadow-tomb*

THE SHADOWS

Through the endless shadow-air,
From the Shadow sitting there,
On a moveless shadow-throne,
Glooming through the ages gone,
North and south, and in and out,
East and west, and all about,
Flinging Shadows everywhere
On the shadow-painted air.
Shadow-man, thou hast no story,
Nothing but a shadow-glory."

But Ralph Rinkelmann said to himself, "They are but Shadows that sing thus; for a Shadow can see but Shadows. A man sees a man where a Shadow sees only a Shadow."

And he was comforted in himself.

THE GIANT'S HEART

* * *

THERE was once a giant who lived on the borders of Giantland where it touched on the country of common people.

Everything in Giantland was so big that the common people saw only a mass of awful mountains and clouds; and no living man had ever come from it, as far as anybody knew, to tell what he had seen in it.

Somewhere near the borders, on the other side, by the edge of a great forest, lived a labourer with his wife and a great many children. One day Tricksey-Wee, as they called her, teased her brother Buffy-Bob, till he could not bear it any longer, and gave her a box on the ear. Tricksey-Wee cried; and Buffy-Bob was so sorry and so ashamed of himself that he cried too, and ran off into the wood. He was so long gone that Tricksey-Wee began to be frightened, for she was very fond of her brother; and she was so distressed that she had first teased him and then cried, that at last she ran into the wood to look for him, though there was more chance of losing herself than of finding him. And, indeed, so it seemed likely to turn out; for, running on without looking, she at length found herself in a valley she knew nothing about. And no wonder; for what she thought was a valley with round, rocky sides, was no other than the space between two of the roots of a great tree that grew on the borders of

Giantland. She climbed over the side of it, and went towards what she took for a black, round-topped mountain, far away; but which she soon discovered to be close to her, and to be a hollow place so great that she could not tell what it was hollowed out of. Staring at it, she found that it was a doorway; and going nearer and staring harder, she saw the door, far in, with a knocker of iron upon it, a great many yards above her head, and as large as the anchor of a big ship. Now nobody had ever been unkind to Tricksey-Wee, and therefore she was not afraid of anybody. For Buffy-Bob's box on the ear she did not think worth considering. So spying a little hole at the bottom of the door which had been nibbled by some giant mouse, she crept through it, and found herself in an enormous hall. She could not have seen the other end of it at all, except for the great fire that was burning there, diminished to a spark in the distance. Towards this fire she ran as fast as she could, and was not far from it when something fell before her with a great clatter, over which she tumbled, and went rolling on the floor. She was not much hurt, however, and got up in a moment. Then she saw that what she had fallen over was not unlike a great iron bucket. When she examined it more closely, she discovered that it was a thimble; and looking up to see who had dropped it beheld a huge face, with spectacles as big as the round windows in a church, bending over her, and looking everywhere for the thimble. Tricksey-Wee immediately laid hold of it in both her arms, and lifted it about an inch nearer to the nose of the peering giantess. This movement made the old lady see where it was, and, her finger popping into it, it vanished from the eyes of Tricksey-Wee, buried in the folds of a white stocking like a cloud in the sky, which Mrs. Giant was busy darning. For it was Saturday night and her husband would wear nothing but white stockings on Sunday. To be sure, he did eat little children, but only *very* little ones; and if ever it crossed his mind that it was wrong to do so, he always said to himself that he wore whiter stockings on Sunday than any other giant in all Giantland.

At the same instant Tricksey-Wee heard a sound like the wind in a tree full of leaves, and could not think what it could be; till, looking up, she found that it was the giantess whispering to her; and when she tried very hard she could hear what she said well enough.

"Run away, dear little girl," she said, "as fast as you can; for my husband will be home in a few minutes."

"But I've never been naughty to your husband," said Tricksey-Wee, looking up in the giantess's face.

"That doesn't matter. You had better go. He is fond of little children, particularly little girls."

"Oh, then he won't hurt me."

"I am not sure of that. He is so fond of them that he eats them up; and I am afraid he couldn't help hurting you a little. He's a very good man, though."

"Oh! Then—" began Tricksey-Wee, feeling rather frightened; but before she could finish her sentence she heard the sound of footsteps very far apart and very heavy. The next moment, who should come running towards her, full speed, and as pale as death, but Buffy-Bob. She held out her arms, and he ran into them. But when she tried to kiss him, she only kissed the back of his head; for his white face and round eyes were turned to the door.

"Run, children; run and hide," said the giantess.

"Come, Buffy," said Tricksey; "yonder's a great brake; we'll hide in it."

The brake was a big broom; and they had just got into the bristles of it when they heard the door open with a sound of thunder, and in stalked the giant. You would have thought you saw the whole earth through the door when he opened it so wide was it; and when he closed it, it was like nightfall.

"Where is that little boy?" he cried, with a voice like the bellowing of a cannon. "He looked a very nice boy indeed. I am almost sure he crept through the mousehole at the bottom of the door. Where is he, my dear?"

"I don't know," answered the giantess.

"But you know it is wicked to tell lies; don't you, my dear?" retorted the giant.

"Now, you ridiculous old Thunderthump!" said his wife, with a smile as broad as the sea in the sun, "How can I mend your white stockings and look after little boys? You have got plenty to last you over Sunday, I am sure. Just look what good little boys they are!"

Tricksey-Wee and Buffy-Bob peered through the bristles, and discovered a row of little boys, about a dozen, with very fat faces and goggle eyes, sitting before the fire, and looking stupidly into it. Thunderthump intended the most of these for pickling, and was feeding them well before salting them. Now and then, however, he could not keep his teeth off them, and would eat one by the bye, without salt.

He strode up to the wretched children. Now what made them very wretched indeed was that they knew if they could only keep from eating, and grow thin, the giant would dislike them, and turn them out to find their way home; but notwithstanding this, so greedy were they, that they ate as much as ever they could hold. The giantess, who fed them, comforted herself with thinking that they were not real boys and girls, but only little pigs pretending to be boys and girls.

"Now tell me the truth," cried the giant, bending his face down over them. They shook with terror, and everyone hoped it was somebody else the giant liked best. "Where is the little boy that ran into the hall just now? Whoever tells me a lie shall be instantly boiled."

"He's in the broom," cried one dough-faced boy. "He's in there, and a little girl with him."

THE GIANT'S HEART

"The naughty children," cried the giant, "to hide from me!" And he made a stride towards the broom.

"Catch hold of the bristles, Bobby. Get right into a tuft, and hold on," cried Tricksey-Wee, just in time.

The giant caught up the broom, and seeing nothing under it set it down again with a force that threw them both on the floor. He then made two strides to the boys, caught the dough-faced one by the neck, took the lid off a great pot that was boiling on the fire, popped him in as if he had been a trussed chicken, put the lid on again, and saying, "There, boys! See what comes of lying!" asked no more questions; for, as he always kept his word, he was afraid he might have to do the same to them all; and he did not like boiled boys. He liked to eat them crisp, as radishes, whether forked or not, ought to be eaten. He then sat down, and asked his wife if his supper was ready. She looked into the pot, and throwing the boy out with the ladle, as if he had been a black beetle that had tumbled in and had had the worst of it, answered that she thought it was. Whereupon he rose to help her; and taking the pot from the fire, poured the whole contents, bubbling and splashing, into a dish like a vat. Then they sat down to supper. The children in the broom could not see what they had; but it seemed to agree with them; for the giant talked like thunder, and the giantess answered like the sea, and they grew chattier and chattier. At length the giant said, "I don't feel quite comfortable about that heart of mine." And as he spoke, instead of laying his hand on his bosom, he waved it away towards the corner where the children were peeping from the broom bristles, like frightened little mice.

"Well, you know, my darling Thunderthump," answered his wife, "I always thought it ought to be nearer home. But you know best, of course."

"Ha! Ha! You don't know where it is, wife. I moved it a month ago."

"What a man you are, Thunderthump! You trust any creature alive rather than your own wife."

Here the giantess gave a sob which sounded exactly like a wave going flop into the mouth of a cave up to the roof.

"Where have you got it now?" she resumed, checking her emotion.

"Well, Doodlem, I don't mind telling *you*," answered the giant soothingly. "The great she-eagle has got it for a nest egg. She sits on it night and day, and thinks she will bring the greatest eagle out of it that ever sharpened his beak on the rocks of Mount Skycrack. I can warrant no one else will touch it while she has got it. But she is rather capricious, and I confess I am not easy about it; for the least scratch of one of her claws would do for me at once. And she *has* claws."

I refer anyone who doubts this part of my story to certain chronicles of Giantland preserved among the Celtic nations. It was quite a common thing for a giant to put his heart out to nurse, because he did not like the trouble and responsibility of doing it himself; although I must confess it was a dangerous sort of plan to take, especially with such a delicate viscus as the heart.

All this time Buffy-Bob and Tricksey-Wee were listening with long ears.

"Oh!" thought Tricksey-Wee, "If I could but find the giant's cruel heart, wouldn't I give it a squeeze!"

The giant and giantess went on talking for a long time. The giantess kept advising the giant to hide his heart somewhere in the house; but he seemed afraid of the advantage it would give her over him.

"You could hide it at the bottom of the flour barrel," said she.

"That would make me feel chokey," answered he.

"Well, in the coal-cellar. Or in the dust-hole—that's the place! No one would think of looking for your heart in the dust-hole."

"Worse and worse!" cried the giant.

"Well, the water-butt," suggested she.

"No, no; it would grow spongy there," said he.

"Well, what *will* you do with it?"

"I will leave it a month longer where it is, and then I will give it to the Queen of the Kangaroos, and she will carry it in her pouch for me. It is best to change its place, you know, lest my enemies should scent it out. But dear Doodlem, it's a fretting care to have a heart of one's own to look after. The responsibility is too much for me. If it were not for a bite of a radish now and then, I never could bear it."

Here the giant looked lovingly towards the row of little boys by the fire, all of whom were nodding, or asleep on the floor.

"Why don't you trust it to me, dear Thunderthump?" said his wife. "I would take the best possible care of it."

"I don't doubt it, my love. But the responsibility would be too much for you. You would no longer be my darling, light-hearted, airy, laughing Doodlem. It would transform you into a heavy, oppressed woman, weary of life—as I am."

The giant closed his eyes and pretended to go to sleep. His wife got his stockings, and went on with her darning. Soon the giant's pretence became reality, and the giantess began to nod over her work.

"Now, Buffy," whispered Tricksey-Wee, "now's our time. I think it's moonlight, and we had better be off. There's a door with a hole for the cat just behind us."

"All right," said Bob; "I'm ready."

So they got out of the broom-brake and crept to the door. But to their great disappointment, when they got through it, they found themselves in a sort of shed. It was full of tubs and things, and, though it was built of wood only, they could not find a crack.

"Let us try this hole," said Tricksey; for the giant and giantess were sleeping behind them, and they dared not go back.

"All right," said Bob.

He seldom said anything else than *All right*.

Now this hole was in a mound that came in through the wall of the shed, and went along the floor for some distance. They crawled into it, and found it very dark. But groping their way along, they soon came to a small crack, through which they saw grass, pale in the moonshine. As they crept on, they found the hole began to get wider and lead upwards.

"What is that noise of rushing?" said Buffy-Bob.

"I can't tell," replied Tricksey; "for, you see, I don't know what we are in."

The fact was they were creeping along a channel in the heart of a giant tree; and the noise they heard was the noise of the sap rushing along in its wooden pipes. When they laid their ears to the wall, they heard it gurgling along with a pleasant noise.

"It sounds kind and good," said Tricksey. "It is water running. Now it must be running from somewhere to somewhere. I think we had better go on, and we shall come somewhere."

It was now rather difficult to go on, for they had to climb as if they were climbing a hill; and now the passage was wide. Nearly worn out, they saw light overhead at last, and creeping through a crack into the open air, found themselves on the fork of a huge tree. A great, broad, uneven space lay around them, out of which spread boughs in every direction, the smallest of them as big as the biggest tree in the country of common people. Overhead were leaves enough to supply all the trees they had ever seen. Not much moonlight could come through, but the leaves would glimmer white in the wind at times. The tree was full of giant birds. Every now and then, one would sweep through, with a great noise. But, except an occasional chirp, sounding like a shrill pipe in a great organ, they made no noise. All at once an owl began to hoot. He thought he was singing. As soon as he began, other birds replied, making rare game of him. To their astonishment, the children found they could understand every word they sang. And what they sang was something like this:

> "*I will sing a song.*
>   *I'm the owl.*"
> "*Sing a song, you sing-song*
>   *Ugly fowl!*
> *What will you sing about,*
>   *Night in and Day out?*"
>
> "*Sing about the night.*
>   *I'm the owl.*"
> "*You could not see for the light,*
>   *Stupid fowl.*'"
> "*Oh! The moon! And the dew!*
>   *And the shadows!—tu-whoo!*"

The owl spread out his silent, soft, sly wings, and lighting between Tricksey-Wee and Buffy-Bob, nearly smothered them, closing up one under each wing. It was like being buried in a down bed. But the owl did not like anything between his sides and his wings, so he opened his wings again, and the children made haste to get out. Tricksey-Wee immediately went in front of the bird, and looking up into his huge face, which was as round as the eyes of the giantess's spectacles, and much bigger, dropped a pretty curtsy, and said, "Please, Mr. Owl, I want to whisper to you."

"Very well, small child," answered the owl, looking important and stooping his ear towards her. "What is it?"

"Please tell me where the eagle lives that sits on the giant's heart."

"Oh, you naughty child! That's a secret. For shame!"

And with a great hiss that terrified them, the owl flew into the tree. All birds are fond of secrets; but not many of them can keep them so well as the owl.

So the children went on because they did not know what else to do. They found the way very rough and difficult, the tree was so full of humps and hollows. Now and then they plashed into a pool of rain; now and then they came upon twigs growing out of the trunk where they had no business, and they were as large as full-grown poplars. Sometimes they came upon great cushions of soft moss, and on one of them they lay down and rested. But they had not lain long before they spied a large nightingale sitting on a branch, with its bright eyes looking up at the moon. In a moment more he began to sing, and the birds about him began to reply, but in a very different tone from that in which they had replied to the owl. Oh, the birds did call the nightingale such pretty names! The nightingale sang, and the birds replied like this:

"*I will sing a song.*
I'm the nightingale."
"*Sing a song, long, long,*
Little Neverfail!
What will you sing about,
Light in or light out?"

"*Sing about the light*
Gone away,
Down, away, and out of sight—
Poor lost day!
Mourning for the day dead,
O'er his dim bed."

The nightingale sang so sweetly, that the children would have fallen asleep but for fear of losing any of the song. When the nightingale stopped they got up and wandered on. They did not know where they were going, but they thought it best to keep going on, because then they might come upon something or other. They were very sorry they had forgotten to ask the nightingale about the eagle's nest, but his music had put everything else out of their heads. They resolved, however, not to forget the next time they had a chance. So they went on and on, till they were both tired, and Tricksey-Wee said at last, trying to laugh, "I declare my legs feel just like a Dutch doll's."

"Then here's the place to go to bed in," said Buffy-Bob.

They stood at the edge of a last year's nest, and looked down with delight into the round, mossy cave. Then they crept gently in, and lying down in each other's arms, found it so deep, and warm, and comfortable, and soft, that they were soon fast asleep.

Now close beside them, in a hollow, was another nest, in which lay a lark and his wife; and the children were awakened, very early in the morning, by a dispute between Mr. and Mrs. Lark.

"Let me up," said the lark.

"It is not time," said the lark's wife.

"It is," said the lark, rather rudely. "The darkness is quite thin. I can almost see my own beak."

"Nonsense!" said the lark's wife. "You know you came home yesterday morning quite worn out—you had to fly so very high before you saw him. I am sure he would not mind if you took it a little easier. Do be quiet and go to sleep again."

"That's not it at all," said the lark. "He doesn't want me. I want him. Let me up, I say."

He began to sing; and Tricksey-Wee and Buffy-Bob, having now learned the way, answered him:

"I will sing a song,
   I'm the Lark."
"Sing, sing, Throat-strong,
   Little Kill-the-dark.
What will you sing about,
   Now the night is out?"

"I can only call,
   I can't think.
Let me up—that's all.
Let me drink!
Thirsting all the long night
   For a drink of light."

By this time the lark was standing on the edge of his nest and looking at the children.

"Poor little things! You can't fly," said the lark.

"No; but we can look up," said Tricksey.

"Ah, you don't know what it is to see the very first of the sun."

"But we know what it is to wait till he comes. He's no worse for your seeing him first, is he?"

"Oh no, certainly not," answered the lark, with condescension; and then, bursting into his *Jubilate*, he sprang aloft, clapping his wings like a clock running down.

"Tell us where—" began Buffy-Bob.

But the lark was out of sight. His song was all that was left of him. That was everywhere, and he was nowhere.

"Selfish bird!" said Buffy. "It's all very well for larks to go hunting the sun, but they have no business to despise their neighbors, for all that."

"Can I be of any use to you?" said a sweet voice out of the nest.

This was the lark's wife, who stayed at home with the young larks while her husband went to church.

"Oh! Thank you. If you please," answered Tricksey-Wee.

And up popped a pretty brown head; and then up came a brown feathery body; and last of all came the slender legs on to the edge of the nest. There she turned, and, looking down into the nest from which came a whole litany of chirpings for breakfast said, "Lie still, little ones." Then she turned to the children.

"My husband is King of the Larks," she said.

Buffy-Bob took off his cap, and Tricksey-Wee curtsied very low.

"Oh, it's not me," said the bird, looking very shy. "I am only his wife. It's my husband."

She looked up after him into the sky, whence his song was still falling like a shower of musical hailstones. Perhaps *she* could see him.

"He's a splendid bird," said Buffy-Bob; "only you know he *will* get up a little too early."

"Oh, no! He doesn't. It's only his way, you know. But tell me what I can do for you."

"Tell us, please, Lady Lark, where the she-eagle lives that sits on Giant Thunderthump's heart."

"Oh! That is a secret."

"Did you promise not to tell?"

"No; but larks ought to be discreet. They see more than other birds."

"But you don't fly up high like your husband, do you?"

"Not often. But it's no matter. I come to know things for all that."

"Do tell me, and I will sing you a song," said Tricksey-Wee.

"Can you sing too? You have got no wings!"

"Yes. And I will sing you a song I learned the other day about a lark and his wife."

"Please do," said the lark's wife. "Be quiet children, and listen."

Tricksey-Wee was very glad she happened to know a song which would please the lark's wife, at least whatever the lark himself might have thought of it if he had heard it. So she sang:

"'Good-morrow, my lord!' in the sky alone,
Sang the lark, as the sun ascended his throne.
'Shine on me, my lord, I only am come,
Of all your servants, to welcome you home.
I have flown a whole hour, right up, I swear,
To catch the first shine of your golden hair!'

"'Must I thank you, then,' said the king, 'Sir Lark,
For flying so high, and hating the dark?
You ask a full cup for half a thirst:
Half is love of me, and half love to be first.
There's many a bird that makes no haste,
But waits till I come. That's as much to my taste.'

"And the king hid his head in a turban of cloud,
And the lark stopped singing, quite vexed and cowed.
But he flew up higher, and thought, 'Anon,
The wrath of the king will be over and gone,
And his crown, shining out of its cloudy fold,
Will change my brown feathers to a glory of gold.'

"So he flew, with the strength of a lark he flew.
But as he rose the cloud rose too,
And not a gleam of the golden hair
Came through the depth of the misty air,
Till, weary with flying, with sighing sore,
The strong sun-seeker could do no more.

THE GIANT'S HEART

"*His wings had had no chrism of gold,*
And his feathers felt withered and worn and old,
So he quivered and sank, and dropped like a stone.
And there on his nest, where he left her, alone,
Sat his little wife on her little eggs,
Keeping them warm with wings and legs.

"*Did I say alone? Ah, no such thing!*
Full in her face was shining the king.
'Welcome, Sir Lark! You look tired,' said he.
'Up is not always the best way to me.
While you have been singing so high and away,
I've been shining to your little wife all day.'

"*He had set his crown all about the nest,*
And out of the midst shone her little brown breast,
And so glorious was she in russet gold,
That for wonder and awe Sir Lark grew cold.
He popped his head under her wing, and lay
As still as a stone, till the king was away."

As soon as Tricksey-Wee had finished her song, the lark's wife began a low, sweet, modest little song of her own; and after she had piped away for two or three minutes, she said, "You dear children, what can I do for you?"

"Tell us where the she-eagle lives, please," said Tricksey-Wee.

"Well, I don't think there can be much harm in telling such wise, good children," said Lady Lark; "I am sure you don't want to do any mischief."

"Oh, no; quite the contrary," said Buffy-Bob.

"Then I'll tell you. She lives on the very topmost peak of Mount

Skycrack; and the only way to get up is to climb on the spiders' webs that cover it from top to bottom."

"That's rather serious," said Tricksey-Wee.

"But you don't want to go up, you foolish little thing! You can't go. And what do you want to go up for?"

"That is a secret," said Tricksey-Wee.

"Well, it's no business of mine," rejoined Lady Lark, a little offended, and quite vexed that she had told them. So she flew away to find some breakfast for her little ones, who by this time were chirping very impatiently. The children looked at each other, joined hands, and walked off.

In a minute more the sun was up, and they soon reached the outside of the tree. The bark was so knobby and rough, and full of twigs, that they managed to get down, though not without great difficulty. Then, far away to the north they saw a huge peak, like the spire of a church, going right up into the sky. They thought this must be Mount Skycrack, and turned their faces towards it. As they went on, they saw a giant or two, now and then, striding about the fields or through the woods, but they kept out of their way. Nor were they in much danger; for it was only one or two of the border giants that were so very fond of children.

At last they came to the foot of Mount Skycrack. It stood in a plain alone, and shot right up, I don't know how many thousand feet, into the air, a long, narrow, spear-like mountain. The whole face of it, from top to bottom, was covered with a network of spiders' webs, the threads of various sizes, from that of silk to that of whipcord. The webs shook, and quivered, and waved in the sun, glittering like silver. All about ran huge greedy spiders, catching huge silly flies, and devouring them.

Here they sat down to consider what could be done. The spiders did not heed them, but ate away at the flies. Now at the foot of the

THE GIANT'S HEART

mountain, and all round it, was a ring of water, not very broad, but very deep. As they sat watching them, one of the spiders, whose web was woven across this water, somehow or other lost his hold, and fell in on his back. Tricksey-Wee and Buffy-Bob ran to his assistance, and laying hold each of one of his legs, succeeded, with the help of the other legs, which struggled spiderfully, in getting him out upon dry land. As soon as he had shaken himself, and dried himself a little, the spider turned to the children, saying, "And now, what can I do for you?"

"Tell us, please," said they, "how we can get up the mountain to the she-eagle's nest."

"Nothing is easier," answered the spider. "Just run up there, and tell them all I sent you, and nobody will mind you."

"But we haven't got claws like you, Mr. Spider," said Buffy.

"Ah! No more you have, poor unprovided creatures! Still, I think we can manage it. Come home with me."

"You won't eat us, will you?" said Buffy.

"My dear child," answered the spider, in a tone of injured dignity, "I eat nothing but what is mischievous or useless. You have helped me, and now I will help you."

The children rose at once, and climbing as well as they could, reached the spider's nest in the centre of the web. Nor did they find it very difficult; for whenever too great a gap came, the spider spinning a strong cord stretched it just where they would have chosen to put their feet next. He left them in his nest after bringing them two enormous honey-bags, taken from bees that he had caught but presently about six of the wisest of the spiders came back with him. It was horrible to look up and see them all round the mouth of the nest looking down on them in contemplation, as if wondering whether they would be nice eating. At length one of them said, "Tell us truly what you want with the eagle, and we will try to help you."

Then Tricksey-Wee told them that there was a giant on the borders who treated little children no better than radishes, and that they had narrowly escaped being eaten by him; that they had found out that the great she-eagle of Mount Skycrack was at present sitting on his heart; and that, if they could only get hold of his heart, they would soon teach the giant better behaviour.

"But," said their host, "if you get at the heart of the giant, you will find it as large as one of your elephants. What can you do with it?"

"The least scratch will kill it," replied Buffy-Bob.

"Ah! But you might do better than that," said the spider. "Now we have resolved to help you. Here is a little bag of spider-juice. The giants cannot bear spiders, and this juice is dreadful poison to them. We are all ready to go up with you, and drive the eagle away. Then you must put the heart into this other bag, and bring it down with you; for then the giant will be in your power."

"But how can we do that?" said Buffy. "The bag is not much bigger than a pudding-bag."

"But it is as large as you will be able to carry."

"Yes; but what are we to do with the heart?"

"Put it into the bag, to be sure. Only, first, you must squeeze out a drop of the other bag upon it. You will see what will happen."

"Very well; we will do as you tell us," said Tricksey-Wee. "And now, if you please, how shall we go?"

"Oh, that's our business," said the first spider. "You come with me, and my grandfather will take your brother. Get up."

So Tricksey-Wee mounted on the narrow part of the spider's back, and held fast. And Buffy-Bob got on the grandfather's back. And up they scrambled, over one web after another, up and up—so fast! And every spider followed; so that when Tricksey-Wee looked back, she saw a whole army of spiders scrambling after them.

THE GIANT'S HEART

"What can we want with so many?" she thought; but she said nothing.

The moon was now up, and it was a splendid sight below and around them. All Giantland was spread out under them, with its great hills, lakes, trees, and animals. And all above them was the clear heaven, and Mount Skycrack rising into it with its endless ladders of spiderwebs, glittering like cords made of moonbeams. And up the moonbeams went, crawling and scrambling, and racing, a huge army of spiders.

At length they reached all but the very summit, where they stopped. Tricksey-Wee and Buffy-Bob could see above them a great globe of feathers, that finished off the mountain like an ornamental knob.

"But how shall we drive her off?" said Buffy.

"We'll soon manage that," answered the grandfather-spider. "Come on you, down there."

Up rushed the whole army, past the children, over the edge of the nest, on to the she-eagle, and buried themselves in her feathers. In a moment she became very restless, and went pecking about with her beak.

All at once she spread out her wings, with a sound like a whirlwind, and flew off to bathe in the sea; and then the spiders began to drop from her in all directions on their gossamer-wings. The children had to hold fast to keep the wind of the eagle's flight from blowing them off. As soon as it was over, they looked into the nest, and there lay the giant's heart—an awful and ugly thing.

"Make haste, child!" said Tricksey's spider.

So Tricksey took her bag, and squeezed a drop out of it upon the heart. She thought she heard the giant give a far-off roar of pain, and she nearly fell from her seat with terror. The heart instantly began to shrink. It shrank and shrivelled till it was nearly gone; and

Buffy-Bob caught it up and put it into his bag. Then the two spiders turned and went down again as fast as they could. Before they got to the bottom, they heard the shrieks of the she-eagle over the loss of her egg; but the spiders told them not to be alarmed, for her eyes were too big to see them. By the time they reached the foot of the mountain, all the spiders had got home, and were busy again catching flies, as if nothing had happened.

After renewed thanks to their friends, the children set off, carrying the giant's heart with them.

"If you should find it at all troublesome, just give it a little more spider-juice directly," said the grandfather, as they took their leave.

Now the giant had given an awful roar of pain the moment they anointed his heart, and had fallen down in a fit, in which he lay so long that all the boys might have escaped if they had not been so fat. One did, and got home in safety. For days the giant was unable to speak. The first words he uttered were, "Oh, my heart! My heart!"

"Your heart is safe enough, dear Thunderthump," said his wife. "Really, a man of your size ought not to be so nervous and apprehensive. I am ashamed of you."

"You have no heart, Doodlem," answered he. "I assure you that at this moment mine is in the greatest danger. It has fallen into the hands of foes, though who they are I cannot tell."

Here he fainted again; for Tricksey-Wee, finding the heart beginning to swell a little, had given it the least touch of spider-juice.

Again he recovered, and said, "Dear Doodlem, my heart is coming back to me. It is coming nearer and nearer."

After lying silent for hours, he exclaimed, "It is in the house, I know!"

And he jumped up and walked about, looking in every corner.

As he rose, Tricksey-Wee and Buffy-Bob came out of the hole in the tree-root, and through the cat-hole in the door, and walked

THE GIANT'S HEART

boldly towards the giant. Both kept their eyes busy watching him. Led by the love of his own heart, the giant soon spied them, and staggered furiously towards them.

"I will eat you, you vermin!" he cried. "Here with my heart!"

Tricksey gave the heart a sharp pinch. Down fell the giant on his knees, blubbering, and crying, and begging for his heart.

"You shall have it if you behave yourself properly," said Tricksey.

"How shall I behave myself properly?" asked he, whimpering.

"Take all those boys and girls, and carry them home at once."

"I'm not able; I'm too ill. I should fall down."

"Take them up directly."

"I can't, till you give me my heart."

"Very well!" said Tricksey; and she gave the heart another pinch.

The giant jumped to his feet and catching up all the children, thrust some into his waistcoat-pockets, some into his breast-pocket, put two or three into his hat, and took a bundle of them under each arm. Then he staggered to the door.

All this time poor Doodlem was sitting in her armchair, crying, and mending a white stocking.

The giant led the way to the borders. He could not go fast but that Buffy and Tricksey managed to keep up with him. When they reached the borders, they thought it would be safer to let the children find their own way home. So they told him to set them down. He obeyed.

"Have you put them all down, Mr. Thunderthump?" asked Tricksey-Wee.

"Yes," said the giant.

"That's a lie!" squeaked a little voice; and out came a head from his waistcoat pocket.

Tricksey-Wee pinched the heart till the giant roared with pain.

"You're not a gentleman. You tell stories," she said.

"He was the thinnest of the lot," said Thunderthump, crying.

"Are you all there now, children?" asked Tricksey.

"Yes, ma'am," returned they, after counting themselves very carefully, and with some difficulty; for they were all stupid children.

"Now," said Tricksey-Wee to the giant, "will you promise to carry off no more children, and never to eat a child again all your life?"

"Yes, yes! I promise," answered Thunderthump, sobbing.

"And you will never cross the borders of Giantland?"

"Never."

"And you shall never again wear white stockings on a Sunday, all your life long. Do you promise?"

The giant hesitated at this, and began to expostulate; but Tricksey-Wee, believing it would be good for his morals, insisted; and the giant promised.

Then she required of him, that, when she gave him back his heart, he should give it to his wife to take care of for him forever after. The poor giant fell on his knees, and began again to beg. But Tricksey-Wee giving the heart a slight pinch, he bawled out, "Yes, yes! Doodlem shall have it, I swear. Only she must not put it in the flour barrel, or in the dust-hole."

"Certainly not. Make your own bargain with her. And you promise not to interfere with my brother and me, or to take any revenge for what we have done?"

"Yes, yes, my dear children; I promise everything. Do, pray, make haste and give me back my poor heart."

"Wait there, then, till I bring it to you."

"Yes, yes. Only make haste, for I feel very faint."

Tricksey-Wee began to undo the mouth of the bag.

But Buffy-Bob, who had got very knowing on his travels, took out his knife with the pretence of cutting the string; but, in reality, to be prepared for any emergency.

No sooner was the heart out of the bag, than it expanded to the size of a bullock; and the giant, with a yell of rage and vengeance, rushed on the two children, who had stepped sideways from the terrible heart. But Buffy-Bob was too quick for Thunderthump. He sprang to the heart, and buried his knife in it, up to the hilt. A fountain of blood spouted from it; and with a dreadful groan the giant fell dead at the feet of little Tricksey-Wee, who could not help being sorry for him, after all.

THE CRUEL PAINTER

* * *

AMONG the young men assembled at the University of Prague, in the year 159–, was one called Karl von Wolkenlicht. A somewhat careless student, he yet held a fair position in the estimation of both professors and men, because he could hardly look at a proposition without understanding it. Where such proposition, however, had to do with anything relating to the deeper insights of the nature, he was quite content that for him, it should remain a proposition; which, however, he laid up in one of his mental cabinets, and was ready to reproduce at a moment's notice. This mental agility was more than matched by the corresponding corporeal excellence, and both aided in producing results in which his remarkable strength was equally apparent. In all games depending upon the combination of muscle and skill, he had scarce rivalry enough to keep him in practice. His strength, however, was embodied in such a softness of muscular outline, such a rare Greek-like style of beauty, and associated with such gentleness of manner and behaviour, that partly from the truth of the resemblance, partly from the absurdity of the contrast, he was known throughout the university by the diminutive of the feminine form of his name, and was always called Lottchen.

"I say, Lottchen," said one of his fellow-students, called Richter, across the table in a wine cellar they were in the habit of frequenting, "do you know, Heinrich Höllenrachen here says that he saw this morning, with mortal eyes, whom do you think? Lilith."

"Adam's first wife?" asked Lottchen, with an attempt at carelessness, while his face flushed like a maiden's.

"None of your chaff!" said Richter. "Your face is honester than your tongue, and confesses what you cannot deny, that you would give your chance of salvation—a small one to be sure, but all you've got—for one peep at Lilith. Wouldn't you now, Lottchen?"

"Go to the devil!" was all Lottchen's answer to his tormentor; but he turned to Heinrich, to whom the students had given the surname above mentioned, because of the enormous width of his jaws, and said with eagerness and envy, disguising them as well as he could, under the appearance of curiosity:

"You don't mean it, Heinrich? You've been taking the beggar in! Confess now."

"Not I. I saw her with my two eyes."

"Notwithstanding the different planes of their orbits," suggested Richter.

"Yes, notwithstanding the fact that I can get a parallax to any of the fixed stars in a moment, with only the breadth of my nose for the base," answered Heinrich, responding at once to the fun, and careless of the personal defect insinuated. "She was near enough for even me to see her perfectly."

"When? Where? How?" asked Lottchen.

"Two hours ago. In the churchyard of St. Stephen's. By a lucky chance. Anymore little questions, my child?" answered Höllenrachen.

"What could have taken her there, who is seen nowhere?" said Richter.

"She was seated on a grave. After she left, I went to the place; but it was a new-made grave. There was no stone up. I asked the sexton about her. He said he supposed she was the daughter of the woman buried there last Thursday week. I knew it was Lilith."

"Her mother dead?" said Lottchen, musingly. Then he thought with himself—"She will be going there again, then!" But he took care that this ghost-thought should wander unembodied. "But how did you know her, Heinrich? You never saw her before."

"How do you come to be over head and ears in love with her, Lottchen, and you haven't seen her at all?" interposed Richter.

"Will you or will you not go to the devil?" rejoined Lottchen, with a comic *crescendo*; to which the other replied with a laugh.

"No one could miss knowing her," said Heinrich.

"Is she so very like, then?"

"It is always herself, her very self."

A fresh flask of wine, turning out to be not up to the mark, brought the current of conversation against itself; not much to the dissatisfaction of Lottchen, who had already resolved to be in the churchyard of St. Stephen's at sun-down the following day, in the hope that he too might be favoured with a vision of Lilith.

This resolution he carried out. Seated in a porch of the church, not knowing in what direction to look for the apparition he hoped to see, and desirous as well of not seeming to be on the watch for one, he was gazing at the fallen rose-leaves of the sunset withering away upon the sky; when, glancing aside by an involuntary movement, he saw a woman seated upon a new-made grave, not many yards from where he sat with her face buried in her hands, and apparently weeping bitterly. Karl was in the shadow of the porch, and could see her perfectly, without much danger of being discovered by her; so he sat and watched her. She raised her head for a moment and the rose-flush of the west fell over it, shining on the tears with which it was wet, and giving the whole a bloom which did not belong to it, for it was always pale, and now pale as death. It was indeed the face of Lilith, the most celebrated beauty of Prague.

Again she buried her face in her hands; and Karl sat with a strange feeling of helplessness, which grew as he sat; and the longing to help her whom he could not help, drew his heart towards her with a trembling reverence which was quite new to him. She wept on. The western roses withered slowly away, and the clouds blended with the sky, and the stars gathered like drops of glory sinking through the vault of night, and the trees about the churchyard grew black, and Lilith almost vanished in the wide darkness. At length she lifted her head, and seeing the night around her, gave a little broken cry of dismay. The minutes had swept over her head, not through her mind, and she did not know that the dark had come.

Hearing her cry, Karl rose and approached her. She heard his footsteps, and started to her feet Karl spoke—

"Do not be frightened," he said. "Let me see you home. I will walk behind you."

"Who are you?" she rejoined.

"Karl Wolkenlicht"

"I have heard of you. Thank you. I can go home alone."

Yet as if in a half-dreamy, half-unconscious mood, she accepted his offered hand to lead her through the graves, and allowed him to walk beside her, till, reaching the corner of a narrow street, she suddenly bade him good night and vanished. He thought it better not to follow her, so he returned her good night and went home.

How to see her again was his first thought the next day; as, in fact how to see her at all had been his first thought for many days. She went nowhere that ever he heard of; she knew nobody that he knew; she was never seen at church, or at market; never seen in the street. Her home had a dreary, desolate aspect. It looked as if no one ever went out or in. It was like a place on which decay had fallen because there was no indwelling spirit. The mud of years was baked upon its door, and no faces looked out of its dusty windows.

How then could she be the most celebrated beauty of Prague? How, then, was it that Heinrich Höllenrachen knew her the moment he saw her? Above all, how was it that Karl Wolkenlicht had, in fact fallen in love with her before ever he saw her? It was thus:

Her father was a painter. Belonging thus to the public, it had taken the liberty of re-naming him. Everyone called him Teufelsbürst, or Devilsbrush. It was a name with which, to judge from the nature of his representations, he could hardly fail to be pleased. For, not as a nightmare-dream, which may alternate with the loveliest visions, but as his ordinary everyday work, he delighted to represent human suffering.

Not an aspect of human woe or torture, as expressed in countenance or limb, came before his willing imagination, but he bore it straightway to his easel. In the moments that precede sleep, when the black space before the eyes of the poet teems with lovely faces, or dawns into a spirit-landscape, face after face of suffering, in all varieties of expression, would crowd, as if compelled by the accompanying fiends, to present themselves, in awful levée, before the inner eye of the expectant master. Then he would rise, light his lamp, and, with rapid hand, make notes of his visions; recording with swift successive sweeps of his pencil, every individual face which had rejoiced his evil fancy. Then he would return to his couch, and, well satisfied, fall asleep, to dream yet further embodiments of human ill.

What wrong could man or mankind have done him, to be thus fearfully pursued by the vengeance of the artist's hate?

Another characteristic of the faces and forms which he drew was that they were all beautiful in the original idea. The lines of each face, however distorted by pain, would have been, in rest, absolutely beautiful; and the whole of the execution bore witness to the fact that upon this original beauty the painter had directed the artillery of anguish, to bring down the sky-soaring heights of its divinity to the level of a hated existence. To do this, he worked in perfect accordance with artistic law, falsifying no line of the original forms. It was the suffering, rather than his pencil, that wrought the change. The latter was the willing instrument to record what the imagination conceived with a cruelty composed enough to be correct.

To enhance the beauty he had thus distorted, and so to enhance yet further the suffering that produced the distortion, he would often represent attendant demons, whom he made as ugly as his imagination could compass; avoiding, however, all grotesqueness beyond what was sufficient to indicate that they were demons, and not men. Their ugliness rose from hate, envy, and all evil passions; amongst which he especially delighted to represent a gloating exultation over human distress. And often in the midst of his clouds of demon faces, would someone who knew him recognise the painter's own likeness, such as the mirror might have presented it to him when he was busiest over the incarnation of some exquisite torture.

But, apparently with the wish to avoid being supposed to choose such representations for their own sakes, he always found a story, often in the histories of the church, whose name he gave to the painting, and which he pretended to have inspired the pictorial conception. No one, however, who looked upon his suffering martyrs, could suppose for a moment that he honoured their martyrdom. They were but the vehicles for his hate of humanity. He was the torturer, and not Diocletian or Nero.

But, stranger yet to tell, there was no picture, whatever its subject, into which he did not introduce one form of placid and harmonious loveliness. In this, however, his fierceness was only more fully displayed. For in no case did this form manifest any relation either to the actors or the endurers in the picture. Hence its very loveliness became almost hateful to those who beheld it. Not a shade crossed the still sky of that brow, not a ripple disturbed the still sea of that cheek. She did not hate, she did not love the sufferers: the painter would not have her hate, for that would be to the injury of her loveliness; would not have her love, for he hated. Sometimes she floated above, as a still, unobservant angel, her gaze turned upward, dreaming along, careless as a white summer cloud, across the blue. If she looked down on the scene below, it was only that the beholder might see that she saw and did not care—that not a feather of her outspread pinions would quiver at the sight. Sometimes she would stand in the crowd, as if she had been copied there from another picture, and had nothing to do with this one, nor any right to be in it at all. Or when the red blood was trickling drop by drop from the crushed limb, she might be seen standing nearest smiling over a primrose or the bloom on a peach. Some had said that she was the painter's wife; that she had been false to him; that he had killed her; and, finding that that was no sufficing revenge, thus half in love, and half in deepest hate, immortalized his vengeance. But it was now universally understood that it was his daughter, of whose loveliness extravagant reports went abroad; though all said, doubtless reading this from her father's pictures, that she was a beauty without a heart. Strange theories of something else supplying its place were rife among the anatomical students. With the girl in the pictures, the wild imagination of Lottchen, probably in part from her apparently absolute unattainableness and her undisputed heartlessness, had fallen in love, as far as the mere imagination can fall in love.

But again, how was he to see her? He haunted the house night after night. Those blue eyes never met his. No step responsive to his came from that door. It seemed to have been so long unopened that it had grown as fixed and hard as the stones that held its bolts in their passive clasp. He dared not watch in the daytime, and with all his watching at night, he never saw father or daughter or domestic cross the threshold. Little he thought that, from a shot-window near the door, a pair of blue eyes, like Lilith's, but paler and colder, were watching him, just as a spider watches the fly that is likely ere long to fall into his toils. And into those toils Karl soon fell. For her form darkened the page; her form stood on the threshold of sleep; and when, overcome with watching, he did enter its precincts, her form entered with him, and walked by his side. He must find her; or the world might go to the bottomless pit for him. But how?

Yes. He would be a painter. Teufelsbürst would receive him as a humble apprentice. He would grind his colours, and Teufelsbürst would teach him the mysteries of the science which is the handmaiden of art. Then he might see *her*, and that was all his ambition.

In the clear morning light of a day in autumn, when the leaves were beginning to fall seared from the hand of that Death which has his dance in the chapels of nature as well as in the cathedral aisles of men—he walked up and knocked at the dingy door. The spider painter opened it himself. He was a little man, meagre and pallid, with those faded blue eyes, a low nose in three distinct divisions, and thin, curveless, cruel lips. He wore no hair on his face; but long grey locks, long as a woman's, were scattered over his shoulders, and hung down on his breast. When Wolkenlicht had explained his errand, he smiled a smile in which hypocrisy could not hide the cunning, and, after many difficulties, consented to receive him as a pupil, on condition that he would become an inmate of his house. Wolkenlicht's heart bounded with delight, which he tried to hide: the second smile of Teufelsbürst might have shown him that he had ill succeeded. The fact that he was not a native of Prague, but, coming from a distant part of the country, was entirely his own master in the city, rendered this condition perfectly easy to fulfil; and that very afternoon, he entered the studio of Teufelsbürst as his scholar and servant.

It was a great room, filled with the appliances and results of art. Many pictures, festooned with cobwebs, were hung carelessly on the dirty walls. Others, half finished, leaned against them on the floor. Several, in different stages of progress, stood upon easels. But all spoke the cruel bent of the artist's genius. In one corner a lay-figure was extended on a couch, covered with a pall of black velvet. Through its folds, the form beneath was easily discernible; and one hand and forearm protruded from beneath it at right angles to the rest of the frame. Lottchen could not help shuddering when he saw it. Although he overcame the feeling in a moment, he felt a great repugnance to seating himself with his back towards it, as the arrangement of an easel, at which Teufelsbürst wished him to draw, rendered necessary. He contrived to edge himself round, so that when he lifted his eyes he should see the figure, and be sure that it could not rise without his being aware of it. But his master saw and understood his altered position; and under some pretence about the light, compelled him to resume the position in which he had placed him at first; after which he sat watching, over the top of his picture, the expression of his countenance as he tried to draw; reading in it the horrid fancy that the figure under the pall had risen, and was stealthily approaching to look over his shoulder. But Lottchen resisted the feeling, and, being already no contemptible draughtsman, was soon interested enough to forget it. And then, any moment, *she* might enter.

Now began a system of slow torture, for the chance of which the painter had been long on the watch—especially since he had first seen Karl lingering about the house. His opportunities of seeing physical suffering were nearly enough even for the diseased necessities of his art; but now he had one in his power, on whom, his own will fettering him, he could try any experiments he pleased for the production of a kind of suffering, in the observation of which he did not consider that he had yet had sufficient experience. He would hold the very heart of the youth in his hand, and wring it and torture it to his own content. And lest Karl should be strong enough to prevent those expressions of pain for which he lay on the watch, he would make use of further means, known to himself, and known to few besides.

All that day Karl saw nothing of Lilith; but he heard her voice once—and that was enough for one day. The next, she was sitting for her father the greater part of the day, and he could see her as often as he dared glance up from his drawing. She had looked at him when she entered, but had shown no sign of recognition; and all day long she took no further notice of him. He hoped, at first, that this came of the intelligence of love; but he soon began to doubt it. For he saw that with the holy shadow of sorrow, all that distinguished the expression of her countenance from that which the painter so constantly reproduced, had vanished likewise. It was the very face of the unheeding angel whom, as often as he lifted his eyes higher than hers, he saw on the wall above her, playing on a psaltery in the smoke of the torment ascending forever from burning Babylon. The power of the painter had not merely wrought for the representation of the woman of his imagination: it had had scope as well in realizing her.

Karl soon began to see that communication, other than of the eyes, was all but hopeless; and to any attempt in that way she seemed altogether indisposed to respond. Nor, if she had wished it, would it have been safe; for as often as he glanced towards her, instead of hers, he met the blue eyes of the painter, gleaming upon him like winter-lightning. His tones, his gestures, his words, seemed kind: his glance and his smile refused to be disguised.

The first day he dined alone in the studio, waited upon by an old woman; the next he was admitted to the family table, with

Teufelsbürst and Lilith. The room offered a strange contrast to the study. As far as handicraft, directed by a sumptuous taste, could construct a house-paradise, this was one. But it seemed rather a paradise of demons; for the walls were covered with Teufelsbürst's paintings. During the dinner Lilith's gaze scarcely met that of Wolkenlicht; and once or twice, when their eyes did meet, her glance was so perfectly unconcerned, that Karl wished he might look at her forever without the fear of her looking at him again. She seemed like one whose love had rushed out glowing with seraphic fire, to be frozen to death in a more than wintry cold: she now walked lonely without her love. In the evenings, he was expected to continue his drawing by lamplight; and at night he was conducted by Teufelsbürst to his chamber. Not once did he leave him there without locking and bolting the door on the outside. But he felt nothing except the coldness of Lilith.

Day after day she sat for her father, in every variety of costume that could best show the variety of her beauty. How much greater that beauty might be, if it ever blossomed into a beauty of soul, Wolkenlicht never imagined; for he soon loved her enough to attribute to her all the possibilities of her face as actual possessions of her being. To account for everything that seemed to contradict this perfection, his brain was prolific in inventions; till he was compelled at last to see that she was in the condition of a rosebud, which, on the point of blossoming, has been chilled into a changeless bud by the cold of an untimely frost. For one day, after the father and daughter had become a little more accustomed to his silent presence, a conversation began between them, which went on until he saw that Teufelsbürst believed in nothing except his art. How much of his feeling for that could be dignified by the name of belief, seeing its objects were such as they were, might have been questioned. It seemed to Wolkenlicht to amount only to this: that amidst a thousand distastes, it was a pleasant thing to re-produce on the canvas the forms he beheld around him, modifying them to express the prevailing feelings of his own mind.

A more desolate communication between souls than that which then passed between father and daughter could hardly be imagined. The father spoke of humanity and all its experiences in a tone of the bitterest scorn. He despised men and himself amongst them; and rejoiced to think that the generations rose and vanished, brood after brood, as the crops of corn grew and disappeared. Lilith, who listened to it all unmoved, taking only an intellectual interest in the question, remarked that even the corn had more life than that; for, after its death, it rose again in the new crop. Whether she meant that the corn was therefore superior to man, forgetting that the superior can produce being without losing its own, or only advanced an objection to her father's argument, Wolkenlicht could not tell. But Teufelsbürst laughed like the sound of a saw, and said: "Follow out the analogy, my Lilith, and you will see that man is like the corn that springs again after it is buried; but unfortunately the only result we know of is a vampire."

Wolkenlicht looked up, and saw a shudder pass through the frame, and over the pale thin face of the painter. This he could not account for. But Teufelsbürst could have explained it, for there were strange whispers abroad, and they had reached his ear; and his philosophy was not quite enough for them. But the laugh with which Lilith met this frightful attempt at wit, grated dreadfully on Wolkenlicht's feeling. With her, too, however, a reaction seemed to follow. For, turning round a moment after, and looking at the picture on which her father was working, the tears rose in her eyes, and she said: "Oh! Father, how like my mother you have made me this time!" "Child!" retorted the painter with a cold fierceness, "you have no mother. That which is gone out is gone out. Put no name in my hearing on that which is not. Where no substance is, how can there be a name?"

Lilith rose and left the room. Wolkenlicht now understood that Lilith was a frozen bud, and could not blossom into a rose. But pure love lives by faith. It loves the vaguely beheld and unrealized ideal. It dares believe that the loved is not all that she ever seemed. It is in virtue of this that love lives on. And it was in virtue of this, that Wolkenlicht loved Lilith yet more after he discovered what a grave of misery her unbelief was digging for her within her own soul. For her sake he would bear anything—bear even with calmness the torments of his own love; he would stay on, hoping and hoping. The text, that we know not what a day may bring forth, is just as true of good things as of evil things; and out of Time's womb the facts must come.

But with the birth of this resolution to endure, his suffering abated; his face grew more calm; his love, no less earnest, was less imperious; and he did not look up so often from his work when Lilith was present. The master could see that his pupil was more at ease, and that he was making rapid progress in his art. This did not suit his designs, and he would betake himself to his further schemes.

For this purpose he proceeded first to simulate a friendship for Wolkenlicht the manifestations of which he gradually increased, until, after a day or two, he asked him to drink wine with him in the evening. Karl readily agreed. The painter produced some of his best; but took care not to allow Lilith to taste it; for he had cunningly prepared and mingled with it a decoction of certain herbs and other ingredients, exercising specific actions upon the brain, and tending to the inordinate excitement of those portions of it which are principally under the rule of the imagination. By the reaction of the brain during the operation of these stimulants, the imagination is filled with suggestions and images. The nature of these determined by the prevailing mood of the time. They are such as the imagination would produce of itself; but increased in number and intensity. Teufelsbürst, without philosophizing about it, called his preparation simply a love-philtre, a concoction well known by name, but the composition of which was the secret of only a few. Wolkenlicht had, of course, not the least suspicion of the treatment to which he was subjected.

Teufelsbürst was, however, doomed to fresh disappointment. Not that his potion failed in the anticipated effect for now Karl's real sufferings began; but that such was the strength of Karl's will, and his fear of doing anything that might give a pretext for banishing him from the presence of Lilith, that he was able to conceal his feelings far too successfully for the satisfaction of Teufelsbürst's art. Yet he had to fetter himself with all the restraints that self-exhortation could load him with, to refrain from falling at the feet of Lilith and kissing the hem of her garment. For that as the lowliest part of all that surrounded her, itself kissing the earth, seemed to come nearest within the reach of his ambition, and therefore to draw him the most.

No doubt the painter had experience and penetration enough to perceive that he was suffering intensely; but he wanted to see the suffering embodied in outward signs, bringing it within the region over which his pencil held sway. He kept on, therefore, trying one thing after another, and rousing the poor youth to agony; till to his other sufferings were added, at length, those of failing health; a fact which notified itself evidently enough even for Teufelsbürst, though its signs were not of the sort he chiefly desired. But Karl endured all bravely.

Meantime, for various reasons, he scarcely ever left the house.

I must now interrupt the course of my story to introduce another element.

A few years before the period of my tale, a certain shoemaker of the city had died under circumstances more than suggestive of suicide. He was buried, however, with such precautions, that six weeks elapsed before the rumour of the facts broke out; upon which rumour, not before, the most fearful reports began to be circulated, supported by what seemed to the people of Prague incontestable evidence. A *spectrum* of the deceased appeared to multitudes of persons, playing horrible pranks, and occasioning indescribable consternation throughout the whole town. This went on till at last, about eight months after his burial, the magistrates caused his body to be dug up; when it was found in just the condition of the bodies of those who in the eastern countries of Europe are called *vampires*. They buried the corpse under the gallows; but neither the digging up nor the re-burying were of avail to banish the spectre. Again the spade and pickaxe were set to work, and the dead man, being found considerably improved in *condition* since his last interment, was, with various horrible indignities, burnt to ashes, "after which the *spectrum* was never seen more."

And a second epidemic of the same nature had broken out a little before the period to which I have brought my story.

About midnight, after a calm frosty day, for it was now winter, a terrible storm of wind and snow came on. The tempest howled frightfully about the house of the painter, and Wolkenlicht found some solace in listening to the uproar, for his troubled thoughts would not allow him to sleep. It raged on all the next three days, till about noon on the fourth day, when it suddenly fell, and all was calm. The following night, Wolkenlicht, lying awake, heard unaccountable noises in the next house, as of things thrown about, of kicking and fighting horses, and of opening and shutting gates. Flinging wide his lattice and looking out, the noise of howling dogs came to him from every quarter of the town. The moon was bright and the air was still. In a little while he heard the sounds of a horse going at full gallop round the house, so that it shook as if it would fall; and flashes of light shone into his room. How much of this may have been owing to the effect of the drugs on poor Lottchen's brain, I leave my readers to determine. But when the family met at breakfast in the morning, Teufelsbürst who had been already out of doors, reported that he had found the marks of strange feet in the snow, all about the house and through the garden at the back; stating, as his belief, that the tracks must be continued over the roofs, for there was no passage otherwise. There was a wicked gleam in his eye as he spoke; and Lilith believed that he was only trying an experiment on Karl's nerves. He persisted that he had never seen any footprints of the sort before. Karl informed him of his experiences during the night; upon which Teufelsbürst looked a little graver still, and proceeded to tell them that the storm, whose snow was still covering the ground, had arisen the very moment that their next-door neighbour died, and had ceased as suddenly the moment he was buried, though it had raved furiously all the time of the funeral, so that "it made men's bodies quake and their teeth chatter in their heads." Karl had heard that the man, whose name was John Kuntz, was dead and buried. He knew that he had been a very wealthy, and therefore most respectable, alderman of the town; that he had been very fond of horses; and that he had died in consequence of a kick received from one of his own, as he was looking at his hoof. But he had not heard that, just before he died, a black cat "opened the casement with her nails, ran to his bed, and violently scratched his face and the bolster, as if she endeavoured by force to remove him out of the place where he lay. But the cat afterwards was suddenly gone, and she was no sooner gone, but he breathed his last."

So said Teufelsbürst, as the reporter of the town-talk. Lilith looked very pale and terrified; and it was perhaps owing to this that the painter brought no more tales home with him. There were plenty to bring, but he heard them all and said nothing. The fact was that the philosopher himself could not resist the infection of the fear that was literally raging in the city; and perhaps the reports that he himself had sold himself to the devil, had sufficient response from his own evil conscience to add to the influence of the epidemic upon him. The whole place was infested with the presence of the dead Kuntz, till scarce a man or woman would dare to be alone. He strangled old men; insulted women; squeezed children to death; knocked out the brains of dogs against the ground; pulled up posts; turned milk into blood; nearly killed a worthy clergyman by breathing upon him the intolerable airs of the grave, cold and malignant and noisome; and, in short, filled the city with a perfect madness of fear, so that every report was believed without the smallest doubt or investigation.

Though Teufelsbürst brought home no more of the town-talk, the old servant was a faithful purveyor, and frequented the news-mart assiduously. Indeed she had some nightmare experiences of her own that she was proud to add to the stock of horrors which the city enjoyed with such a hearty community of goods. For those regions were not far removed from the very birth-place and home of the vampire. The belief in vampires is the quintessential concentration and embodiment of all the passion of fear in Hungary and the adjacent regions. Nor of all the other inventions of the human imagination, has there ever been one so perfect in crawling terror as this. Lilith and Karl were quite familiar with the popular ideas on the subject. It did not require to be explained to them, that a vampire was a body retaining a kind of animal life after the soul had departed. If any relation continued between it and the vanished ghost, it was only sufficient to make it restless in its grave. Possessed of vitality enough to keep it uncorrupted and pliant, its only instinct was a blind hunger for the sole food which could keep its awful life persistent—living human blood. Hence it, or if not it, a sort of semi-material exhalation of essence of it, retaining its form and material relations, crept from its tomb, and went roaming about till it found someone asleep, towards whom it had an attraction, founded on old affection. It sucked the blood of this unhappy being, transferring so much of its life to itself as a vampire could assimilate. Death was the certain consequence. If suspicion conjectured aright, and they opened the proper grave, the body of the vampire would be found perfectly fresh and plump, sometimes indeed of rather florid complexion; with grown hair, eyes half open, and the stains of recent blood about its greedy leechlike lips. Nothing remained but to consume the corpse to ashes, upon which the vampire would show itself no more. But what added infinitely to the horror was the certainty that whoever died from the mouth of the vampire, wrinkled grandsire, or delicate maiden, must in turn rise from the grave, and go forth a vampire, to suck the blood of the dearest left behind. This was the generation of the vampire brood. Lilith trembled at the very name of the creature. Karl was too much in love to be afraid of anything. Yet the evident fear of the unbelieving painter took a hold of his imagination; and, under the influence of the potions of which he still partook unwittingly—when he was not thinking about Lilith, he was thinking about the vampire.

Meantime, the condition of things in the painter's household continued much the same for Wolkenlicht—work all day; no communication between the young people; the dinner and the wine; silent reading when work was done, with stolen glances many over the top of the book, glances that were never returned; the cold good night; the locking of the door, the wakeful night and the drowsy morning. But at length a change came, and sooner than any of the party had expected. For, whether it was that the impatience of Teufelsbürst had urged him to yet more dangerous experiments, or that the continuance of those he had been so long employing had overcome at length the vitality of Wolkenlicht—one afternoon, as he was sitting at his work, he suddenly dropped from his chair, and his master hurrying to him in some alarm, found him rigid and apparently lifeless. Lilith was not in the study when this took place. Injustice to Teufelsbürst, it must be confessed that he employed all the skill he was master of, which for beneficent purposes was not very great, to restore the youth; but without avail. At last, hearing the footsteps of Lilith, he desisted in some consternation; and that she might escape being shocked by the sight of a dead body where she had been accustomed to see a living one, he removed the lay figure from the couch, and laid Karl in its place, covering him with the black velvet pall. He was just in time. She started at seeing no one in Karl's place, and said:

"Where is your pupil, father?"

"Gone home," he answered, with a kind of convulsive grin.

She glanced round the room, caught sight of the lay figure where it had not been before, looked at the couch, and saw the pall yet heaved up from beneath, opened her eyes till the entire white sweep around the iris suggested a new expression of consternation to Teufelsbürst, though from a quarter whence he did not desire or look for it; and then, without a word, sat down to a drawing she had been busy upon the day before. But her father, glancing at her now, as Wolkenlicht had used to do, could not help seeing that she was frightfully pale. She showed no other sign of uneasiness. As soon as he released her, she withdrew, with one more glance, as she passed, at the couch and the figure blocked out in black upon it. She hastened to her chamber, shut and locked the door, sat down on the side of the couch, and fell, not a-weeping, but a-thinking. Was he dead? What did it matter? They would all be dead soon. Her mother was dead already. It was only that earth could not bear more children, except she devoured those to whom she had already given birth. But what if they had to come back in another form, and live another sad, hopeless, loveless life over again? And so she went on questioning, and receiving no replies; while through all her thoughts passed and repassed the eyes of Wolkenlicht, which she had often felt to be upon her when she did not see them, wild with repressed longing, the light of their love shining through the veil of diffused tears, ever gathering and never overflowing. Then came the pale face, so worshiping, so distant in its self-withdrawn devotion, slowly dawning out of the vapours of her reverie. When it vanished, she tried to see it again. It would not come when she called it; but when her thoughts left knocking at the door of the lost and wandered away, out came the pale, troubled, silent face again, gathering itself up from some unknown nook in her world of phantasy, and once more, when she tried to steady it by the fixedness of her own regard, fading back into the mist. So the phantasm of the dead drew near and wooed, as the living had never dared. What if there were any good in loving? What if men and women did not die all out, but some dim shade of each, like that pale, mind-ghost of Wolkenlicht floated through the eternal vapours of chaos? And what if they might sometimes cross each other's path, meet, know that they met, love on? Would not that revive the withered memory, fix the fleeting ghost, give a new habitation, a body even, to the poor, unhoused wanderers, frozen by the eternal frosts, no longer thinking beings, but thoughts wandering through the brain of the "Melancholy Mass"? Back with the thought came the face of the dead Karl, and the maiden threw herself on her bed in a flood of bitter tears. She could have loved him if he had only lived: she did love him, for he was dead. But even in the midst of the remorse that followed, for had she not killed him? Life seemed a less hard and hopeless thing than before. For it is love itself and not its responses or results that is the soul of life and its pleasures.

Two hours passed ere she could again show herself to her father, from whom she seemed in some new way divided by the new feeling in which he did not, and could not share. But at last, lest he should seek her, and finding her, should suspect her thoughts, she descended and sought him. For there is a maidenliness in sorrow, that wraps her garments close around her. But he was not to be seen; the door of the study was locked. A shudder passed through her as she thought of what her father, who lost no opportunity of furthering his all but perfect acquaintance with the human form and structure, might be about with the figure which she knew lay dead beneath that velvet pall, but which had arisen to haunt the hollow caves and cells of her living brain. She rushed away, and up once more to her silent room, through the darkness which had now settled down in the house; threw herself again on her bed, and lay almost paralysed with horror and distress.

But Teufelsbürst was not about anything so frightful as she supposed, though something frightful enough. I have already implied that Wolkenlicht was, in form, as fine an embodiment of youthful manhood as any old Greek republic could have provided one of its sculptors with as model for an Apollo. It is true, that to the eye of a Greek artist he would not have been more acceptable in consequence of the regimen he had been going through for the last few weeks; but the emaciation of Wolkenlicht's frame, and the consequent prominence of the muscles, indicating the pain he had gone through, were peculiarly attractive to Teufelsbürst. He was busy preparing to take a cast of the body of his dead pupil, that it might aid to the perfection of his future labours.

He was deep in the artistic enjoyment of a form, at the same time so beautiful and strong, yet with the lines of suffering in every limb and feature, when his daughter's hand was laid on the latch. He started, flung the velvet drapery over the body, and went to the door. But Lilith had vanished. He returned to his labours. The operation took a long time, for he performed it very carefully. Towards midnight, he had finished encasing the body in a close-clinging shell of plaster, which, when broken off, and fitted together, would be the matrix to the form of the dead Wolkenlicht. Before leaving it to harden till the morning, he was just proceeding to strengthen it with an additional layer all over, when a flash of lightning, reflected in all its dazzle from the snow without, almost blinded him. A peal of long-drawn thunder followed; the wind rose; and just such a storm came on as had risen some time before at the death of Kuntz, whose spectre was still tormenting the city. The gnomes of terror, deep hidden in the caverns of Teufelsbürst's nature, broke out jubilant. With trembling hands he tried to cast the pall over the awful white chrysalis, failed, and fled to his chamber. And there lay the studio naked to the eyes of the lightning, with its tortured forms throbbing out of the dark, and quivering, as with life, in the almost continuous palpitations of the light; while on the couch lay the motionless mass of whiteness, gleaming blue in the lightning, almost more terrible in its crude indications of the human form, than that which it enclosed. It lay there as if dropped from some tree of chaos, haggard with the snows of eternity—a huge misshapen nut, with a corpse for its kernel.

But the lightning would soon have revealed a more terrible sight still, had there been any eyes to behold it. At midnight while a peal of thunder was just dying away in the distance, the crust of death flew asunder, rending in all directions; and, pale as his investiture, staring with ghastly eyes, the form of Karl started up, sitting on the couch. Had he not been far beyond ordinary men in strength, he could not thus have rent his sepulchre. Indeed, had Teufelsbürst been able to finish his task by the additional layer of gypsum which he contemplated, he must have died the moment life revived; although, so long

THE CRUEL PAINTER

as the trance lasted, neither the exclusion from the air, nor the practical solidification of the walls of his chest, could do him any injury. He had lain unconscious throughout the operations of Teufelsbürst, but now the catalepsy had passed away, possibly under the influence of the electric condition of the atmosphere. Very likely the strength he now put forth was intensified by a convulsive reaction of all the powers of life, as is not unfrequently the case in sudden awakenings from similar interruptions of vital activity. The coming to himself and the bursting of his case were simultaneous. He sat staring about him, with of all his mental faculties, only his imagination awake, from which the thoughts that occupied it when he fell senseless had not yet faded. These thoughts had been compounded of feelings about Lilith, and speculations about the vampire that haunted the neighbourhood; and the fumes of the last drug of which he had partaken, still hovering in his brain, combined with these thoughts and fancies to generate the delusion that he had just broken from the embrace of his coffin, and risen, the last-born of the vampire-race. The sense of unavoidable obligation to fulfil his doom, was yet mingled with a faint flutter of joy, for he knew that he must go to Lilith. With a deep sigh, he rose, gathered up the pall of black velvet, flung it around him, stepped from the couch, and left the study to find her.

Meantime, Teufelsbürst had sufficiently recovered to remember that he had left the door of the studio unfastened, and that anyone entering would discover in what he had been engaged, which, in the case of his getting into any difficulty about the death of Karl, would tell powerfully against him. He was at the farther end of a long passage, leading from the house to the studio, on his way to make all secure, when Karl appeared at the door, and advanced towards him. The painter, seized with invincible terror, turned and fled. He reached his room, and fell senseless on the floor. The phantom held on its way, heedless.

Lilith, on gaining her room the second time, had thrown herself on her bed as before, and had wept herself into a troubled slumber. She lay dreaming—and dreadful dreams. Suddenly she awoke in one of those peals of thunder which tormented the high regions of the air, as a storm billows the surface of the ocean. She lay awake and listened. As it died away, she thought she heard, mingling with its last muffled murmurs, the sound of moaning. She turned her face towards the room in keen terror. But she saw nothing. Another light, long-drawn sigh reached her ear, and at the same moment a flash of lightning illumined the room. In the corner farthest from her bed, she spied a white face, nothing more. She was dumb and motionless with fear. Utter darkness followed, a darkness that seemed to enter into her very brain. Yet she felt that the face was slowly crossing the black gulf of the room, and drawing near to where she lay. The next flash revealed, as it bended over her, the ghastly face of Karl, down which flowed fresh tears. The rest of his form was lost in blackness. Lilith did not faint, but it was the very force of her fear that seemed to keep her alive. It became for the moment the atmosphere of her life. She lay trembling and staring at the spot in the darkness where she supposed the face of Karl still to be. But the next flash showed her the face far off, looking at her through the panes of her lattice-window.

For Lottchen, as soon as he saw Lilith, seemed to himself to go through a second stage of awaking. Her face made him doubt whether he could be a vampire after all; for instead of wanting to bite her arm and suck the blood, he all but fell down at her feet in a passion of speechless love. The next moment he became aware that his presence must be at least very undesirable to her; and in an instant he had reached her window, which he knew looked upon a lower roof that extended between two different parts of the house, and before the next flash came, he had stepped through the lattice and closed it behind him.

Believing his own room to be attainable from this quarter, he proceeded along the roof in the direction he judged best. The cold winter air by degrees restored him entirely to his right mind, and he soon comprehended the whole of the circumstances in which he found himself. Peeping through a window he was passing, to see whether it belonged to his room, he spied Teufelsbürst who, at the very moment was lifting his head from the faint into which he had fallen at the first sight of Lottchen. The moon was shining clear, and in its light the painter saw, to his horror, the pale face staring in at his window. He thought it had been there ever since he had fainted, and dropped again in a deeper swoon than before. Karl saw him fall, and the truth flashed upon him that the wicked artist took him for what he had believed himself to be when first he recovered from his trance—namely, the vampire of the former Karl Wolkenlicht. The moment he comprehended it, he resolved to keep up the delusion if possible. Meantime he was innocently preparing a new ingredient for the popular dish of horrors to be served at the ordinary of the city the next day. For the old servant's were not the only eyes that had seen him besides those of Teufelsbürst. What could be more like a vampire, dragging his pall after him, than this apparition of poor, half-frozen Lottchen, crawling across the roof? Karl remembered afterwards that he had heard the dogs howling awfully in every direction, as he crept along; but this was hardly necessary to make those who saw him conclude that it was the same phantasm of John Kuntz, which had been infesting the whole city, and especially the house next door to the painter's, which had been the dwelling of the respectable alderman who had degenerated into this most disreputable of moneyless vagabonds. What added to the consternation of all who heard of it was the sickening conviction that the extreme measures which they had resorted to in order to free the city from the ghoul, beyond which nothing could be done, had been utterly unavailing, successful as they had proved in every other known case of the kind. For, urged as well by various horrid signs about his grave, which not even its close proximity to the altar could render a place of repose, they had opened it, had found in the body every peculiarity belonging to a vampire, had pulled it out with the greatest difficulty on account of a quite supernatural ponderosity; which rendered the horse which had killed him—a strong animal—all but unable to drag it along, and had at last, after cutting it in pieces, and expending on the fire two hundred and sixteen great billets, succeeded in conquering its incombustibleness, and reducing it to ashes. Such, at least, was the story which had reached the painter's household, and was believed by many; and if all this did not compel the perturbed corpse to rest, what more could be done?

When Karl had reached his room, and was dressing himself, the thought struck him that something might be made of the report of the extreme weight of the body of old Kuntz, to favour the continuance of the delusion of Teufelsbürst, although he hardly knew yet to what use he could turn this delusion. He was convinced that he would have made no progress however long he might have remained in his house; and that he would have more chance of favour with Lilith if he were to meet her in any other circumstances whatever, than those in which he invariably saw her—namely, surrounded by her father's influences, and watched by her father's cold blue eyes.

As soon as he was dressed, he crept down to the studio, which was now quiet enough, the storm being over, and the moon filling it with her steady shine. In the corner lay in all directions the fragments of the mould which his own body had formed and filled. The bag of plaster and the bucket of water which the painter had been using stood beside. Lottchen gathered all the pieces together, and then making his way to an out-house where he had seen various odds and ends of rubbish lying, chose from the heap as many pieces of old iron and other metal as he could find. To these he added a few large stones from the garden. When he had got all into the studio, he locked the door, and proceeded to fit together the parts of the mould, filling up the hollow as he went on with the heaviest things he could get into it, and solidifying the whole by pouring in plaster; till, having at length completed it, and obliterated, as much as possible, the marks of joining, he left it to harden, with the conviction that now it would make a considerable impression on Teufelsbürst's imagination, as well as on his muscular sense. He then left everything else as nearly undisturbed as he could; and, knowing all the ways of the house, was soon in the street, without leaving any signs of his exit.

Karl soon found himself before the house in which his friend Höllenrachen resided. Knowing his studious habits, he had hoped to see his light still burning, nor was he disappointed. He contrived to bring him to his window, and a moment after, the door was cautiously opened.

"Why, Lottchen, where do you come from?"

"From the grave, Heinrich, or next door to it."

"Come in, and tell me all about it. We thought the old painter had made a model of you, and tortured you to death."

"Perhaps you were not far wrong. But get me a horn of ale, for even a vampire is thirsty, you know."

"A vampire!" exclaimed Heinrich, retreating a pace, and involuntarily putting himself upon his guard.

Karl laughed.

"My hand was warm, was it not old fellow?" he said. "Vampires are cold, all but the blood."

"What a fool I am!" rejoined Heinrich. "But you know we have been hearing such horrors lately that a fellow may be excused for shuddering a little when a pale-faced apparition tells him at two o'clock in the morning that he is a vampire, and thirsty, too."

Karl told him the whole story; and the mental process of regarding it for the sake of telling it, revealed to him pretty clearly some of the treatment of which he had been unconscious at the time. Heinrich was quite sure that his suspicions were correct. And now the question was, what was to be done next.

"At all events," said Heinrich, "we must keep you out of the way for some time. I will represent to my landlady that you are in hiding from enemies, and her heart will rule her tongue. She can let you have a garret-room, I know; and I will do as well as I can to bear you company. We shall have time then to invent some plan of operation."

To this proposal Karl agreed with hearty thanks, and soon all was arranged. The only conclusion they could yet arrive at was, that somehow or other the old demon-painter must be tamed.

Meantime, how fared it with Lilith? She too had no doubt that she had seen the body-ghost of poor Karl, and that the vampire had, according to rule, paid her the first visit because he loved her best. This was horrible enough if the vampire were not really the person he represented; but if in any sense it were Karl himself, at least it gave some expectation of a more prolonged existence than her father had taught her to look for; and if love anything like her mother's still lasted, even along with the habits of a vampire, there was something to hope for in the future. And then, though he had visited her, he had not, as far as she was aware, deprived her of a drop of blood. She could not be certain that he had not bitten her, for she had been in such a strange condition of mind that she might not have felt it, but she believed that he had restrained the impulses of his vampire nature, and had left her, lest he should yet yield to them. She fell fast asleep; and, when morning came, there was not, as far as she could judge, one of those triangular leech-like perforations to be found upon her whole body. Will it be believed that the moment she was satisfied of this, she was seized by a terrible jealousy, lest Karl should have gone and bitten someone else? Most people will wonder that she should not have gone out of her senses at once; but there was all the difference between a visit from a real vampire and a visit from a man she had begun to love, even although she took him for a vampire. All the difference does *not* lie in a name. They were very different causes, and the effects must be different.

When Teufelsbürst came down in the morning, he crept into the studio like a murderer. There lay the awful white block, seeming to his eyes just the same as he had left it. What was to be done with it? He dared not open it. Mould and model must go together. But whither? If inquiry should be made after Wolkenlicht and this were discovered anywhere on his premises, would it not be enough to bring him at once to the gallows? Therefore it would be dangerous to bury it in the garden; or in the cellar.

"Besides," thought he, with a shudder, "that would be to fix the vampire as a guest forever." And the horrors of the past night rushed back upon his imagination with renewed intensity. What would it be to have the dead Karl crawling about his house forever, now inside, now out, now sitting on the stairs, now staring in at the windows?

He would have dragged it to the bottom of his garden, past which the Moldau flowed, and plunged it into the stream; but then, should the spectre continue to prove troublesome, it would be almost impossible to reach the body so as to destroy it by fire; besides which, he could not do it without assistance, and the probability of discovery. If, however, the apparition should turn out to be no vampire, but only a respectable ghost, they might manage to endure its presence, till it should be weary of haunting them.

He resolved at last to convey the body for the meantime into a concealed cellar in the house, seeing something must be done before his daughter came down. Proceeding to remove it, his consternation was greatly increased when he discovered how the body had grown in weight since he had thus disposed of it, leaving on his mind scarcely a hope that it could turn out not to be a vampire after all. He could scarcely stir it, and there was but one whom he could call to his assistance—the old woman who acted as his housekeeper and servant.

He went to her room, roused her, and told her the whole story. Devoted to her master for many years, and not quite so sensitive to fearful influences as when less experienced in horrors, she showed immediate readiness to render him assistance. Utterly unable, however, to lift the mass between them, they could only drag and push it along; and such a slow toil was it that there was no time to remove the traces of its track, before Lilith came down and saw a broad white line leading from the door of the studio down the cellar-stairs. She knew in a moment what it meant; but not a word was uttered about the matter, and the name of Karl Wolkenlicht seemed to be entirely forgotten.

But how could the affairs of a house go on all the same when everyone of the household knew that a dead body lay in the cellar? Nay more, that, although it lay still and dead enough all day, it would come half alive at nightfall, and, turning the whole house into a sepulchre by its presence, go creeping about like a cat all over it in the dark—perhaps with phosphorescent eyes? So it was not surprising that the painter abandoned his studio early, and that the three found themselves together in the gorgeous room formerly described, as soon as twilight began to fall.

Already Teufelsbürst had begun to experience a kind of shrinking from the horrid faces in his own pictures, and to feel disgusted at the abortions of his own mind. But all that he and the old woman now felt was an increasing fear as the night drew on, a kind of sickening and paralysing terror. The thing down there would not lie quiet—at least its phantom in the cellars of their imagination would not. As much as possible, however, they avoided alarming Lilith, who, knowing all they knew, was as silent as they. But her mind was in a strange state of excitement partly from the presence of a new sense of love, the pleasure of which all the atmosphere of grief into which it grew could not totally quench. It comforted her somehow, as a child may comfort when his father is away.

Bedtime came, and no one made a move to go. Without a word spoken on the subject, the three remained together all night; the elders nodding and slumbering occasionally, and Lilith getting some share of repose on a couch. All night the shape of death might be somewhere about the house; but it did not disturb them. They heard no sound, saw no sight; and when the morning dawned, they separated, chilled and stupid, and for the time beyond fear, to seek repose in their private chambers. There they remained equally undisturbed.

But when the painter approached his easel a few hours after, looking more pale and haggard still than he was wont, from the fears of the night, a new bewilderment took possession of him. He had been busy with a fresh embodiment of his favourite subject, into which he had sketched the form of the student as the sufferer. He had represented poor Wolkenlicht as just beginning to recover from a trance, while a group of surgeons, unaware of the signs of returning life, were absorbed in a minute dissection of one of the limbs. At an open door he had painted Lilith passing, with her face buried in a bunch of sweet-peas. But when he came to the picture, he found, to his astonishment and terror, that the face of one of the group was now turned towards that of the victim, regarding his revival with demoniac satisfaction, and taking pains to prevent the others from discovering it. The face of this prince of torturers was that of Teufelsbürst himself. Lilith had altogether vanished, and in her place stood the dim vampire reiteration of the body that lay extended on the table, staring greedily at the assembled company. With trembling hands the painter removed the picture from the easel, and turned its face to the wall.

Of course this was the work of Lottchen. When he left the house, he took with him the key of a small private door, which was so seldom used that, while it remained closed, the key would not be missed, perhaps for many months. Watching the windows, he had chosen a safe time to enter, and had been hard at work all night on these alterations. Teufelsbürst attributed them to the vampire, and left the picture as he found it, not daring to put brush to it again.

The next night was passed much after the same fashion. But the fear had begun to die away a little in the hearts of the women, who did not know what had taken place in the study on the previous night. It burrowed, however, with gathered force in the vitals of Teufelsbürst. But this night likewise passed in peace; and before it was over, the old woman had taken to speculating in her own mind as to the best way of disposing of the body, seeing it was not at all likely to be troublesome. But when the painter entered his study in trepidation the next morning, he found that the form of the lovely Lilith was painted out of every picture in the room. This could not be concealed; and Lilith and the servant became aware that the studio was the portion of the house in haunting which the vampire left the rest in peace.

Karl recounted all the tricks he had played to his friend Heinrich, who begged to be allowed to bear him company the following night. To this Karl consented, thinking it would be considerably more agreeable to have a companion. So they took a couple of bottles of wine and some provisions with them, and before midnight found themselves snug in the study. They sat very quiet for some time, for they knew that if they were seen, two vampires would not be so terrible as one, and might occasion discovery. But at length Heinrich could bear it no longer.

"I say, Lottchen, let's go and look for your dead body. What has the old beggar done with it?"

"I think I know. Stop; let me peep out. All right! Come along."

With a lamp in his hand, he led the way to the cellars, and after searching about a little, they discovered it.

"It looks horrid enough," said Heinrich, "but I think a drop or two of wine would brighten it up a little."

So he took a bottle from his pocket and after they had had a glass apiece, he dropped a third in blots all over the plaster. Being red wine, it had the effect Höllenrachen desired.

"When they visit it next, they will know that the vampire can find the food he prefers," said he.

In a corner close by the plaster, they found the clothes Karl had worn.

"Hillo!" said Heinrich, "we'll make something of this find."

So he carried them with him to the study. There he got hold of the lay-figure.

"What are you about, Heinrich?"

"Going to make a scarecrow to keep the ravens off old Teufel's pictures," answered Heinrich, as he went on dressing the lay-figure in Karl's clothes. He next seated the creature at an easel with its back to the door, so that it should be the first thing the painter should see when he entered. Karl meant to remove this before he went, for it was too comical to fall in with the rest of his proceedings. But the two sat down to their supper, and by the time they had finished the wine, they thought they should like to go to bed. So they got up and went home, and Karl forgot the lay-figure, leaving it in busy motionlessness all night before the easel.

When Teufelsbürst saw it, he turned and fled with a cry that brought his daughter to his help. He rushed past her, able only to articulate:

"The vampire! The vampire! Painting!"

Far more courageous than he, because her conscience was more peaceful, Lilith passed on to the studio. She too recoiled a step or two when she saw the figure; but with the sight of the back of Karl, as she supposed it to be, came the longing to see the face that was on the other side. So she crept round and round by the wall, as far off as she could. The figure remained motionless. It was a strange kind of shock that she experienced when she saw the face, disgusting from its inanity. The absurdity next struck her; and with the absurdity flashed into her mind the conviction that this was not the doing of a vampire; for of all creatures under the moon, he could not be expected to be a humourist. A wild hope sprang up in her mind that Karl was not dead. Of this she soon resolved to make herself sure.

She closed the door of the studio; in the strength of her new hope, undressed the figure, put it in its place, concealed the garments—all the work of a few minutes; and then, finding her father just recovering from the worst of his fear, told him there was nothing in the studio but what ought to be there, and persuaded him to go and see. He not only saw no one, but found that no further liberties had been taken with his pictures. Reassured, he soon persuaded himself that the spectre in this case had been the offspring of his own terror-haunted brain. But he had no spirit for painting now. He wandered about the house, himself haunting it like a restless ghost.

When night came, Lilith retired to her own room. The waters of fear had begun to subside in the house; but the painter and his old attendant did not yet follow her example.

As soon, however, as the house was quite still, Lilith glided noiselessly down the stairs, went into the studio, where as yet there assuredly was no vampire, and concealed herself in a corner.

As it would not do for an earnest student like Heinrich to be away from his work very often, he had not asked to accompany Lottchen this time. And indeed Karl himself, a little anxious about the result of the scarecrow, greatly preferred going alone.

While she was waiting for what might happen, the conviction grew upon Lilith, as she reviewed all the past of the story, that these phenomena were the work of the real Karl, and of no vampire. In a few moments she was still more sure of this. Behind the screen where she had taken refuge, hung one of the pictures out of which her portrait had been painted the night before last. She had taken a lamp with her into the study, with the intention of extinguishing it the moment she heard any sign of approach; but as the vampire lingered, she began to occupy herself with examining the picture beside her. She had not looked at it long, before she wetted the tip of her forefinger, and began to rub away at the obliteration. Her suspicions were instantly confirmed: the substance employed was only a gummy wash over the paint. The delight she experienced at the discovery threw her into a mischievous humour.

"I will see," she said to herself, "whether I cannot match Karl Wolkenlicht at this game."

In a closet in the room hung a number of costumes, which Lilith had at different times worn for her father. Among them was a large white drapery, which she easily disposed as a shroud. With the help of some chalk, she soon made herself ghastly enough, and then placing her lamp on the floor behind the screen, and setting a chair over it, so that it should throw no light in any direction, she waited once more for the vampire. Nor had she much longer to wait. She soon heard a door move, the sound of which she hardly knew, and then the studio door opened. Her heart beat dreadfully, not with fear lest it should be a vampire after all, but with hope that it was Karl. To see him once more was too great joy. Would she not make up to him for all her coldness! But would he care for her now? Perhaps he had been quite cured of his longing for a hard heart like hers. She peeped. It was he sure enough, looking as handsome as ever. He was holding his light to look at her last work, and the expression of his face, even in regarding her handiwork, was enough to let her know that he loved her still. If she had not seen this, she dared not have shown herself from her hiding-place. Taking the lamp in her hand, she got upon the chair, and looked over the screen, letting the light shine from below upon her face. She then made a slight noise to attract Karl's attention. He looked up, evidently rather startled, and saw the face of Lilith in the air. He gave a stifled cry, threw himself on his knees, with his arms stretched towards her, and moaned—

"I have killed her! I have killed her!"

Lilith descended, and approached him noiselessly. He did not move. She came close to him and said:

"Are you Karl Wolkenlicht?"

His lips moved, but no sound came.

"If you are a vampire, and I am a ghost," she said—but a low happy laugh alone concluded the sentence.

Karl sprang to his feet Lilith's laugh changed into a burst of sobbing and weeping, and in another moment the ghost was in the arms of the vampire.

Lilith had no idea how far her father had wronged Karl, and though, from thinking over the past, he had no doubt that the painter had drugged him, he did not wish to pain her by imparting this conviction. But Lilith was afraid of a reaction of rage and hatred in her father after the terror was removed; and Karl saw that he might thus be deprived of all further intercourse with Lilith, and all chance of softening the old man's heart towards him; while Lilith would not hear of forsaking him who had banished all the human race but herself. They managed at length to agree upon a plan of operation.

The first thing they did was to go to the cellar where the plaster mass lay, Karl carrying with him a great axe used for cleaving wood. Lilith shuddered when she saw it, stained as it was with the wine Heinrich had spilt over it, and almost believed herself the midnight companion of a vampire after all, visiting with him the terrible corpse in which he lived all day. But Karl soon reassured her; and a few good blows of the axe revealed a very different core to that which Teufelsbürst supposed to be in it. Karl broke it into pieces, and with Lilith's help, who insisted on carrying her share, the whole was soon at the bottom of the Moldau, and every trace of its ever having existed removed. Before morning, too, the form of Lilith had dawned anew in every picture. There was no time to restore to its former condition the one Karl had first altered; for in it the changes were all that they seemed; nor indeed was he capable of restoring it in the master's style; but they put it quite out of the way, and hoped that sufficient time might elapse before the painter thought of it again.

When they had done, and Lilith, for all his entreaties, would remain with him no longer, Karl took his former clothes with him, and having spent the rest of the night in his old room, dressed in them in the morning. When Teufelsbürst entered his studio next day, there sat Karl, as if nothing had happened, finishing the drawing on which he had been at work when the fit of insensibility came upon him. The painter started, stared, rubbed his eyes, thought it was another spectral illusion, but was on the point of yielding to his terror, when Karl rose, and approached him with a smile. The healthy, sunshiny countenance of Karl, let him be ghost or goblin, could not fail to produce somewhat of a tranquillizing effect on

Teufelsbürst. He took his offered hand mechanically, his countenance utterly vacant with idiotic bewilderment Karl said:

"I was not well, and thought it better to pay a visit to a friend for a few days; but I shall soon make up for lost time, for I am all right now."

He sat down at once, taking no notice of his master's behaviour, and went on with his drawing. Teufelsbürst stood staring at him for some minutes without moving, then suddenly turned and left the room. Karl heard him hurrying down the cellar stairs. In a few moments he came up again. Karl stole a glance at him. There he stood in the same spot, no doubt more full of bewilderment than ever; but it was not possible that his face should express more. At last he went to his easel, and sat down with a long-drawn sigh as if of relief. But though he sat at his easel, he painted none that day; and as often as Karl ventured a glance, he saw him still staring at him. The discovery that his pictures were restored to their former condition aided, no doubt, in leading him to the same conclusion as the other facts, whatever that conclusion might be—probably that he had been the sport of some evil power, and had been for the greater part of a week utterly bewitched. Lilith had taken care to instruct the old woman, with whom she was all-powerful; and as neither of them showed the smallest traces of the astonishment which seemed to be slowly vitrifying his own brain, he was at last perfectly satisfied that things had been going on all right everywhere but in his inner man; and in this conclusion he certainly was not far wrong in more senses than one. But when all was restored again to the old routine, it became evident that the peculiar direction of his art in which he had hitherto indulged had ceased to interest him. The shock had acted chiefly upon that part of his mental being which had been so absorbed. He would sit for hours without doing anything, apparently plunged in meditation. Several weeks elapsed without any change, and both Lilith and Karl were getting dreadfully anxious about him. Karl paid him every attention; and the old man, for he now looked much older than before, submitted to receive his services as well as those of Lilith. At length, one morning, he said in a slow thoughtful tone:

"Karl Wolkenlicht, I should like to paint you."

"Certainly, sir," answered Karl, jumping up, "where would you like me to sit?"

So the ice of silence and inactivity was broken, and the painter drew and painted; and the spring of his art flowed once more; and he made a beautiful portrait of Karl—a portrait without evil or suffering. And as soon as he had finished Karl, he began once more to paint Lilith; and when he had painted her, he composed a picture for the very purpose of introducing them together; and in this picture there was neither ugliness nor torture, but human feeling and human hope instead. Then Karl knew that he might speak to him of Lilith; and he spoke, and was heard with a smile. But he did not dare to tell him the truth of the vampire story till one day that Teufelsbürst was lying on the floor of a room in Karl's ancestral castle, half smothered in grand-children; when the only answer it drew from the old man was a kind of shuddering laugh, and the words—"Don't speak of it, Karl, my boy!"

CROSS PURPOSES

* * *

I.

ONCE upon a time, the Queen of Fairyland, finding her own subjects far too well-behaved to be amusing, took a sudden longing to have a mortal or two at her Court. So, after looking about her for some time, she fixed upon two to bring to Fairyland.

But how were they to be brought?

"Please your majesty," said at last the daughter of the prime minister, "I will bring the girl."

The speaker, whose name was Peaseblossom, after her great-great-grandmother, looked so graceful, and hung her head so apologetically, that the Queen said at once, "How will you manage it, Peaseblossom?"

"I will open the road before her, and close it behind her."

"I have heard that you have pretty ways of doing things; so you may try."

The court happened to be held in an open forest glade of smooth turf, upon which there was just one mole-heap. As soon as the Queen had given her permission to Peaseblossom, up through the mole-heap came the head of a goblin, which cried out, "Please your majesty, I will bring the boy."

"You!" exclaimed the Queen. "How will you do it?"

The goblin began to wriggle himself out of the earth, as if he had been a snake, and the whole world his skin, till the court was convulsed with laughter. As soon as he got free, he began to roll over and over, in every possible manner, rotatory and cylindrical, all at once, until he reached the wood. The courtiers followed, holding their sides, so that the Queen was left sitting upon her throne in solitary state. When they reached the wood, the goblin, whose name was Toadstool, was nowhere to be seen. While they were looking for him, out popped his head from the mole-heap again, with the words, "So, your majesty."

"You have taken your own time to answer," said the Queen, laughing.

"And my own way too, eh, Your majesty?" rejoined Toadstool, grinning.

"No doubt. Well, you may try."

And the goblin, making as much of a bow as he could with only half his neck above ground, disappeared under it.

II.

NO mortal, or fairy either, can tell where Fairyland begins and where it ends. But somewhere on the border of Fairyland there was a nice country village, in which lived some nice country people.

Alice was the daughter of the squire, a pretty, good-natured girl, whom her friends called fairy-like, and others called silly. One rosy summer evening, when the wall opposite her window was flaked all over with rosiness, she threw herself on her bed, and lay gazing at the wall. The rose-colour sank through her eyes and eyed her brain, and she began to feel as if she were reading a story-book. She thought she was looking at a western sea, with the waves all red with sunset. But when the colour died out, Alice gave a sigh to see how commonplace the wall grew. "I wish it was always sunset!" she said, half aloud. "I don't like gray things."

"I will take you where the sun is always setting, if you like, Alice," said a sweet, tiny voice near her. She looked down on the coverlet of the bed, and there, looking up at her, stood a lovely little creature. It seemed quite natural that the little lady should be there; for many things we never could believe, have only to happen, and then there is nothing strange about them. She was dressed in white, with a cloak of sunset-red—the colours of the sweetest of sweetpeas. On her head was a crown of twisted tendrils, with a little gold beetle in front.

"Are you a fairy?" said Alice.

"Yes. Will you go with me to the sunset?"

"Yes, I will."

When Alice proceeded to rise, she found that she was no bigger than the fairy; and when she stood up on the counterpane, the bed looked like a great hall with a painted ceiling. As she walked towards Peaseblossom, she stumbled several times over the tufts that made the pattern. But the fairy took her by the hand and led her towards the foot of the bed. Long before they reached it, however, Alice saw that the fairy was a tall, slender lady, and that she herself was quite her own size. What she had taken for tufts on the counterpane were really bushes of furze, and broom, and heather, on the side of a slope.

"Where are we?" asked Alice.

"Going on," answered the fairy.

Alice, not liking the reply, said, "I want to go home."

"Goodbye, then," answered the fairy.

Alice looked round. A wide, hilly country lay all about them. She could not even tell from what quarter they had come.

"I must go with you, I see," she said.

Before they reached the bottom, they were walking over the loveliest meadow-grass. A little stream went cantering down beside them, without channel or bank, sometimes running between the blades, sometimes sweeping the grass all one way under it. And it made a great babbling for such a little stream and such a smooth course.

Gradually the slope grew gentler, and the stream flowed more softly and spread out wider. At length they came to a wood of long, straight poplars, growing out of the water, for the stream ran into the wood, and there stretched out into a lake. Alice thought they could go no farther; but Peaseblossom led her straight on, and they walked through.

It was now dark; but everything under the water gave out a pale, quiet light. There were deep pools here and there, but there was no mud, or frogs, or water-lizards, or eels. All the bottom was pure, lovely grass, brilliantly green. Down the banks of the pools she saw, all under water, primroses and violets and pimpernels. Any flower she wished to see she had only to look for, and she was sure to find it. When a pool came in their way, the fairy swam, and Alice swam by her; and when they got out they were quite dry, though the water was as delightfully wet as water should be. Besides the trees, tall, splendid lilies grew out of it and hollyhocks and irises and sword-plants, and many other long-stemmed flowers. From every leaf and petal of these, from every branch-tip and tendril, dropped bright water. It gathered slowly at each point, but the points were so many that there was a constant musical plashing of diamond rain upon the still surface of the lake. As they went on, the moon rose and threw a pale mist of light over the whole, and the diamond drops turned to half-liquid pearls, and round every tree-top was a halo of moonlight, and the water went to sleep, and the flowers began to dream.

"Look," said the fairy; "those lilies are just dreaming themselves into a child's sleep. I can see them smiling. This is the place out of which go the things that appear to children every night."

"Is this dreamland, then?" asked Alice.

"If you like," answered the fairy.

"How far am I from home?"

"The farther you go, the nearer home you are."

Then the fairy lady gathered a bundle of poppies and gave it to Alice. The next deep pool that they came to, she told her to throw it in. Alice did so, and following it, laid her head upon it. That moment she began to sink. Down and down she went till at last she felt herself lying on the long, thick grass at the bottom of the pool, with the poppies under her head and the clear water high over it. Up through it she saw the moon, whose bright face looked sleepy too, disturbed only by the little ripples of the rain from the tall flowers on the edges of the pool.

She fell fast asleep, and all night dreamed about home.

III.

RICHARD—which is name enough for a fairy story—was the son of a widow in Alice's village. He was so poor that he did not find himself generally welcome; so he hardly went anywhere, but read books at home, and waited upon his mother. His manners, therefore, were shy, and sufficiently awkward to give an unfavourable impression to those who looked at outsides. Alice would have despised him; but he never came near enough for that.

Now Richard had been saving up his few pence in order to buy an umbrella for his mother; for the winter would come, and the one she had was almost torn to ribands. One bright summer evening, when he thought umbrellas must be cheap, he was walking across the marketplace to buy one; there, in the middle of it, stood an odd-looking little man, actually selling umbrellas. Here was a chance for him! When he drew nearer, he found that the little man, while vaunting his umbrellas to the skies, was asking such absurdly small prices for them, that no one would venture to buy one. He had opened and laid them all out in full stretch on the marketplace—about five-and-twenty of them, stick downwards, like little tents—and he stood beside, haranguing the people. But he would not allow one of the crowd to touch his umbrellas. As soon as his eye fell upon Richard, he changed his tone, and said, "Well, as nobody seems inclined to buy, I think, my dear umbrellas, we had better be going home." Whereupon the umbrellas got up, with some difficulty, and began hobbling away. The people stared at each other with open mouths, for they saw that what they had taken for a lot of umbrellas, was in reality a flock of black geese. A great turkey-cock went gobbling behind them, driving them all down a lane towards the forest. Richard thought with himself, "There is more in this than I can account for. But an umbrella that could lay eggs would be a very jolly umbrella." So by the time the people were beginning to laugh at each other, Richard was halfway down the lane at the heels of the geese. There he stopped and caught one of them, but instead of a goose he had a huge hedgehog in his hands, which he dropped in dismay; whereupon it waddled away a goose as before, and the whole of them began cackling and hissing in a way that he could not mistake. For the turkey cock, he gobbled and gabbled and choked himself and got right again in the most ridiculous manner. In fact, he seemed sometimes to forget that he was a turkey, and laughed like a fool. All at once, with a simultaneous long-necked hiss, they flew into the wood, and the turkey after them. But Richard soon got up with them again, and found them all hanging by their feet from the trees, in two rows, one on each side of the path, while the turkey was walking on. Him Richard followed; but the moment he reached the middle of the suspended geese, from every side arose the most frightful hisses, and their necks grew longer and longer, till there were nearly thirty broad bills close to his head, blowing in his face, in his ears, and at the back of his neck. But the turkey, looking round and seeing what was going on, turned and walked back. When he reached the place, he looked up at the first and gobbled at him in the wildest manner. That goose grew silent and dropped from the tree. Then he went to the next, and the next, and so on, till he had gobbled them all off the trees, one after another. But when Richard expected to see them go after the turkey, there was nothing there but a flock of huge mushrooms and puff-balls.

"I have had enough of this," thought Richard. "I will go home again."

"Go home, Richard," said a voice close to him.

Looking down, he saw, instead of the turkey, the most comical-looking little man he had ever seen.

"Go home, Master Richard," repeated he, grinning.

"Not for your bidding," answered Richard.

"Come on then, Master Richard."

"Nor that either, without a good reason."

"I will give you *such* an umbrella for your mother."

"I don't take presents from strangers."

"Bless you, I'm no stranger here! Oh no! Not at all." And he set off in the manner usual with him, rolling every way at once.

Richard could not help laughing and following. At length Toadstool plumped into a great hole full of water. "Served him right!" thought Richard. "Served him right!" bawled the goblin, crawling out again, and shaking the water from him like a spaniel. "This is the very place I wanted, only I rolled too fast." However, he went on rolling again faster than before, though it was now up hill, till he came to the top of a considerable height, on which grew a number of palm trees.

"Have you a knife, Richard?" said the goblin, stopping all at once, as if he had been walking quietly along, just like other people.

Richard pulled out a pocket-knife and gave it to the creature, who instantly cut a deep gash in one of the trees. Then he bounded to another and did the same, and so on, till he had gashed them all. Richard, following him, saw that a little stream, clearer than the clearest water, began to flow from each, increasing in size the longer it flowed. Before he had reached the last there was quite a tinkling and rustling of little rills that run down the stems of the palms. This grew and grew, till Richard saw that a full rivulet was flowing down the side of the hill.

"Here is your knife, Richard," said the goblin; but by the time he had put it in his pocket, the rivulet had grown to a small torrent.

"Now, Richard, come along," said Toadstool, and threw himself into the torrent.

"I would rather have a boat," returned Richard.

"Oh, you stupid!" cried Toadstool, crawling up the side of the hill, down which the stream had already carried him some distance.

With every contortion that labour and difficulty could suggest, yet with incredible rapidity, he crawled to the very top of one of the trees, and tore down a huge leaf, which he threw on the ground, and himself after it rebounding like a ball. He then laid the leaf on the water, held it by the stem, and told Richard to get upon it. He did so. It went down deep in the middle with his weight. Toadstool let it go, and it shot down the stream like an arrow. Thus began the strangest and most delightful voyage. The stream rushed careering and curveting down the hill-side, bright as a diamond, and soon reached a meadow plain. The goblin rolled alongside of the boat like a bundle of weeds; but Richard rode in triumph through the low grassy country upon the back of his watery steed. It went straight as an arrow, and, strange to tell, was heaped up on the ground, like a ridge of water or a wave, only rushing on endways. It needed no channel, and turned aside for no opposition. It flowed over everything that crossed its path, like a great serpent of water, with folds fitting into all the ups and downs of the way. If a wall came in its course it flowed against it, heaping itself up on itself till it reached the top, whence it plunged to the foot on the other side, and flowed on. Soon he found that it was running gently up a grassy hill. The waves kept curling back as if the wind blew them, or as if they could hardly keep from running down again. But still the stream mounted and flowed, and the waves with it. It found it difficult, but it could do it. When they reached the top, it bore them across a heathy country, rolling over purple heather, and blue harebells, and delicate ferns, and tall foxgloves crowded with bells purple and white. All the time, the palm-leaf curled its edges away from the water, and made a delightful boat for Richard, while Toadstool tumbled along in the stream like a porpoise. At length the water began to run very fast, and went faster and faster, till suddenly it plunged them into a deep lake, with a great splash, and stopped there. Toadstool went out of sight, and came up gasping and grinning, while Richard's boat tossed and heaved like a vessel in a storm at sea; but not a drop of water came in. Then the goblin began to swim, and pushed and tugged the boat along. But the lake was so still, and the motion so pleasant, that Richard fell fast asleep.

IV.

WHEN he woke, he found himself still afloat upon the broad palm-leaf. He was alone in the middle of a lake, with flowers and trees growing in and out of it everywhere. The sun was just over the tree-tops. A drip of water from the flowers greeted him with music; the mists were dissolving away; and where the sunlight fell on the lake the water was clear as glass. Casting his eyes downward, he saw, just beneath him, far down at the bottom, Alice—drowned, as he thought. He was in the act of plunging in, when he saw her open her eyes, and at the same moment begin to float up. He held out his hand, but she repelled it with disdain; and swimming to a tree, sat down on a low branch, wondering how ever the poor widow's son could have found his way into Fairyland. She did not like it. It was an invasion of privilege.

"How did you come here, young Richard?" she asked, from six yards off.

"A goblin brought me."

"Ah, I thought so. A fairy brought me."

"Where is your fairy?"

"Here I am," said Peaseblossom, rising slowly to the surface, just by the tree on which Alice was seated.

"Where is your goblin?" retorted Alice.

"Here I am," bawled Toadstool, rushing out of the water like a salmon, and casting a sumersault in the air before he fell in again with a tremendous splash. His head rose again close beside Peaseblossom, who being used to such creatures only laughed.

"Isn't he handsome?" he grinned.

"Yes, very. He wants polishing though."

"You could do that for yourself, you know. Shall we change?"

"I don't mind. You'll find her rather silly."

"That's nothing. The boy's too sensible for me."

He dived, and rose at Alice's feet. She shrieked with terror. The fairy floated away like a water-lily towards Richard. "What a lovely creature!" thought he, but hearing Alice shriek again, he said, "Don't leave Alice, she's frightened at that queer creature. I don't think there's any harm in him, though, Alice."

"Oh, no. He won't hurt her," said Peaseblossom. "I'm tired of her. He's going to take her to the court, and I will take you."

"I don't want to go."

"But you must. You can't go home again. You don't know the way."

"Richard! Richard!" cried Alice, in an agony.

Richard sprang from his boat, and was by her side in a moment.

"He pinched me," cried Alice.

Richard hit the goblin a terrible blow on the head; but it took no more effect upon him than if his head had been a round ball of India rubber. He gave Richard a furious look, however, and bawling out, "You'll repent that, Dick!" vanished under the water.

"Come along, Richard, make haste; he will murder you," cried the fairy.

"It is all your fault," said Richard. "I won't leave Alice."

Then the fairy saw it was all over with her and Toadstool; for they can do nothing with mortals against their will. So she floated away across the water in Richard's boat, holding her robe for a sail, and vanished, leaving the two alone in the lake.

"You have driven away my fairy!" cried Alice. "I shall never get home now. It is all your fault, you naughty young man."

"I drove away the goblin," remonstrated Richard.

"Will you please to sit on the other side of the tree. I wonder what my papa would say if he saw me talking to you!"

"Will you come to the next tree, Alice?" said Richard, after a pause.

Alice, who had been crying all the time that Richard was thinking, said, "I won't." Richard, therefore, plunged into the water without her, and swam for the tree. Before he had got halfway, however, he heard Alice crying, "Richard! Richard!" This was just what he wanted. So he turned back, and Alice threw herself into the water. With Richard's help she swam pretty well, and they reached the tree. "Now for the next!" said Richard; and they swam to the next, and then to the third. Every tree they reached was larger than the last, and every tree before them was larger still. So they swam from tree to tree, till they came to one that was so large that they could not see round it. What was to be done? Clearly, to climb this tree. It was a dreadful prospect for Alice, but Richard proceeded to climb; and by putting her feet where he put his, and now and then getting hold of his ankle, she managed to make her way up. There were a great many stumps where branches had withered off, and the bark was nearly as rough as a hill-side, so there was plenty of foothold for them. When they had climbed a long time, and were getting very tired indeed, Alice cried out, "Richard, I shall drop—I shall. Why did you come this way?" And she began once more to cry. But at that moment Richard caught hold of a branch above his head, and reaching down his other hand got hold of Alice, and held her till she had recovered a little. In a few moments they reached the fork of the tree, and there they sat and rested. "This is capital!" said Richard, cheerily.

"What is?" asked Alice, sulkily.

"Why, we have room to rest, and there's no hurry for a minute or two. I'm tired."

"You selfish creature!" said Alice. "If you are tired, what must I be?"

"Tired too," answered Richard. "But we've got on bravely. And look! What's that?"

By this time the day was gone, and the night so near, that in the shadows of the tree all was dusky and dim. But there was still light enough to discover that in a niche of the tree sat a huge horned owl, with green spectacles on his beak, and a book in one foot. He took no heed of the intruders, but kept muttering to himself. And what do you think the owl was saying? I will tell you. He was talking about the book that he held upside down in his foot.

"Stupid book this-s-s-s! Nothing in it at all! Everything upside down! Stupid ass-s-s-s! Says owls can't read! *I* can read backwards!"

"I think that is the goblin again," said Richard, in a whisper. "However, if you ask a plain question, he must give you a plain answer, for they are not allowed to tell downright lies in Fairyland."

"Don't ask him, Richard; you know you gave him a dreadful blow."

"I gave him what he deserved, and he owes me the same. Hallo! Which is the way out?"

He wouldn't say *if you please*, because then it would not have been a plain question.

"Downstairs," hissed the owl, without ever lifting his eyes from the book, which all the time he read upside down, so learned was he.

"On your honour, as a respectable old owl?" asked Richard.

"No," hissed the owl; and Richard was almost sure that he was not really an owl. So he stood staring at him for a few moments, when all at once, without lifting his eyes from the book, the owl said, "I will sing a song," and began:

> "*Nobody knows the world but me.*
> *When they're all in bed, I sit up to see.*
> *I'm a better student than students all,*
> *For I never read till the darkness fall,*
> *And I never read without my glasses,*
> *And that is how my wisdom passes.*
> *Howlowlwhoolhoolwoolool.*

> "*I can see the wind. Now who can do that?*
> *I see the dreams that he has in his hat,*

> *I see him snorting them out as he goes—*
> *Out at his stupid old trumpet-nose.*
> *Ten thousand things that you couldn't think*
> *I write them down with pen and ink.*
>   *Howlowlwhooloolwhitit that's wit.*
>
> *"You may call it learning—'tis mother-wit.*
> *No one else sees the lady-moon sit*
> *On the sea, her nest, all night, but the owl,*
> *Hatching the boats and the long-legged fowl.*
> *When the oysters gape to sing by rote,*
> *She crams a pearl down each stupid throat.*
>   *Howlowlwhitit that's wit, there's a fowl!"*

And so singing, he threw the book in Richard's face, spread out his great, silent, soft wings, and sped away into the depths of the tree. When the book struck Richard, he found that it was only a lump of wet moss.

While talking to the owl he had spied a hollow behind one of the branches. Judging this to be the way the owl meant, he went to see, and found a rude, ill-defined staircase going down into the very heart of the trunk. But so large was the tree that this could not have hurt it in the least. Down this stair, then, Richard scrambled as best he could, followed by Alice—not of her own will, she gave him clearly to understand, but because she could do no better. Down, down they went slipping and falling sometimes, but never very far, because the stair went round and round. It caught Richard when he slipped, and he caught Alice when she did. They had begun to fear that there was no end to the stair, it went round and round so steadily, when, creeping through a crack, they found themselves in a great hall, supported by thousands of pillars of gray stone. Where the little light came from they could not tell. This hall they began to cross in a straight line, hoping to reach one side, and intending to walk along it till they came to some opening. They kept straight by going from pillar to pillar, as they had done before by the trees. Any honest plan will do in Fairyland, if you only stick to it. And no plan will do if you do not stick to it.

It was very silent, and Alice disliked the silence more than the dimness, so much, indeed, that she longed to hear Richard's voice. But she had always been so cross to him when he had spoken, that he thought it better to let her speak first; and she was too proud to do that. She would not even let him walk alongside of her, but always went slower when he wanted to wait for her; so that at last he strode on alone. And Alice followed. But by degrees the horror of silence grew upon her, and she felt at last as if there was no one in the universe but herself. The hall went on widening around her; their footsteps made no noise; the silence grew so intense that it seemed on the point of taking shape. At last she could bear it no longer. She ran after Richard, got up with him, and laid hold of his arm.

He had been thinking for some time what an obstinate, disagreeable girl Alice was, and wishing he had her safe home to be rid of her, when, feeling a hand, and looking round, he saw that it was the disagreeable girl. She soon began to be companionable after a fashion, for she began to think, putting everything together, that Richard must have been several times in Fairyland before now. "It is very strange," she said to herself; "for he is quite a poor boy, I am sure of that. His arms stick out beyond his jacket like the ribs of his mother's umbrella. And to think of me wandering about Fairyland with *him*!"

The moment she touched his arm, they saw an arch of blackness before them. They had walked straight to a door—not a very inviting one, for it opened upon an utterly dark passage. Where there was only one door, however, there was no difficulty about choosing. Richard walked straight through it; and from the greater fear of being left behind, Alice faced the lesser fear of going on. In a moment they were in total darkness. Alice clung to Richard's arm, and murmured, almost against her will, "Dear Richard!" It was strange that fear should speak like love; but it was in Fairyland. It was strange, too, that as soon as she spoke thus, Richard should fall in love with her all at once. But what was more curious still was, that at the same moment, Richard saw her face. In spite of her fear, which had made her pale, she looked very lovely.

"Dear Alice!" said Richard, "How pale you look!"

"How can you tell that, Richard, when all is as black as pitch?"

"I can see your face. It gives out light. Now I see your hands. Now I can see your feet. Yes, I can see every spot where you are going to—No, don't put your foot there. There is an ugly toad just there."

The fact was that the moment he began to love Alice, his eyes began to send forth light. What he thought came from Alice's face, really came from his eyes. All about her and her path he could see, and every minute saw better; but to his own path he was blind. He could not see his hand when he held it straight before his face, so dark was it. But he could see Alice, and that was better than seeing the way—ever so much.

At length Alice too began to see a face dawning through the darkness. It was Richard's face: but it was far handsomer than when she saw it last. Her eyes had begun to give light too. And she said to herself—"Can it be that I love the poor widow's son? I suppose that must be it," she answered herself, with a smile; for she was not disgusted with herself at all. Richard saw the smile, and was glad. Her paleness had gone, and a sweet rosiness had taken its place. And now she saw Richard's path as he saw hers, and between the two sights they got on well.

They were now walking on a path betwixt two deep waters, which never moved, shining as black as ebony where the eyelight fell. But they saw ere long that this path kept growing narrower and narrower. At last, to Alice's dismay, the black waters met in front of them.

"What is to be done now, Richard?" she said.

When they fixed their eyes on the water before them, they saw that it was swarming with lizards, and frogs, and black snakes, and all kinds of strange and ugly creatures, especially some that had neither heads, nor tails, nor legs, nor fins, nor feelers, being, in fact, only living lumps. These kept jumping out and in, and sprawling upon the path. Richard thought for a few moments before replying to Alice's question, as, indeed, well he might. But he came to the conclusion that the path could not have gone on for the sake of stopping there; and that it must be a kind of finger that pointed on where it was not allowed to go itself. So he caught up Alice in his strong arms, and jumped into the middle of the horrid swarm. And just as minnows vanish if you throw anything amongst them, just so these wretched creatures vanished, right and left and every way.

He found the water broader than he had expected; and before he got over, he found Alice heavier than he could have believed; but upon a firm, rocky bottom, Richard waded through in safety. When he reached the other side, he found that the bank was a lofty, smooth, perpendicular rock, with some rough steps cut in it. By-and-by the steps led them right into the rock, and they were in a narrow passage once more, but this time, leading up. It wound round and round, like the thread of a great screw. At last Richard knocked his head against something, and could go no farther. The place was close and hot. He put up his hands, and pushed what felt like a warm stone: it moved a little.

"Go down, you brutes!" growled a voice above, quivering with anger. "You'll upset my pot and my cat, and my temper, too, if you push that way. Go down!"

Richard knocked very gently, and said: "Please let us out."

"O yes, I dare say! Very fine and soft-spoken! Go down, you goblin brutes! I've had enough of you. I'll scald the hair off your ugly heads if you do that again. Go down, I say!"

Seeing fair speech was of no avail, Richard told Alice to go down a little, out of the way; and, setting his shoulders to one end of the stone, heaved it up; whereupon down came the other end, with a pot, and a fire, and a cat which had been asleep beside it. She frightened Alice dreadfully as she rushed past her, showing nothing but her green lamping eyes.

Richard, peeping up, found that he had turned a hearthstone upside down. On the edge of the hole stood a little crooked old man, brandishing a mop-stick in a tremendous rage, and hesitating only where to strike him. But Richard put him out of his difficulty by springing up and taking the stick from him. Then, having lifted Alice out, he returned it with a bow, and, heedless of the maledictions of the old man, proceeded to get the stone and the pot up again. For puss, she got out of herself.

Then the old man became a little more friendly, and said: "I beg your pardon, I thought you were goblins. They never will let me alone. But you must allow, it was rather an unusual way of paying a morning call." And the creature bowed conciliatingly.

"It was, indeed," answered Richard. "I wish you had turned the door to us instead of the hearthstone." For he did not trust the old man. "But," he added, "I hope you will forgive us."

"Oh, certainly, certainly, my dear young people. Use your freedom. But such young people have no business to be out alone. It is against the rules."

"But what is one to do—I mean two to do—when they can't help it?"

"Yes, yes, of course; but now, you know, I must take charge of you. So you sit there, young gentleman; and you sit there, young lady."

He put a chair for one at one side of the hearth, and for the other at the other side, and then drew his chair between them. The cat got upon his hump, and then set up her own. So here was a wall that would let through no moonshine. But although both Richard and Alice were very much amused, they did not like to be parted in this peremptory manner. Still they thought it better not to anger the old man anymore—in his own house, too.

But he had been once angered, and that was once too often, for he had made it a rule never to forgive without taking it out in humiliation.

It was so disagreeable to have him sitting there between them, that they felt as if they were far asunder. In order to get the better of the fancy, they wanted to hold each other's hand behind the dwarf's back. But the moment their hands began to approach, the back of the cat began to grow long, and its hump to grow high; and, in a moment more, Richard found himself crawling wearily up a steep hill, whose ridge rose against the stars, while a cold wind blew drearily over it. Not a habitation was in sight; and Alice had vanished from his eyes. He felt however, that she must be somewhere on the other side, and so climbed and climbed, to get over the brow of the hill, and down to where he thought she must be. But the longer he climbed, the farther off the top of the hill seemed; till at last he sank quite exhausted, and—must I confess it?—very nearly began to cry. To think of being separated from Alice, all at once, and in such a disagreeable way! But he fell a-thinking instead, and soon said to himself: "This must be some trick of that wretched old man. Either this mountain is a cat or it is not. If it is a mountain, this won't hurt it; if it is a cat, I hope it will." With that, he pulled out his pocket-knife, and feeling for a soft place, drove it at one blow up to the handle in the side of the mountain.

A terrific shriek was the first result; and the second, that Alice and he sat looking at each other across the old man's hump, from which the cat-a-mountain had vanished. Their host sat staring at the blank fireplace, without ever turning round, pretending to know nothing of what had taken place.

"Come along, Alice," said Richard, rising. "This won't do. We won't stop here."

Alice rose at once, and put her hand in his. They walked towards the door. The old man took no notice of them. The moon was shining brightly through the window; but instead of stepping out into the moonlight when they opened the door, they stepped into a great beautiful hall, through the high gothic windows of which the same moon was shining. Out of this hall they could find no way, except by a staircase of stone which led upwards. They ascended it together. At the top Alice let go Richard's hand to peep into a little room, which looked all the colours of the rainbow, just like the inside of a diamond. Richard went a step or two along a corridor, but finding she had left him, turned and looked into the chamber. He could see her nowhere. The room was full of doors; and she must have mistaken the door. He heard her voice calling him, and hurried in the direction of the sound. But he could see nothing of her. "More tricks," he said to himself. "It is of no use to stab this one. I must wait till I see what can be done." Still he heard Alice calling him, and still he followed, as well as he could. At length he came to a doorway, open to the air, through which the moonlight fell. But when he reached it, he found that it was high up in the side of a tower, the wall of which went straight down from his feet, without stair or descent of any kind. Again he heard Alice call him, and lifting his eyes, saw her, across a wide castle-court, standing at another door just like the one he was at, with the moon shining full upon her.

"All right, Alice!" he cried. "Can you hear me?"

"Yes," answered she.

"Then listen. This is all a trick It is all a lie of that old wretch in the kitchen. Just reach out your hand, Alice dear."

Alice did as Richard asked her; and, although they saw each other many yards off across the court, their hands met.

"There! I thought so!" exclaimed Richard, triumphantly. "Now, Alice, I don't believe it is more than a foot or two down to the court below, though it looks like a hundred feet. Keep fast hold of my hand, and jump when I count three." But Alice drew her hand from him in sudden dismay; whereupon Richard said, "Well, I will try first," and jumped. The same moment his cheery laugh came to Alice's ears, and she saw him standing safe on the ground, far below.

"Jump, dear Alice, and I will catch you," said he.

"I can't; I am afraid," answered she.

"The old man is somewhere near you. You had better jump," said Richard.

Alice jumped from the wall in terror, and only fell a foot or two into Richard's arms. The moment she touched the ground, they found themselves outside the door of a little cottage which they knew very well, for it was only just within the wood that bordered on their village. Hand in hand they ran home as fast as they could. When they reached a little gate that led into her father's grounds, Richard bade Alice goodbye. The tears came in her eyes. Richard and she seemed to have grown quite man and woman in Fairyland, and they did not want to part now. But they felt that they must. So Alice ran in the back way, and reached her own room before anyone had missed her. Indeed, the last of the red had not quite faded from the west.

As Richard crossed the marketplace on his way home, he saw an umbrella-man just selling the last of his umbrellas. He thought the man gave him a queer look as he passed, and felt very much inclined to punch his head. But remembering how useless it had been to punch the goblin's head, he thought it better not.

In reward of their courage, the Fairy Queen sent them permission to visit Fairyland as often as they pleased; and no goblin or fairy was allowed to interfere with them.

For Peaseblossom and Toadstool, they were both banished from court, and compelled to live together, for seven years, in an old tree that had just one green leaf upon it.

Toadstool did not mind it much, but Peaseblossom did.

THE GOLDEN KEY

* * *

THERE was a boy who used to sit in the twilight and listen to his great-aunt's stories.

She told him that if he could reach the place where the end of the rainbow stands he would find there a golden key.

"And what is the key for?" the boy would ask. "What is it the key of? What will it open?"

"That nobody knows," his aunt would reply. "He has to find that out."

"I suppose, being gold," the boy once said, thoughtfully, "that I could get a good deal of money for it if I sold it."

"Better never find it than sell it," returned his aunt.

And then the boy went to bed and dreamed about the golden key.

Now all that his great-aunt told the boy about the golden key would have been nonsense, had it not been that their little house stood on the borders of Fairyland. For it is perfectly well known that out of Fairyland nobody ever can find where the rainbow stands. The creature takes such good care of its golden key, always flitting from place to place, lest anyone should find it! But in Fairyland it is quite different. Things that look real in this country look very thin indeed in Fairyland, while some of the things that here cannot stand still for a moment will not move there. So it was not in the least absurd of the old lady to tell her nephew such things about the golden key.

"Did you ever know anybody to find it?" he asked, one evening.

"Yes. Your father, I believe, found it."

"And what did he do with it, can you tell me?"

"He never told me."

"What was it like?"

"He never showed it to me."

"How does a new key come there always?"

"I don't know. There it is."

"Perhaps it is the rainbow's egg."

"Perhaps it is. You will be a happy boy if you find the nest."

"Perhaps it comes tumbling down the rainbow from the sky."

"Perhaps it does."

One evening, in summer, he went into his own room, and stood at the lattice-window, and gazed into the forest which fringed the outskirts of Fairyland. It came close up to his great-aunt's garden, and, indeed, sent some straggling trees into it. The forest lay to the east and the sun, which was setting behind the cottage, looked straight into the dark wood with his level red eye. The trees were all old, and had few branches below, so that the sun could see a great way into the forest; and the boy, being keen-sighted, could see almost as far as the sun. The trunks stood like rows of red columns in the shine of the red sun, and he could see down aisle after aisle in the vanishing distance. And as he gazed into the forest he began to feel as if the trees were all waiting for him, and had something they could not go on with till he came to them. But he was hungry, and wanted his supper. So he lingered.

Suddenly, far among the trees, as far as the sun could shine, he saw a glorious thing. It was the end of a rainbow, large and brilliant.

He could count all the seven colours, and could see shade after shade beyond the violet; while before the red stood a colour more gorgeous and mysterious still. It was a colour he had never seen before. Only the spring of the rainbow-arch was visible. He could see nothing of it above the trees.

"The golden key!" he said to himself, and darted out of the house, and into the wood.

He had not gone far before the sun set. But the rainbow only glowed the brighter. For the rainbow of Fairyland is not dependent upon the sun as ours is. The trees welcomed him. The bushes made way for him. The rainbow grew larger and brighter; and at length he found himself within two trees of it.

It was a grand sight, burning away there in silence, with its gorgeous, its lovely, its delicate colours, each distinct, all combining. He could now see a great deal more of it. It rose high into the blue heavens, but bent so little that he could not tell how high the crown of the arch must reach. It was still only a small portion of a huge bow.

He stood gazing at it till he forgot himself with delight—even forgot the key which he had come to seek. And as he stood it grew more wonderful still. For in each of the colours, which was as large as the column of a church, he could faintly see beautiful forms slowly ascending as if by the steps of a winding stair. The forms appeared irregularly—now one, now many, now several, now none—men and women and children—all different, all beautiful.

He drew nearer to the rainbow. It vanished. He started back a step in dismay. It was there again, as beautiful as ever. So he contented himself with standing as near it as he might, and watching the forms that ascended the glorious colours towards the unknown height of the arch, which did not end abruptly, but faded away in the blue air, so gradually that he could not say where it ceased.

When the thought of the golden key returned, the boy very wisely proceeded to mark out in his mind the space covered by the foundation of the rainbow, in order that he might know where to search, should the rainbow disappear. It was based chiefly upon a bed of moss.

Meantime it had grown quite dark in the wood. The rainbow alone was visible by its own light. But the moment the moon rose the rainbow vanished. Nor could any change of place restore the vision to the boy's eyes. So he threw himself down upon the mossy bed, to wait till the sunlight would give him a chance of finding the key. There he fell fast asleep.

When he woke in the morning the sun was looking straight into his eyes. He turned away from it, and the same moment saw a brilliant little thing lying on the moss within a foot of his face. It was the golden key. The pipe of it was of plain gold, as bright as gold could be. The handle was curiously wrought and set with sapphires. In a terror of delight he put out his hand and took it, and had it.

He lay for a while, turning it over and over, and feeding his eyes upon its beauty. Then he jumped to his feet, remembering that the pretty thing was of no use to him yet. Where was the lock to which the key belonged? It must be somewhere, for how could anybody be so silly as make a key for which there was no lock? Where should he go to look for it? He gazed about him, up into the air, down to the earth, but saw no keyhole in the clouds, in the grass, or in the trees.

Just as he began to grow disconsolate, however, he saw something glimmering in the wood. It was a mere glimmer that he saw, but he took it for a glimmer of rainbow, and went towards it. And now I will go back to the borders of the forest.

Not far from the house where the boy had lived, there was another house, the owner of which was a merchant who was much away from home. He had lost his wife some years before, and had only one child, a little girl, whom he left to the charge of two servants, who were very idle and careless. So she was neglected and left untidy, and was sometimes ill-used besides.

Now it is well known that the little creatures commonly called fairies, though there are many different kinds of fairies in Fairyland, have an exceeding dislike to untidiness. Indeed, they are quite spiteful to slovenly people. Being used to all the lovely ways of the trees and flowers, and to the neatness of the birds and all woodland creatures, it makes them feel miserable, even in their deep woods and on their grassy carpets, to think that within the same moonlight lies a dirty, uncomfortable, slovenly house. And this makes them angry with the people that live in it, and they would gladly drive them out of the world if they could. They want the whole earth nice and clean. So they pinch the maids black and blue, and play them all manner of uncomfortable tricks.

But this house was quite a shame, and the fairies in the forest could not endure it. They tried everything on the maids without effect, and at last resolved upon making a clean riddance, beginning with the child. They ought to have known that it was not her fault, but they have little principle and much mischief in them, and they thought that if they got rid of her the maids would be sure to be turned away.

So one evening, the poor little girl having been put to bed early, before the sun was down, the servants went off to the village, locking the door behind them. The child did not know she was alone, and lay contentedly looking out of her window towards the forest, of which, however, she could not see much, because of the ivy and other creeping plants which had straggled across her window. All at once she saw an ape making faces at her out of the mirror, and the heads carved upon a great old wardrobe grinning fearfully. Then two old spider-legged chairs came forward into the middle of the room, and began to dance a queer, old-fashioned dance. This set her laughing, and she forgot the ape and the grinning heads. So the fairies saw they had made a mistake, and sent the chairs back to their places. But they knew that she had been reading the story of Silverhair all day. So the next moment she heard the voices of the three bears upon the stair, big voice, middle voice, and little voice, and she heard their soft, heavy tread, as if they had had stockings over their boots, coming nearer and nearer to the door of her room, till she could bear it no longer. She did just as Silverhair did, and as the fairies wanted her to do: she darted to the window, pulled it open, got upon the ivy, and so scrambled to the ground. She then fled to the forest as fast as she could run.

Now, although she did not know it, this was the very best way she could have gone; for nothing is ever so mischievous in its own place as it is out of it; and, besides, these mischievous creatures were only the children of Fairyland, as it were, and there are many other beings there as well; and if a wanderer gets in among them, the good ones will always help him more than the evil ones will be able to hurt him.

The sun was now set, and the darkness coming on, but the child thought of no danger but the bears behind her. If she had looked round, however, she would have seen that she was followed by a very different creature from a bear. It was a curious creature, made like a fish, but covered, instead of scales, with feathers of all colours, sparkling like those of a humming-bird. It had fins, not wings, and swam through the air as a fish does through the water. Its head was like the head of a small owl.

After running a long way, and as the last of the light was disappearing, she passed under a tree with drooping branches. It dropped its branches to the ground all about her, and caught her as in a trap. She struggled to get out, but the branches pressed her closer and closer to the trunk. She was in great terror and distress, when the air-fish, swimming into the thicket of branches, began tearing them with its beak. They loosened their hold at once, and the creature went on attacking them, till at length they let the child go. Then the air-fish came from behind her, and swam on in front, glittering and sparkling all lovely colours; and she followed.

It led her gently along till all at once it swam in at a cottage door. The child followed still. There was a bright fire in the middle of the floor, upon which stood a pot without a lid, full of water that boiled and bubbled furiously. The air-fish swam straight to the pot and into the boiling water, where it lay quietly. A beautiful woman rose from the opposite side of the fire and came to meet the girl. She took her up in her arms, and said, "Ah, you are come at last! I have been looking for you a long time."

She sat down with her on her lap, and there the girl sat staring at her. She had never seen anything so beautiful. She was tall and strong, with white arms and neck, and a delicate flush on her face. The child could not tell what was the colour of her hair, but could not help thinking it had a tinge of dark green. She had not one ornament upon her, but she looked as if she had just put off quantities of diamonds and emeralds. Yet here she was in the simplest, poorest little cottage, where she was evidently at home. She was dressed in shining green.

The girl looked at the lady, and the lady looked at the girl.

"What is your name?" asked the lady.

"The servants always called me Tangle."

"Ah, that was because your hair was so untidy. But that was their fault, the naughty women! Still it is a pretty name, and I will call you Tangle too. You must not mind me asking you questions, for you may ask me the same questions, every one of them, and any others that you like. How old are you?"

"Ten," answered Tangle.

"You don't look like it," said the lady.

"How old are you, please?" returned Tangle.

"Thousands of years old," answered the lady.

"You don't look like it," said Tangle.

"Don't I? I think I do. Don't you see how beautiful I am?"

And her great blue eyes looked down on the little Tangle, as if all the stars in the sky were melted in them to make their brightness.

"Ah! But," said Tangle, "when people live long they grow old. At least I always thought so."

"I have no time to grow old," said the lady. "I am too busy for that. It is very idle to grow old. But I cannot have my little girl so untidy. Do you know I can't find a clean spot on your face to kiss?"

"Perhaps," suggested Tangle, feeling ashamed, but not too much so to say a word for herself, "perhaps that is because the tree made me cry so."

"My poor darling!" said the lady, looking now as if the moon were melted in her eyes, and kissing her little face, dirty as it was, "the naughty tree must suffer for making a girl cry."

"And what is your name, please?" asked Tangle.

"Grandmother," answered the lady.

"Is it really?"

"Yes, indeed. I never tell stories, even in fun."

"How good of you!"

"I couldn't if I tried. It would come true if I said it, and then I should be punished enough."

And she smiled like the sun through a summer-shower.

"But now," she went on, "I must get you washed and dressed, and then we shall have some supper."

"Oh! I had supper long ago," said Tangle.

"Yes, indeed you had," answered the lady, "three years ago. You don't know that it is three years since you ran away from the bears. You are thirteen and more now."

Tangle could only stare. She felt quite sure it was true.

"You will not be afraid of anything I do with you—will you?" said the lady.

"I will try very hard not to be; but I can't be certain, you know," replied Tangle.

"I like your saying so, and I shall be quite satisfied," answered the lady.

She took off the girl's night-gown, rose with her in her arms and going to the wall of the cottage, opened a door. Then Tangle saw a deep tank, the sides of which were filled with green plants, which had flowers of all colours. There was a roof over it like the roof of the cottage. It was filled with beautiful clear water, in which swam a multitude of such fishes as the one that had led her to the cottage. It was the light their colours gave that showed the place in which they were.

The lady spoke some words Tangle could not understand, and threw her into the tank.

The fishes came crowding about her. Two or three of them got under her head and kept it up. The rest of them rubbed themselves all over her, and with their wet feathers washed her quite clean. Then the lady, who had been looking on all the time, spoke again; whereupon some thirty or forty of the fishes rose out of the water underneath Tangle, and so bore her up to the arms the lady held out to her. She carried her back to the fire, and, having dried her well, opened a chest, and taking out the finest linen garments, smelling of grass and lavender, put them upon her, and over all a green dress, just like her own, shining like hers, and soft like hers, and going into just such lovely folds from the waist, where it was tied with a brown cord, to her bare feet.

"Won't you give me a pair of shoes too, Grandmother?" said Tangle.

"No, my dear; no shoes. Look here. I wear no shoes."

So saying, she lifted her dress a little, and there were the loveliest white feet, but no shoes. Then Tangle was content to go without shoes too. And the lady sat down with her again, and combed her hair, and brushed it, and then left it to dry while she got the supper.

First she got bread out of one hole in the wall; then milk out of another; then several kinds of fruit out of a third; and then she went to the pot on the fire, and took out the fish, now nicely cooked, and, as soon as she had pulled off its feathered skin, ready to be eaten.

"But," exclaimed Tangle. And she stared at the fish, and could say no more.

"I know what you mean," returned the lady. "You do not like to eat the messenger that brought you home. But it is the kindest return you can make. The creature was afraid to go until it saw me put the pot on, and heard me promise it should be boiled the moment it returned with you. Then it darted out of the door at once. You saw it go into the pot of itself the moment it entered, did you not?"

"I did," answered Tangle, "and I thought it very strange; but then I saw you, and forgot all about the fish."

"In Fairyland," resumed the lady, as they sat down to the table, "the ambition of the animals is to be eaten by the people; for that is their highest end in that condition. But they are not therefore destroyed. Out of that pot comes some thing more than the dead fish, you will see."

Tangle now remarked that the lid was on the pot. But the lady took no further notice of it till they had eaten the fish, which Tangle found nicer than any fish she had ever tasted before. It was as white as snow, and as delicate as cream. And the moment she had swallowed a mouthful of it, a change she could not describe began to take place in her. She heard a murmuring all about her, which became more and more articulate, and at length, as she went on eating, grew intelligible. By the time she had finished her share, the sounds of all the animals in the forest came crowding through the door to her ears; for the door still stood wide open, though it was pitch dark outside; and they were no longer sounds only; they were speech, and speech that she could understand. She could tell what the insects in the cottage were saying to each other too. She had even a suspicion that the trees and flowers all about the cottage were holding midnight communications with each other; but what they said she could not hear.

As soon as the fish was eaten, the lady went to the fire and took the lid off the pot. A lovely little creature in human shape, with large white wings, rose out of it, and flew round and round the roof of the cottage; then dropped, fluttering, and nestled in the lap of the lady. She spoke to it some strange words, carried it to the door, and threw it out into the darkness. Tangle heard the flapping of its wings die away in the distance.

"Now have we done the fish any harm?" she said, returning.

"No," answered Tangle, "I do not think we have. I should not mind eating one every day."

"They must wait their time, like you and me too, my Tangle."

And she smiled a smile which the sadness in it made more lovely.

"But," she continued, "I think we may have one for supper tomorrow."

So saying she went to the door of the tank, and spoke; and now Tangle understood her perfectly.

"I want one of you," she said, "the wisest."

Thereupon the fishes got together in the middle of the tank, with their heads forming a circle above the water, and their tails a larger circle beneath it. They were holding a council, in which their relative wisdom should be determined. At length one of them flew up into the lady's hand, looking lively and ready.

"You know where the rainbow stands?" she asked.

"Yes, Mother, quite well," answered the fish.

"Bring home a young man you will find there, who does not know where to go."

The fish was out of the door in a moment. Then the lady told Tangle it was time to go to bed; and, opening another door in the side of the cottage, showed her a little arbour, cool and green, with a bed of purple heath growing in it upon which she threw a large wrapper made of the feathered skins of the wise fishes, shining gorgeous in the firelight. Tangle was soon lost in the strangest loveliest dreams. And the beautiful lady was in every one of her dreams.

In the morning she awoke to the rustling of leaves over her head, and the sound of running water. But to her surprise, she could find no door—nothing but the moss-grown wall of the cottage. So she crept through air opening in the arbour, and stood in the forest. Then she bathed in a stream that ran merrily through the trees, and felt happier; for having once been in her grandmother's pond, she must be clean and tidy ever after; and, having put on her green dress, felt like a lady.

She spent that day in the wood, listening to the birds and beasts and creeping things. She understood all that they said, though she could not repeat a word of it; and every kind had a different language, while there was a common though more limited understanding between all the inhabitants of the forest. She saw nothing of the beautiful lady, but she felt that she was near her all the time; and she took care not to go out of sight of the cottage. It was round, like a snow-hut or a wigwam; and she could see neither door nor window in it. The fact was, it had no windows; and though it was full of doors, they all opened from the inside, and could not even be seen from the outside.

She was standing at the foot of a tree in the twilight, listening to a quarrel between a mole and a squirrel, in which the mole told the squirrel that the tail was the best of him, and the squirrel called the mole Spade-fists, when, the darkness having deepened around her, she became aware of something shining in her face, and looking round, saw that the door of the cottage was open, and the red light of the fire flowing from it like a river through the darkness. She left Mole and Squirrel to settle matters as they might, and darted off to the cottage. Entering, she found the pot boiling on the fire, and the grand, lovely lady sitting on the other side of it.

"I've been watching you all day," said the lady. "You shall have something to eat by-and-by, but we must wait till our supper comes home."

She took Tangle on her knee, and began to sing to her—such songs as made her wish she could listen to them forever. But at length in rushed the shining fish, and snuggled down in the pot. It was followed by a youth who had outgrown his worn garments. His face was ruddy with health, and in his hand he carried a little jewel, which sparkled in the firelight.

The first words the lady said were, "What is that in your hand, Mossy?"

Now Mossy was the name his companions had given him, because he had a favourite stone covered with moss, on which he used to sit whole days reading; and they said the moss had begun to grow upon him too.

Mossy held out his hand. The moment the lady saw that it was the golden key, she rose from her chair, kissed Mossy on the forehead, made him sit down on her seat, and stood before him like a servant. Mossy could not bear this, and rose at once. But the lady begged him, with tears in her beautiful eyes, to sit and let her wait on him.

"But you are a great, splendid, beautiful lady," said Mossy.

"Yes, I am. But I work all day long—that is my pleasure; and you will have to leave me so soon!"

"How do you know that if you please, madam?" asked Mossy.

"Because you have got the golden key."

"But I don't know what it is for. I can't find the keyhole. Will you tell me what to do?"

"You must look for the keyhole. That is your work. I cannot help you. I can only tell you that if you look for it you will find it."

"What kind of box will it open? What is there inside?"

"I do not know. I dream about it, but I know nothing."

"Must I go at once?"

"You may stop here tonight, and have some of my supper. But you must go in the morning. All I can do for you is to give you clothes. Here is a girl called Tangle, whom you must take with you."

"That will be nice," said Mossy.

"No, no!" said Tangle. "I don't want to leave you, please, Grandmother."

"You must go with him, Tangle. I am sorry to lose you, but it will be the best thing for you. Even the fishes, you see, have to go into the pot, and then out into the dark. If you fall in with the Old Man of the Sea, mind you ask him whether he has not got some more fishes ready for me. My tank is getting thin."

So saying, she took the fish from the pot, and put the lid on as before. They sat down and ate the fish, and then the winged creature rose from the pot, circled the roof, and settled on the lady's lap. She talked to it, carried it to the door, and threw it out into the dark. They heard the flap of its wings die away in the distance.

The lady then showed Mossy into just such another chamber

as that of Tangle; and in the morning he found a suit of clothes laid beside him. He looked very handsome in them. But the wearer of Grandmother's clothes never thinks about how he or she looks, but thinks always how handsome other people are.

Tangle was very unwilling to go.

"Why should I leave you? I don't know the young man," she said to the lady.

"I am never allowed to keep my children long. You need not go with him except you please, but you must go some day; and I should like you to go with him, for he has the golden key. No girl need be afraid to go with a youth that has the golden key. You will take care of her, Mossy, will you not?"

"That I will," said Mossy.

And Tangle cast a glance at him, and thought she should like to go with him.

"And," said the lady, "if you should lose each other as you go through the—the—I never can remember the name of that country—do not be afraid, but go on and on."

She kissed Tangle on the mouth and Mossy on the forehead, led them to the door, and waved her hand eastward. Mossy and Tangle took each other's hand and walked away into the depth of the forest. In his right hand Mossy held the golden key.

They wandered thus a long way, with endless amusement from the talk of the animals. They soon learned enough of their language to ask them necessary questions. The squirrels were always friendly, and gave them nuts out of their own hoards; but the bees were selfish and rude, justifying themselves on the ground that Tangle and Mossy were not subjects of their queen, and charity must begin at home, though indeed they had not one drone in their poorhouse at the time. Even the blinking moles would fetch them an earth-nut or a truffle now and then, talking as if their mouths, as well as their eyes and ears, were full of cotton wool, or their own velvety fur. By the time they got out of the forest they were very fond of each other, and Tangle was not in the least sorry that her grandmother had sent her away with Mossy.

At length the trees grew smaller, and stood farther apart, and the ground began to rise, and it got more and more steep, till the trees were all left behind, and the two were climbing a narrow path with rocks on each side. Suddenly they came upon a rude doorway, by which they entered a narrow gallery cut in the rock. It grew darker and darker, till it was pitch-dark, and they had to feel their way. At length the light began to return, and at last they came out upon a narrow path on the face of a lofty precipice. This path went winding down the rock to a wide plain, circular in shape, and surrounded on all sides by mountains. Those opposite to them were a great way off, and towered to an awful height, shooting up sharp, blue, ice-enamelled pinnacles. An utter silence reigned where they stood. Not even the sound of water reached them.

Looking down, they could not tell whether the valley below was a grassy plain or a great still lake. They had never seen any space look like it. The way to it was difficult and dangerous, but down the narrow path they went, and reached the bottom in safety. They found it composed of smooth, light-coloured sandstone, undulating in parts, but mostly level. It was no wonder to them now that they had not been able to tell what it was, for this surface was everywhere crowded with shadows. It was a sea of shadows. The mass was chiefly made up of the shadows of leaves innumerable, of all lovely and imaginative forms, waving to and fro, floating and quivering in the breath of a breeze whose motion was unfelt, whose sound was unheard. No forests clothed the mountain-sides, no trees were anywhere to be seen, and yet the shadows of the leaves, branches, and stems of all various trees covered the valley as far as their eyes could reach. They soon spied the shadows of flowers mingled with those of the leaves, and now and then the shadow of a bird with open beak, and throat distended with song. At times would appear the forms of strange, graceful creatures, running up and down the shadow-boles and along the branches, to disappear in the wind-tossed foliage. As they walked they waded knee-deep in the lovely lake. For the shadows were not merely lying on the surface of the ground, but heaped up above it like substantial forms of darkness, as if they had been cast upon a thousand different planes of the air. Tangle and Mossy often lifted their heads and gazed upwards to descry whence the shadows came; but they could see nothing more than a bright mist spread above them, higher than the tops of the mountains, which stood clear against it. No forests, no leaves, no birds were visible.

After a while, they reached more open spaces, where the shadows were thinner; and came even to portions over which shadows only flitted, leaving them clear for such as might follow. Now a wonderful form, half bird-like half human, would float across on outspread sailing pinions. Anon an exquisite shadow group of gambolling children would be followed by the loveliest female form, and that again by the grand stride of a Titanic shape, each disappearing in the surrounding press of shadowy foliage. Sometimes a profile of unspeakable beauty or grandeur would appear for a moment and vanish. Sometimes they seemed lovers that passed linked arm in arm, sometimes father and son, sometimes brothers in loving contest, sometimes sisters entwined in gracefullest community of complex form. Sometimes wild horses would tear across, free, or bestrode by nobel shadows of ruling men. But some of the things which pleased them most they never knew how to describe.

About the middle of the plain they sat down to rest in the heart of a heap of shadows. After sitting for a while, each, looking up, saw the other in tears: they were each longing after the country whence the shadows fell.

"We *must* find the country from which the shadows come," said Mossy.

"We must, dear Mossy," responded Tangle. "What if your golden key should be the key to it?"

"Ah! That would be grand," returned Mossy. "But we must rest here for a little, and then we shall be able to cross the plain before night."

So he lay down on the ground, and about him on every side, and over his head, was the constant play of the wonderful shadows. He could look through them, and see the one behind the other, till they mixed in a mass of darkness. Tangle, too, lay admiring, and wondering, and longing after the country whence the shadows came. When they were rested they rose and pursued their journey.

How long they were in crossing this plain I cannot tell; but before night Mossy's hair was streaked with grey, and Tangle had got wrinkles on her forehead.

As evening drew on, the shadows fell deeper and rose higher. At length they reached a place where they rose above their heads, and made all dark around them. Then they took hold of each other's hand, and walked on in silence and in some dismay. They felt the gathering darkness, and something strangely solemn besides, and the beauty of the shadows ceased to delight them. All at once Tangle found that she had not a hold of Mossy's hand, though when she lost it she could not tell.

"Mossy, Mossy!" she cried aloud in terror.

But no Mossy replied.

A moment after, the shadows sank to her feet, and down under her feet, and the mountains rose before her. She turned towards the gloomy region she had left, and called once more upon Mossy. There the gloom lay tossing and heaving, a dark, stormy, foamless sea of shadows, but no Mossy rose out of it, or came climbing up the hill on which she stood. She threw herself down and wept in despair.

Suddenly she remembered that the beautiful lady had told them, if they lost each other in a country of which she could not remember the name, they were not to be afraid, but go straight on.

"And besides," she said to herself, "Mossy has the golden key, and so no harm will come to him, I do believe."

She rose from the ground, and went on.

Before long she arrived at a precipice, in the face of which a stair was cut. When she ascended halfway, the stair ceased, and the path led straight into the mountain. She was afraid to enter, and turning again towards the stair, grew giddy at the sight of the depth beneath her, and was forced to throw herself down in the mouth of the cave.

When she opened her eyes, she saw a beautiful little creature with wings standing beside her, waiting.

"I know you," said Tangle. "You are my fish."

"Yes. But I am a fish no longer. I am an aëranth now."

"What is that?" asked Tangle.

"What you see I am," answered the shape. "And I am come to lead you through the mountain."

"Oh! Thank you, dear fish—aëranth, I mean," returned Tangle, rising.

Thereupon the aëranth took to his wings, and flew on through the long, narrow passage, reminding Tangle very much of the way he had swum on before when he was a fish. And the moment his white wings moved, they began to throw off a continuous shower of sparks of all colours, which lighted up the passage before them. All at once he vanished, and Tangle heard a low, sweet sound, quite different from the rush and crackle of his wings. Before her was an open arch, and through it came light, mixed with the sound of sea-waves.

She hurried out, and fell, tired and happy, upon the yellow sand of the shore. There she lay, half asleep with weariness and rest, listening to the low plash and retreat of the tiny waves, which seemed ever enticing the land to leave off being land, and become sea. And as she lay, her eyes were fixed upon the foot of a great rainbow standing far away against the sky on the other side of the sea. At length she fell fast asleep.

When she awoke, she saw an old man with long white hair down to his shoulders, leaning upon a stick covered with green buds, and so bending over her.

"What do you want here, beautiful woman?" he said.

"Am I beautiful? I am so glad!" answered Tangle, rising. "My grandmother is beautiful."

"Yes. But what do you want?" He repeated, kindly.

"I think I want you. Are not you the Old Man of the Sea?"

"I am."

"Then Grandmother says, have you any more fishes ready for her?"

"We will go and see, my dear," answered the Old Man, speaking yet more kindly than before. "And I can do something for you, can I not?"

"Yes—show me the way up to the country from which the shadows fall," said Tangle.

For there she hoped to find Mossy again.

"Ah! Indeed, that would be worth doing," said the Old Man. "But I cannot, for I do not know the way myself. But I will send you to the Old Man of the Earth. Perhaps he can tell you. He is much older than I am."

Leaning on his staff, he conducted her along the shore to a steep rock, that looked like a petrified ship turned upside down. The door of it was the rudder of a great vessel, ages ago at the bottom of the sea. Immediately within the door was a stair in the rock, down which the Old Man went, and Tangle followed. At the bottom the Old Man had his house, and there he lived.

As soon as she entered it, Tangle heard a strange noise, unlike anything she had ever heard before. She soon found that it was the fishes talking. She tried to understand what they said; but their speech was so old-fashioned, and rude, and undefined, that she could not make much of it.

"I will go and see about those fishes for my daughter," said the Old Man of the Sea.

And moving a slide in the wall of his house, he first looked out and then tapped upon a thick piece of crystal that filled the round opening. Tangle came up behind him, and peeping through the window into the heart of the great deep green ocean, saw the most curious creatures, some very ugly, all very odd, and with especially queer mouths, swimming about everywhere, above and below, but all coming towards the window in answer to the tap of the Old Man of the Sea. Only a few could get their mouths against the glass; but those who were floating miles away yet turned their heads towards it. The Old Man looked through the whole flock carefully for some minutes, and then turning to Tangle, said, "I am sorry. I have not got one ready yet. I want more time than she does. But I will send some as soon as I can."

He then shut the slide.

Presently a great noise arose in the sea. The Old Man opened the slide again, and tapped on the glass, whereupon the fishes were all as still as asleep.

"They were only talking about you," he said. "And they do speak such nonsense! Tomorrow," he continued, "I must show you the way to the Old Man of the Earth. He lives a long way from here."

"Do let me go at once," said Tangle.

"No, that is not possible. You must come this way first."

He led her to a hole in the wall, which she had not observed before. It was covered with the green leaves and white blossoms of a creeping plant.

"Only white-blossoming plants can grow under the sea," said the Old Man. "In there you will find a bath, in which you must lie till I call you."

Tangle went in, and found a smaller room or cave, in the further corner of which was a great basin hollowed out of rock, and half-full of the clearest seawater. Little streams were constantly running into it from cracks in the wall of the cavern. It was polished quite smooth inside, and had a carpet of yellow sand in the bottom of it. Large green leaves and white flowers of various plants crowded up and over it draping and covering it almost entirely.

No sooner was she undressed and lying in the bath, than she began to feel as if the water were sinking into her, and she were receiving all the good of sleep without undergoing its forgetfulness. She felt the good coming all the time. And she grew happier and more hopeful than she had been since she lost Mossy. But she could not help thinking how very sad it was for a poor old man to live there all alone, and have to take care of a whole seaful of stupid and riotous fishes.

After about an hour, as she thought, she heard his voice calling her, and rose out of the bath. All the fatigue and aching of her long journey had vanished. She was as whole, and strong, and well as if she had slept for seven days.

Returning to the opening that led into the other part of the house, she started back with amazement, for through it she saw the form of a grand man, with a majestic and beautiful face, waiting for her.

"Come," he said; "I see you are ready."

She entered with reverence.

"Where is the Old Man of the Sea?" she asked, humbly.

"There is no one here but me," he answered, smiling. "Some people call me the Old Man of the Sea. Others have another name for me, and are terribly frightened when they meet me taking a walk by the shore. Therefore I avoid being seen by them, for they are so afraid, that they never see what I really am. You see me now. But I must show you the way to the Old Man of the Earth."

He led her into the cave where the bath was, and there she saw, in the opposite corner, a second opening in the rock.

"Go down that stair, and it will bring you to him," said the Old Man of the Sea.

With humble thanks Tangle took her leave. She went down the winding-stair, till she began to fear there was no end to it. Still down and down it went, rough and broken, with springs of water bursting out of the rocks and running down the steps beside her. It was quite dark about her, and yet she could see. For after being in that bath, people's eyes always give out a light they can see by. There were no creeping things in the way. All was safe and pleasant though so dark and damp and deep.

At last there was not one step more, and she found herself in a glimmering cave. On a stone in the middle of it sat a figure with its back towards her—the figure of an old man bent double with age. From behind she could see his white beard spread out on the rocky floor in front of him. He did not move as she entered, so she passed round that she might stand before him and speak to him.

The moment she looked in his face, she saw that he was a youth of marvellous beauty. He sat entranced with the delight of what he beheld in a mirror of something like silver, which lay on the floor at his feet, and which from behind she had taken for his white beard. He sat on, heedless of her presence, pale with the joy of his vision.

She stood and watched him. At length, all trembling, she spoke. But her voice made no sound. Yet the youth lifted up his head. He showed no surprise, however, at seeing her—only smiled a welcome.

"Are you the Old Man of the Earth?" Tangle had said.

And the youth answered, and Tangle heard him, though not with her ears:

"I am. What can I do for you?"

"Tell me the way to the country whence the shadows fall."

"Ah! That I do not know. I only dream about it myself. I see its shadows sometimes in my mirror: the way to it I do not know. But I think the Old Man of the Fire must know. He is much older than I am. He is the oldest man of all."

"Where does he live?"

"I will show you the way to his place. I never saw him myself."

So saying, the young man rose, and then stood for a while gazing at Tangle.

"I wish I could see that country too," he said. "But I must mind my work."

He led her to the side of the cave, and told her to lay her ear against the wall.

"What do you hear?" he asked.

"I hear," answered Tangle, "the sound of a great water running inside the rock."

"That river runs down to the dwelling of the oldest man of all—the Old Man of the Fire. I wish I could go to see him. But I must mind my work. That river is the only way to him."

Then the Old Man of the Earth stooped over the floor of the cave, raised a huge stone from it, and left it leaning. It disclosed a great hole that went plumb-down.

"That is the way," he said.

"But there are no stairs."

"You must throw yourself in. There is no other way."

She turned and looked him full in the face—stood so for a whole minute, as she thought: it was a whole year—then threw herself headlong into the hole.

When she came to herself, she found herself gliding down fast and deep. Her head was under water, but that did not signify, for, when she thought about it, she could not remember that she had breathed once since her bath in the cave of the Old Man of the Sea. When she lifted up her head a sudden and fierce heat struck her, and she sank it again instantly, and went sweeping on.

Gradually the stream grew shallower. At length she could hardly keep her head under. Then the water could carry her no farther. She rose from the channel, and went step for step down the burning descent. The water ceased altogether. The heat was terrible. She felt scorched to the bone, but it did not touch her strength. It grew hotter and hotter. She said, "I can bear it no longer." Yet she went on.

At the long last the stair ended at a rude archway in an all but glowing rock. Through this archway Tangle fell exhausted into a cool mossy cave. The floor and walls were covered with moss—green, soft, and damp. A little stream spouted from a rent in the rock and fell into a basin of moss. She plunged her face into it and drank. Then she lifted her head and looked around. Then she rose and looked again. She saw no one in the cave. But the moment she stood upright she had a marvellous sense that she was in the secret of the earth and all its ways. Everything she had seen, or learned from books; all that her grandmother had said or sung to her; all the talk of the beasts, birds, and fishes; all that happened to her on her journey with Mossy, and since then in the heart of the earth with the Old Man and the older man—all was plain: she understood it all, and saw that everything meant the same thing, though she could not have put it into words again.

The next moment she descried, in a corner of the cave, a little naked child, sitting on the moss. He was playing with balls of various colours and sizes, which he disposed in strange figures upon the floor beside him. And now Tangle felt that there was something in her knowledge which was not in her understanding. For she knew there must be an infinite meaning in the change and sequence and individual forms of the figures into which the child arranged the balls, as well as in the varied harmonies of their colours, but what it all meant she could not tell.† He went on busily, tirelessly, playing his solitary game, without looking up, or seeming to know that there was a stranger in his deep-withdrawn cell. Diligently as a lace-maker shifts her bobbins, he shifted and arranged his balls. Flashes of meaning would now pass from them to Tangle, and now again all would be not merely obscure, but utterly dark. She stood looking for a long time, for there was fascination in the sight; and the longer she looked the more an indescribable vague intelligence went on rousing itself in her mind. For seven years she had stood there watching the naked child with his coloured balls, and it seemed to her like seven hours, when all at once the shape the balls took, she know not why, reminded her of the Valley of Shadows, and she spoke:

"Where is the Old Man of the Fire?" she said.

"Here I am," answered the child, rising and leaving his balls on the moss. "What can I do for you?"

There was such an awfulness of absolute repose on the face of the child that Tangle stood dumb before him. He had no smile, but the love in his large gray eyes was deep as the centre. And with the repose there lay on his face a shimmer as of moonlight, which seemed as if any moment it might break into such a ravishing smile

---

†   I think I must be indebted to Novalis for these geometrical figures.

as would cause the beholder to weep himself to death. But the smile never came, and the moonlight lay there unbroken. For the heart of the child was too deep for any smile to reach from it to his face.

"Are you the oldest man of all?" Tangle at length, although filled with awe, ventured to ask.

"Yes, I am. I am very, very old. I am able to help you, I know. I can help everybody."

And the child drew near and looked up in her face so that she burst into tears.

"Can you tell me the way to the country the shadows fall from?" she sobbed.

"Yes. I know the way quite well. I go there myself sometimes. But you could not go my way; you are not old enough. I will show you how you can go."

"Do not send me out into the great heat again," prayed Tangle.

"I will not," answered the child.

And he reached up, and put his little cool hand on her heart.

"Now," he said, "you can go. The fire will not burn you. Come."

He led her from the cave, and following him through another archway, she found herself in a vast desert of sand and rock. The sky of it was of rock, lowering over them like solid thunderclouds; and the whole place was so hot that she saw, in bright rivulets, the yellow gold and white silver and red copper trickling molten from the rocks. But the heat never came near her.

When they had gone some distance, the child turned up a great stone, and took something like an egg from under it. He next drew a long curved line in the sand with his finger, and laid the egg in it. He then spoke something Tangle could not understand. The egg broke, a small snake came out and, lying in the line in the sand, grew and grew till he filled it. The moment he was thus full-grown, he began to glide away, undulating like a sea-wave.

"Follow that serpent," said the child. "He will lead you the right way."

Tangle followed the serpent. But she could not go far without looking back at the marvellous child. He stood alone in the midst of the glowing desert beside a fountain of red flame that had burst forth at his feet, his naked whiteness glimmering a pale rosy red in the torrid fire. There he stood, looking after her, till, from the lengthening distance, she could see him no more. The serpent went straight on, turning neither to the right nor left.

Meantime Mossy had got out of the lake of shadows, and, following his mournful, lonely way, had reached the seashore. It was a dark, stormy evening. The sun had set. The wind was blowing from the sea. The waves had surrounded the rock within which lay the Old Man's house. A deep water rolled between it and the shore, upon which a majestic figure was walking alone.

Mossy went up to him and said, "Will you tell me where to find the Old Man of the Sea?"

"I am the Old Man of the Sea," the figure answered.

"I see a strong kingly man of middle age," returned Mossy.

Then the Old Man looked at him more intently, and said, "Your sight young man, is better than that of most who take this way. The night is stormy: come to my house and tell me what I can do for you."

Mossy followed him. The waves flew from before the footsteps of the Old Man of the Sea, and Mossy followed upon dry sand.

When they had reached the cave, they sat down and gazed at each other.

Now Mossy was an old man by this time. He looked much older than the Old Man of the Sea, and his feet were very weary.

After looking at him for a moment, the Old Man took him by the hand and led him into his inner cave. There he helped him to undress, and laid him in the bath. And he saw that one of his hands Mossy did not open.

"What have you in that hand?" he asked.

Mossy opened his hand, and there lay the golden key.

"Ah!" said the Old Man. "That accounts for your knowing me. And I know the way you have to go."

"I want to find the country whence the shadows fall," said Mossy.

"I dare say you do. So do I. But meantime, one thing is certain. What is the key for, do you think?"

"For a keyhole somewhere. But I don't know why I keep it. I never could find the keyhole. And I have lived a good while, I believe," said Mossy, sadly. "I'm not sure that I'm not old. I know my feet ache."

"Do they?" said the Old Man, as if he really meant to ask the question: and Mossy, who was still lying in the bath, watched his feet for a moment before he replied.

"No, they do not," he answered. "Perhaps I am not old either."

"Get up and look at yourself in the water."

He rose and looked at himself in the water, and there was not a gray hair on his head or a wrinkle on his skin.

"You have tasted of death now," said the Old Man. "Is it good?"

"It is good," said Mossy. "It is better than life."

"No," said the Old Man; "it is only more life. Your feet will make no holes in the water now."

"What do you mean?"

"I will show you that presently."

They returned to the outer cave, and sat and talked together for a long time. At length the Old Man of the Sea rose, and said to Mossy, "Follow me."

He led him up the stair again, and opened another door. They stood on the level of the raging sea, looking towards the east. Across the waste of waters, against the bosom of a fierce black cloud, stood the foot of a rainbow, glowing in the dark.

"This indeed is my way," said Mossy, as soon as he saw the rainbow, and stepped out upon the sea. His feet made no holes in the water. He fought the wind, and climbed the waves, and went on towards the rainbow.

The storm died away. A lovely day and a lovelier night followed. A cool wind blew over the wide plain of the quiet ocean. And still Mossy journeyed eastward. But the rainbow had vanished with the storm.

Day after day he held on, and he thought he had no guide. He did not see how a shining fish under the waters directed his steps. He crossed the sea, and came to a great precipice of rock, up which he could discover but one path. Nor did this lead him farther than halfway up the rock, where it ended on a platform. Here he stood and pondered. It could not be that the way stopped here, else what was the path for? It was a rough path, not very plain, yet certainly a path. He examined the face of the rock. It was smooth as glass. But as his eyes kept roving hopelessly over it, something glittered, and he caught sight of a row of small sapphires. They bordered a little hole in the rock.

"The keyhole!" he cried.

He tried the key. It fitted. It turned. A great clang and clash, as of iron bolts on huge brazen caldrons, echoed thunderously within. He drew out the key. The rock in front of him began to fall. He retreated from it as far as the breadth of the platform would allow. A great slab fell at his feet. In front was still the solid rock, with this one slab fallen forward out of it. But the moment he stepped upon it a second fell, just short of the edge of the first making the next step of a stair, which thus kept dropping itself before him as he ascended into the heart of the precipice. It led him into a hall fit for such an approach—irregular and rude in formation, but floor, sides, pillars, and vaulted roof, all one mass of shining stones of every colour that light can show. In the centre stood seven columns, ranged from red to violet. And on the pedestal of one of them sat a woman, motionless, with her face bowed upon her knees. Seven years had she sat there waiting. She lifted her head as Mossy drew near. It was Tangle. Her hair had grown to her feet and was rippled like the windless sea on broad sands. Her face was beautiful, like her grandmother's, and as still and peaceful as that of the Old Man of the Fire. Her form was tall and noble. Yet Mossy knew her at once.

"How beautiful you are, Tangle!" he said, in delight and astonishment.

"Am I?" she returned. "Oh, I have waited for you so long! But you, you are like the Old Man of the Sea. No. You are like the Old Man of the Earth. No, no. You are like the oldest man of all. You are like them all. And yet you are my own old Mossy! How did you come here? What did you do after I lost you? Did you find the keyhole? Have you got the key still?"

She had a hundred questions to ask him, and he a hundred more to ask her. They told each other all their adventures, and were as happy as man and woman could be. For they were younger and better, and stronger and wiser, than they had ever been before.

It began to grow dark. And they wanted more than ever to reach the country whence the shadows fall. So they looked about them for a way out of the cave. The door by which Mossy entered had closed again, and there was half a mile of rock between them and the sea. Neither could Tangle find the opening in the floor by which the serpent had led her thither. They searched till it grew so dark that they could see nothing, and gave it up.

After a while, however, the cave began to glimmer again. The light came from the moon, but it did not look like moonlight, for it gleamed through those seven pillars in the middle, and filled the place with all colours. And now Mossy saw that there was a pillar beside the red one, which he had not observed before. And it was of the same new colour that he had seen in the rainbow when he saw it first in the fairy forest. And on it he saw a sparkle of blue. It was the sapphires round the keyhole.

He took his key. It turned in the lock to the sounds of Aeolian music. A door opened upon slow hinges, and disclosed a winding stair within. The key vanished from his fingers. Tangle went up. Mossy followed. The door closed behind them. They climbed out of the earth; and, still climbing, rose above it. They were in the rainbow. Far abroad, over ocean and land, they could see through its transparent walls the earth beneath their feet. Stairs beside stairs wound up together, and beautiful beings of all ages climbed along with them.

They knew that they were going up to the country whence the shadows fall.

And by this time I think they must have got there.

THE GRAY WOLF

* * *

ONE evening twilight in spring, a young English student, who had wandered northwards as far as the outlying fragments of Scotland called the Orkney and Shetland islands, found himself on a small island of the latter group, caught in a storm of wind and hail, which had come on suddenly. It was in vain to look about for any shelter; for not only did the storm entirely obscure the landscape, but there was nothing around him save a desert moss.

At length, however, as he walked on for mere walking's sake, he found himself on the verge of a cliff, and saw, over the brow of it, a few feet below him, a ledge of rock, where he might find some shelter from the blast, which blew from behind. Letting himself down by his hands, he alighted upon something that crunched beneath his tread, and found the bones of many small animals scattered about in front of a little cave in the rock, offering the refuge he sought. He went in, and sat upon a stone. The storm increased in violence, and as the darkness grew he became uneasy, for he did not relish the thought of spending the night in the cave. He had parted from his companions on the opposite side of the island, and it added to his uneasiness that they must be full of apprehension about him. At last there came a lull in the storm, and the same instant he heard a footfall, stealthy and light as that of a wild beast, upon the bones at the mouth of the cave. He started up in some fear, though the least thought might have satisfied him that there could be no very dangerous animals upon the island. Before he had time to think, however, the face of a woman appeared in the opening. Eagerly the wanderer spoke. She started at the sound of his voice. He could not see her well, because she was turned towards the darkness of the cave.

"Will you tell me how to find my way across the moor to Shielness?" he asked.

"You cannot find it tonight," she answered, in a sweet tone, and with a smile that bewitched him, revealing the whitest of teeth.

"What am I to do then?" he asked.

"My mother will give you shelter, but that is all she has to offer."

"And that is far more than I expected a minute ago," he replied. "I shall be most grateful."

She turned in silence and left the cave. The youth followed.

She was barefooted, and her pretty brown feet went catlike over the sharp stones, as she led the way down a rocky path to the shore. Her garments were scanty and torn, and her hair blew tangled in the wind. She seemed about five and twenty, lithe and small. Her long fingers kept clutching and pulling nervously at her skirts as she went. Her face was very gray in complexion, and very worn, but delicately formed, and smooth-skinned. Her thin nostrils were tremulous as eyelids, and her lips, whose curves were faultless, had no colour to give sign of indwelling blood. What her eyes were like he could not see, for she had never lifted the delicate films of her eyelids.

At the foot of the cliff they came upon a little hut leaning against it and having for its inner apartment a natural hollow within it. Smoke was spreading over the face of the rock, and the grateful odour of food gave hope to the hungry student. His guide opened the door of the cottage; he followed her in, and saw a woman bending over a fire in the middle of the floor. On the fire lay a large fish broiling. The daughter spoke a few words, and the mother turned and welcomed the stranger. She had an old and very wrinkled, but honest face, and looked troubled. She dusted the only chair in the cottage, and placed it for him by the side of the fire, opposite the one window, whence he saw a little patch of yellow sand over which the spent waves spread themselves out listlessly. Under this window there was a bench, upon which the daughter threw herself in an unusual posture, resting her chin upon her hand. A moment after, the youth caught the first glimpse of her blue eyes. They were fixed upon him with a strange look of greed, amounting to craving, but as if aware that they belied or betrayed her, she dropped them instantly. The moment she veiled them, her face, notwithstanding its colourless complexion, was almost beautiful.

When the fish was ready, the old woman wiped the deal table, steadied it upon the uneven floor, and covered it with a piece of fine table-linen. She then laid the fish on a wooden platter, and invited the guest to help himself. Seeing no other provision, he pulled from his pocket a hunting knife, and divided a portion from the fish, offering it to the mother first.

"Come, my lamb," said the old woman; and the daughter approached the table. But her nostrils and mouth quivered with disgust.

The next moment she turned and hurried from the hut.

"She doesn't like fish," said the old woman, "and I haven't anything else to give her."

"She does not seem in good health," he rejoined.

The woman answered only with a sigh, and they ate their fish with the help of a little rye bread. As they finished their supper, the youth heard the sound as of the pattering of a dog's feet upon the sand close to the door, but ere he had time to look out of the window, the door opened and the young woman entered. She looked better, perhaps from having just washed her face. She drew a stool to the corner of the fire opposite him. But as she sat down, to his bewilderment, and even horror, the student spied a single drop of blood on her white skin within her torn dress. The woman brought out a jar of whisky, put a rusty old kettle on the fire, and took her place in front of it. As soon as the water boiled, she proceeded to make some toddy in a wooden bowl.

Meantime the youth could not take his eyes off the young woman, so that at length he found himself fascinated, or rather bewitched. She kept her eyes for the most part veiled with the loveliest eyelids fringed with darkest lashes, and he gazed entranced; for the red glow of the little oil lamp covered all the strangeness of her complexion. But as soon as he met a stolen glance out of those eyes unveiled, his soul shuddered within him. Lovely face and craving eyes alternated fascination and repulsion.

The mother placed the bowl in his hands. He drank sparingly, and passed it to the girl. She lifted it to her lips, and as she tasted— only tasted it—looked at him. He thought the drink must have been drugged and have affected his brain. Her hair smoothed itself back, and drew her forehead backwards with it; while the lower part of her face projected towards the bowl, revealing, ere she sipped, her dazzling teeth in strange prominence. But the same moment the vision vanished; she returned the vessel to her mother, and rising, hurried out of the cottage.

Then the old woman pointed to a bed of heather in one corner with a murmured apology; and the student, wearied both with the fatigues of the day and the strangeness of the night, threw himself upon it, wrapped in his cloak. The moment he lay down, the storm began afresh, and the wind blew so keenly through the crannies of the hut, that it was only by drawing his cloak over his head that he could protect himself from its currents. Unable to sleep, he lay listening to the uproar, which grew in violence, till the spray was dashing against the window. At length the door opened, and the young woman came in, made up the fire, drew the bench before it, and lay down in the same strange posture, with her chin propped on her hand and elbow, and her face turned towards the youth. He moved a little; she dropped her head, and lay on her face, with her arms crossed beneath her forehead. The mother had disappeared.

Drowsiness crept over him. A movement of the bench roused him, and he fancied he saw some four-footed creature as tall as a large dog trot quietly out of the door. He was sure he felt a rush of cold wind. Gazing fixedly through the darkness, he thought he saw the eyes of the damsel encountering his, but a glow from the falling together of the remnants of the fire, revealed clearly enough that the bench was vacant. Wondering what could have made her go out in such a storm, he fell fast asleep.

In the middle of the night he felt a pain in his shoulder, came broad awake, and saw the gleaming eyes and grinning teeth of some animal close to his face. Its claws were in his shoulder, and its mouth in the act of seeking his throat. Before it had fixed its fangs, however, he had its throat in one hand, and sought his knife with the other. A terrible struggle followed; but regardless of the tearing claws, he found and opened his knife. He had made one futile stab, and was drawing it for a surer, when, with a spring of the whole body, and one wildly-contorted effort, the creature twisted its neck from his hold, and with something betwixt a scream and a howl, darted from him. Again he heard the door open; again the wind blew in upon him, and it continued blowing; a sheet of spray dashed across the floor, and over his face. He sprung from his couch and bounded to the door.

It was a wild night—dark, but for the flash of whiteness from the waves as they broke within a few yards of the cottage; the wind was raving, and the rain pouring down the air. A gruesome sound as of mingled weeping and howling came from somewhere in the dark. He turned again into the hut and closed the door, but could find no way of securing it.

The lamp was nearly out and he could not be certain whether the form of the young woman was upon the bench or not. Overcoming a strong repugnance, he approached it, and put out his hands—there was nothing there. He sat down and waited for the daylight: he dared not sleep anymore.

When the day dawned at length, he went out yet again, and looked around. The morning was dim and gusty and gray. The wind had fallen, but the waves were tossing wildly. He wandered up and down the little strand, longing for more light.

At length he heard a movement in the cottage. By-and-by the voice of the old woman called to him from the door.

"You're up early, sir. I doubt you didn't sleep well."

"Not very well," he answered. "But where is your daughter?"

"She's not awake yet," said the mother. "I'm afraid I have but a poor breakfast for you. But you'll take a dram and a bit of fish. It's all I've got."

Unwilling to hurt her, though hardly in good appetite, he sat down at the table. While they were eating, the daughter came in, but turned her face away and went to the further end of the hut. When she came forward after a minute or two, the youth saw that her hair was drenched, and her face whiter than before. She looked ill and faint, and when she raised her eyes, all their fierceness had vanished, and sadness had taken its place. Her neck was now covered with a cotton handkerchief. She was modestly attentive to him, and no longer shunned his gaze. He was gradually yielding to the temptation of braving another night in the hut and seeing what would follow, when the old woman spoke.

"The weather will be broken all day, sir," she said. "You had better be going, or your friends will leave without you."

Ere he could answer, he saw such a beseeching glance on the face of the girl, that he hesitated, confused. Glancing at the mother, he saw the flash of wrath in her face. She rose and approached her daughter, with her hand lifted to strike her. The young woman stooped her head with a cry. He darted round the table to interpose between them. But the mother had caught hold of her; the handkerchief had fallen from her neck; and the youth saw five blue bruises on her lovely throat—the marks of the four fingers and the thumb of a left hand. With a cry of horror he darted from the house, but as he reached the door he turned. His hostess was lying motionless on the floor, and a huge gray wolf came bounding after him.

There was no weapon at hand; and if there had been, his inborn chivalry would never have allowed him to harm a woman even under the guise of a wolf. Instinctively, he set himself firm, leaning a little forward, with half-outstretched arms, and hands curved ready to clutch again at the throat upon which he had left those pitiful marks. But the creature as she sprung eluded his grasp, and just as he expected to feel her fangs, he found a woman weeping on his bosom, with her arms around his neck. The next instant, the gray wolf broke from him, and bounded howling up the cliff. Recovering himself as he best might, the youth followed, for it was the only way to the moor above, across which he must now make his way to find his companions.

All at once he heard the sound of a crunching of bones—not as if a creature was eating them, but as if they were ground by the teeth of rage and disappointment; looking up, he saw close above him the mouth of the little cavern in which he had taken refuge the day before. Summoning all his resolution, he passed it slowly and softly. From within came the sounds of a mingled moaning and growling.

Having reached the top, he ran at full speed for some distance across the moor before venturing to look behind him. When at length he did so, he saw, against the sky, the girl standing on the edge of the cliff, wringing her hands. One solitary wail crossed the space between. She made no attempt to follow him, and he reached the opposite shore in safety.

THE CARASOYN

* * *

I. THE MOUNTAIN STREAM

ONCE upon a time, there lived in a valley in Scotland, a boy about twelve years of age, the son of a shepherd. His mother was dead, and he had no sister or brother. His father was out all day on the hills with his sheep; but when he came home at night, he was as sure of finding the cottage neat and clean, the floor swept, a bright fire, and his supper waiting for him, as if he had had wife and daughter to look after his household, instead of only a boy. Therefore, although Colin could only read and write, and knew nothing of figures, he was ten times wiser, and more capable of learning anything, than if he had been at school all his days. He was never at a loss when anything had to be done. Somehow, he always blundered into the straight road to his end, while another would be putting on his shoes to look for it. And yet all the time that he was busiest working, he was busiest building castles in the air. I think the two ought always to go together.

And so Colin was never over-worked, but had plenty of time to himself. In winter he spent it in reading by the fireside, or carving pieces of wood with his pocket knife; and in summer he always went out for a ramble. His great delight was in a little stream which ran down the valley from the mountains above. Up this *burn* he would wander every afternoon, with his hands in his pockets. He never got far, however—he was so absorbed in watching its antics. Sometimes he would sit on a rock, staring at the water as it hurried through the stones, scolding, expostulating, muttering, and always having its own way. Sometimes he would stop by a deep pool, and watch the crimson-spotted trouts, darting about as if their thoughts and not their tails sent them where they wanted to go. And when he stopped at the little cascade, tumbling smooth and shining over a hollowed rock, he seldom got beyond it.

But there was one thing which always troubled him. It was that when the stream came near the cottage, it could find no other way than through the little yard where stood the cowhouse and the pigsty; and there, not finding a suitable channel, spread abroad in a disconsolate manner, becoming rather a puddle than a brook, all defiled with the treading of the cloven feet of the cow and the pigs. In fact, it looked quite lost and ruined; so that even after it had, with much labour, got out of the yard again, it took a long time to gather itself together, and not quite succeeding, slipped away as if ashamed, with spent forces and poverty-stricken speed; till at length, meeting the friendly help of a rivulet coming straight from the hills, it gathered heart and bounded on afresh.

"It can't be all that the cow drinks that makes the difference," said Colin to himself. "The pigs don't care about it. I do believe it's affronted at being dashed about. The cow isn't dirty, but she's rather stupid and inconsiderate. The pigs are dirty. Something must be done. Let me see."

He reconnoitred the whole ground. Upon the other side of the house all was rock, through which he could not cut; and he was forced to the conclusion that the only other course for the stream to take lay right through the cottage.

To most engineers this would have appeared the one course to be avoided; but Colin's heart danced at the thought of having his dear *burn* running right through the house. How cool it would be all the summer! How convenient for cooking; and how handy at meals! And then the music of it! How it would tell him stories, and sing him to sleep at night! What a companion it would be when his father was away! And then he could bathe in it when he liked. In winter—ah! To be sure! But winter was a long way off.

The very next day his father went to the fair. So Colin set to work at once.

It was not such a very difficult undertaking; for the walls of the cottage, and the floor as well, were of clay—the former nearly sun-dried into a brick, and the latter trampled hard; but still both assailable by pickaxe and spade. He cut through the walls, and dug a channel along the floor, letting in stones in the bottom and sides. After it got out of the cottage and through the small garden in front, it should find its own way to the channel below, for here the hill was very steep.

The same evening his father came home.

"What have you been about, Colin?" he asked, in great surprise, when he saw the trench in the floor.

"Wait a minute, father," said Colin, "till I have got your supper, and then I'll tell you."

So when his father was seated at the table, Colin darted out, and hurrying up to the stream, broke through the bank just in the place whence a natural hollow led straight to the cottage. The stream dashed out like a wild creature from a cage, faster than he could follow, and shot through the wall of the cottage. His father gave a shout; and when Colin went in, he found him sitting with his spoon halfway to his mouth, and his eyes fixed on the muddy water which rushed foaming through his floor.

"It will soon be clean, father," said Colin, "and then it will be so nice!"

His father made no answer, but continued staring. Colin went on with a long list of the advantages of having a brook running through your house. At length his father smiled and said:

"You are a curious creature, Colin. But why shouldn't you have your fancies as well as older people? We'll try it awhile, and then we'll see about it."

The fact was, Colin's father had often thought what a lonely life the boy's was. And it seemed hard to take from him any pleasure he could have. So out rushed Colin at the front, to see how the brook would take the shortest way headlong down the hill to its old channel. And to see it go tumbling down that hill was a sight worth living for.

"It is a mercy," said Colin, "it has no neck to break, or it would break twenty times in a minute. It flings itself from rock to rock right down, just as I should like to do, if it weren't for my neck."

All that evening he was out and in without a moment's rest; now up to the beginning of the cut, now following the stream down to the cottage; then through the cottage, and out again at the front door to see it dart across the garden, and dash itself down the hill.

At length his father told him he must go to bed. He took one more peep at the water, which was running quite clear now, and obeyed. His father followed him presently.

II. THE FAIRY FLEET

THE bed was about a couple of yards from the edge of the brook. And as Colin was always first up in the morning, he slept at the front of the bed. So he lay for some time gazing at the faint glimmer of the water in the dull red light from the sod-covered fire, and listening to its sweet music as it hurried through to the night again, till its murmur changed into a lullaby, and sung him fast asleep.

Soon he found that he was coming awake again. He was lying listening to the sound of the busy stream. But it had gathered more sounds since he went to sleep—amongst the rest, one of boards knocking together, and a tiny chattering and sweet laughter, like the tinkling of heather-bells. He opened his eyes. The moon was shining along the brook, lighting the smoky rafters above with its reflection from the water, which had been dammed back at its outlet from the cottage, so that it lay bank-full and level with the floor. But its surface was hardly to be seen, save by an occasional glimmer, for the crowded boats of a fairy fleet which had just arrived. The sailors were as busy as sailors could be, mooring along the banks, or running their boats high and dry on the shore. Some had little sails which glimmered white in the moonshine—half-lowered, or blowing out in the light breeze that crept down the course of the stream. Some were pulling about through the rest, oars flashing, tiny voices calling, tiny feet running, tiny hands hauling at ropes that ran through blocks of shining ivory. On the shore stood groups of fairy ladies in all colours of the rainbow, green predominating, waited upon by gentlemen all in green, but with red and yellow feathers in their caps. The queen had landed on the side next to Colin, and in a few minutes more twenty dances were going at once along the shores of the fairy river. And there lay great Colin's face, just above the bed-clothes, glowering at them like an ogre.

At last, after a few dances, he heard a clear, sweet, ringing voice say, "I've had enough of this. I'm tired of doing like the big people. Let's have a game of Hey Cockolorum Jig!"

That instant every group sprang asunder, and every fairy began a frolic on his own account. They scattered all over the cottage, and Colin lost sight of most of them.

While he lay watching the antics of two of those near him, who behaved more like clowns at a fair than the gentlemen they had been a little while before, he heard a voice close to his ear; but though he looked everywhere about his pillow, he could see nothing. The voice stopped the moment he began to look, but began again as soon as he gave it up.

"You can't see me. I'm talking to you through a hole in the head of your bed."

"Don't look," said the voice. "If the queen sees me I shall be pinched. Oh, please don't."

The voice sounded as if its owner would cry presently. So Colin took good care not to look. It went on:

"Please, I am a little girl, not a fairy. The queen stole me the minute I was born, seven years ago, and I can't get away. I don't like the fairies. They are so silly. And they never grow any wiser. I grow wiser every year. I want to get back to my own people. They won't let me. They make me play at being somebody else all night long, and sleep all day. That's what they do themselves. And I should so like to be myself. The queen says that's not the way to be happy at all; but I do want very much to be a little girl. Do take me."

"How am I to get you?" asked Colin in a whisper, which sounded, after the sweet voice of the changeling, like the wind in a field of dry beans.

"The queen is so pleased with you that she is sure to offer you something. Choose me. Here she comes."

Immediately he heard another voice, shriller and stronger, in front of him; and, looking about, saw standing on the edge of the bed a lovely little creature, with a crown glittering with jewels, and a rush for a sceptre in her hand, the blossom of which shone like a bunch of garnets.

"You great staring creature!" she said. "Your eyes are much too big to see with. What clumsy hobgoblins you thick folk are!"

So saying, she laid her wand across Colin's eyes.

"Now, then, stupid!" she said and that instant Colin saw the room like a huge barn, full of creatures about two feet high. The beams overhead were crowded with fairies, playing all imaginable tricks, scrambling everywhere, knocking each other over, throwing dust and soot in each other's faces, grinning from behind corners, dropping on each other's necks, and tripping up each other's heels. Two had got hold of an empty egg-shell, and coming behind one sitting on the edge of the table, and laughing at someone on the floor, tumbled it right over him, so that he was lost in the cavernous hollow. But the lady-fairies mingled in none of these rough pranks. Their tricks were always graceful, and they had more to say than to do.

But the moment the queen had laid her wand across his eyes, she went on:

"Know, son of a human mortal, that thou hast pleased a queen of the fairies. Lady as I am over the elements, I cannot have everything I desire. One thing thou hast given me. Years have I longed for a path down this rivulet to the ocean below. Your horrid farm-yard, ever since your great-grandfather built this cottage, was the one obstacle. For we fairies hate dirt, not only in houses, but in fields and woods as well, and above all in running streams. But I can't talk like this any longer. I tell you what, you are a dear good boy, and you shall have what you please. Ask me for anything you like."

"May it please your majesty," said Colin, very deliberately, "I want a little girl that you carried away some seven years ago the moment she was born. May it please your majesty, I want her."

"It does not please my majesty," cried the queen, whose face had been growing very black. "Ask for something else."

"Then, whether it pleases your majesty or not," said Colin, bravely, "I hold your majesty to your word. I want that little girl, and that little girl I *will* have, and nothing else."

"You dare to talk so to me, you thick!"

"Yes, your majesty."

"Then you shan't have her."

"Then I'll turn the brook right through the dunghill," said Colin. "Do you think I'll let you come into my cottage to play at high jinks when you please, if you behave to me like this?"

And Colin sat up in bed, and looked the queen in the face. And as he did so he caught sight of the loveliest little creature peeping round the corner at the foot of the bed. And he knew she was the little girl because she was quiet, and looked frightened, and was sucking her thumb.

Then the queen, seeing with whom she had to deal, and knowing that queens in Fairyland are bound by their word, began to try another plan with him. She put on her sweetest manner and looks; and as she did so, the little face at the foot of the bed grew more troubled, and the little head shook itself, and the little thumb dropped out of the little mouth.

"Dear Colin," said the queen, "you shall have the girl. But you must do something for me first."

The little girl shook her head as fast as ever she could, but Colin was taken up with the queen.

"To be sure I will. What is it?" he said.

And so he was bound by a new bargain, and was in the queen's power.

"You must fetch me a bottle of Carasoyn," said she.

"What is that?" asked Colin.

"A kind of wine that makes people happy."

"Why, are you not happy already?"

"No, Colin," answered the queen, with a sigh.

"You have everything you want."

"Except the Carasoyn," returned the queen.

"You do whatever you like, and go wherever you please."

"That's just it. I want something that I neither like nor please—that I don't know anything about. I want a bottle of Carasoyn."

And here she cried like a spoilt child, not like a sorrowful woman.

"But how am I to get it?"

"I don't know. You must find out."

"Oh! That's not fair," cried Colin.

But the queen burst into a fit of laughter that sounded like the bells of a hundred frolicking sheep, and bounding away to the side of the river, jumped on board of her boat. And like a swarm of bees gathered the courtiers and sailors; two creeping out of the bellows, one at the nozzle and the other at the valve; three out of the basket-hilt of the broadsword on the wall; six all white out of the meal-tub; and so from all parts of the cottage to the river-side. And amongst them Colin spied the little girl creeping on board the queen's boat, with her pinafore to her eyes; and the queen was shaking her fist at her. In five minutes more they had all scrambled into the boats, and the whole fleet was in motion down the stream. In another moment the cottage was empty, and everything had returned to its usual size.

"They'll be all dashed to pieces on the rocks," cried Colin, jumping up, and running into the garden. When he reached the fall, there was nothing to be seen but the swift plunge and rush of the broken water in the moonlight. He thought he heard cries and shouts coming up from below, and fancied he could distinguish the sobs of the little maiden whom he had so foolishly lost. But the sounds might be only those of the water, for to the different voices of a running stream there is no end. He followed its course all the way to its old channel, but saw nothing to indicate any disaster. Then he crept back to his bed, where he lay thinking what a fool he had been, till he cried himself to sleep over the little girl who would never grow into a woman.

III. THE OLD WOMAN AND HER HEN

IN the morning, however, his courage had returned; for the word Carasoyn was always saying itself in his brain.

"People in fairy stories," he said, "always find what they want. Why should not I find this Carasoyn? It does not seem likely. But the world doesn't go round by *likely*. So I will try."

But how was he to begin?

When Colin did not know what to do, he always did something. So as soon as his father was gone to the hill, he wandered up the stream down which the fairies had come.

"But I needn't go on so," he said, "for if the Carasoyn grew in the fairies' country, the queen would know how to get it."

All at once he remembered how he had lost himself on the moor when he was a little boy; and had gone into a hut and found there an old woman spinning. And she had told him such stories! And shown him the way home. So he thought she might be able to help him now; for he remembered that she was very old then, and must be older and still wiser now. And he resolved to go and look for the hut, and ask the old woman what he was to do.

So he left the stream, and climbed the hill, and soon came upon a desolate moor. The sun was clouded and the wind was cold, and everything looked dreary. And there was no sign of a hut anywhere. He wandered on, looking for it; and all at once found that he had forgotten the way back. At the same instant he saw the hut right before him. And then he remembered it was when he had lost himself that he saw it the former time.

"It seems the way to find some things is to lose yourself," said he to himself.

He went up to the cottage, which was like a large beehive built of turf, and knocked at the door.

"Come in, Colin," said a voice; and he entered, stooping low.

The old woman sat by a little fire, spinning, after the old fashion, with a distaff and spindle. She stopped the moment he went in.

"Come and sit down by the fire," she said, "and tell me what you want."

Then Colin saw that she had no eyes.

"I am very sorry you are blind," he said.

"Never you mind that my dear. I see more than you do for all my blindness. Tell me what you want and I shall see at least what I can do for you."

"How do you know I want anything?" asked Colin.

"Now that's what I don't like," said the old woman. "Why do you waste words? Words should not be wasted anymore than crumbs."

"I beg your pardon," returned Colin. "I will tell you all about it."

And so he told her the whole story.

"Oh those children! Those children!" said the old woman. "They are always doing some mischief. They never know how to enjoy themselves without hurting somebody or other. I really must give that queen a bit of my mind. Well, my dear, I like you; and I will tell you what must be done. You shall carry the silly queen her bottle of Carasoyn. But she won't like it when she gets it, I can tell her. That's my business, however. First of all, Colin, you must dream three days without sleeping. Next, you must work three days without dreaming. And last, you must work and dream three days together."

"How am I to do all that?"

"I will help you all I can, but a great deal will depend on yourself. In the meantime you must have something to eat."

So saying, she rose, and going to a corner behind her bed, returned with a large golden-coloured egg in her hand. This she laid on the hearth, and covered over with hot ashes. She then chatted away to Colin about his father, and the sheep, and the cow, and the housework, and showed that she knew all about him. At length she drew the ashes off the egg, and put it on the plate.

"It shines like silver now," said Colin.

"That is a sign it is quite done," said she, and set it before him.

Colin had never tasted anything half so nice. And he had never seen such a quantity of meat in an egg. Before he had finished it he had made a hearty meal. But, in the meantime, the old woman said, "Shall I tell you a story while you have your dinner?"

"Oh, yes, please do," answered Colin. "You told me such stories before!"

"Jenny," said the old woman, "my wool is all done. Get me some more."

And from behind the bed out came a sober-coloured, but large and beautifully-shaped hen. She walked sedately across the floor, putting down her feet daintily, like a prim matron as she was, and stopping by the door, gave a *cluck, cluck*.

"Oh, the door is shut, is it?" said the old woman.

"Let me open it," said Colin.

"Do, my dear."

"What are all those white things?" he asked, for the cottage stood in the middle of a great bed of grass with white tops.

"Those are my sheep," said the old woman. "You will see."

Into the grass Jenny walked, and stretching up her neck, gathered the white woolly stuff in her beak. When she had as much as she could hold, she came back and dropped it on the floor; then picked the seeds out and swallowed them, and went back for more. The old woman took the wool, and fastening it on her distaff, began to spin, giving the spindle a twirl, and then dropping it and drawing out the thread from the distaff. But as soon as the spindle began to twirl, it began to sparkle all the colours of the rainbow, that it was a delight to see. And the hands of the woman, instead of being old and wrinkled, were young and long-fingered and fair, and they drew out the wool, and the spindle spun and flashed, and the hen kept going out and in, bringing wool and swallowing the seeds, and the old woman kept telling Colin one story after another, till he thought he could sit there all his life and listen. Sometimes it seemed the spindle that was flashing them, sometimes the long fingers that were spinning them, and sometimes the hen that was gathering them off the roads of the long dry grass and bringing them in her beak and laying them down on the floor.

All at once the spindle grew slower, and gradually ceased turning; the fingers stopped drawing out the thread, the hen retreated behind the bed, and the voice of the blind woman was silent.

"I suppose it is time for me to go," said Colin.

"Yes, it is," answered his hostess.

"Please tell me, then, how I am to dream three days without sleeping."

"That's over," said the old woman. "You've just finished that part. I told you I would help you all I could."

"Have I been here three days, then?" asked Colin, in astonishment.

"And nights too. And I and Jenny and the spindle are quite tired and want to sleep. Jenny has got three eggs to lay besides. Make haste, my boy."

"Please, then, tell me what I am to do next."

"Jenny will put you in the way. When you come where you are going, you will tell them that the old woman with the spindle desires them to lift Cumberbone Crag a yard higher, and to send a flue under Stonestarvit Moss. Jenny, show Colin the way."

Jenny came out with a surly *cluck* and led him a good way across the heath by a path only a hen could have found. But she turned suddenly and walked home again.

IV. THE GOBLIN BLACKSMITH

COLIN could just perceive something suggestive of a track, which he followed till the sun went down. Then he saw a dim light before him, keeping his eye upon which, he came at last to a smithy, where, looking in at the open door, he saw a huge, humpbacked smith working a forehammer in each hand.

He grinned out of the middle of his breast when he saw Colin, and said, "Come in; come in: my youngsters will be glad of you."

He was an awful looking creature, with a great hare lip, and a red ball for a nose. Whatever he did—speak, or laugh, or sneeze—he did not stop working one moment. As often as the sparks flew in his face, he snapped at them with his eyes (which were the colour of a half-dead coal), now with this one, now with that; and the more sparks they got into them the brighter his eyes grew. The moment Colin entered, he took a huge bar of iron from the furnace, and began laying on it so with his two forehammers that he disappeared in a cloud of sparks, and Colin had to shut his eyes and be glad to escape with a few burns on his face and hands. When he had beaten the iron till it was nearly black, the smith put it in the fire again, and called out a hundred odd names:

"Here Gob, Shag, Latchit, Licker, Freestone, Greywhackit, Mousetrap, Potatoe-pot, Blob, Blotch, Blunker—"

And ever as he called, one dwarf after another came tumbling out of the chimney in the corner of which the fire was roaring. They crowded about Colin and began to make hideous faces and spit fire at him. But he kept a bold countenance. At length one pinched him, and he could not stand that, but struck him hard on the head. He thought he had knocked his own hand to pieces, it gave him such a jar; and the head rung like an iron pot.

"Come, come, young man," cried the smith; "you keep your hands off my children."

"Tell them to keep their hands off me, then," said Colin.

And calling to mind his message, just as they began to crowd about him again with yet more spiteful looks, he added: "Here, you imps! I won't stand it longer. Get to your work directly. The old woman with the spindle says you're to lift Cumberbone Crag a yard higher, and to send a flue under Stonestarvit Moss."

In a moment they had vanished in the chimney. In a moment more the smithy rocked to its foundations. But the smith took no notice, only worked more furiously than ever. Then came a great crack and a shock that threw Colin on the floor. The smith reeled, but never lost hold of his hammers or missed a blow on the anvil.

"Those boys will do themselves a mischief," he said; then turning to Colin, "Here, you sir, take that hammer. This is no safe place for idle people. If you don't work you'll be knocked to pieces in no time."

The same moment there came a wind from the chimney that blew all the fire into the middle of the smithy. The smith dashed up upon the forge, and rushed out of sight. Presently he returned with one of the goblins under his arm kicking and screaming, laid his ugly head down on the anvil, where he held him by the neck, and hit him a great blow with his hammer above the ear. The hammer rebounded, the goblin gave a shriek, and the smith flung him into the chimney, saying: "That's the only way to serve *him*. You'll be more careful for one while, I guess, Slobberkin."

And thereupon he took up his other hammer and began to work again, saying to Colin: "Now, young man, as long as you get a blow with your hammer in for every one of mine, you'll be quite safe; but if you stop, or lose the beat, I won't be answerable to the old woman with the spindle for the consequences."

Colin took up the hammer and did his best. But he soon found that he had never known what it was to work. The smith worked a hammer in each hand, and it was all Colin could do to work his little hammer with both his hands; so it was a terrible exertion to put in blow for blow with the smith. Once, when he lost the time, the smith's forehammer came down on the head of his, beat it flat on the anvil, and flung the handle to the other end of the smithy, where it struck the wall like the report of a cannon.

"I told you," said the smith. "There's another. Make haste, for the boys will be in want of you and me too before they get Cumberbone Crag half a foot higher."

Presently in came the biggest-headed of the family, out of the chimney.

"Six-foot wedges, and a three-yard crowbar!" he said; "or Cumberbone will cumber our bones presently."

The smith rushed behind the bellows, brought out a bar of iron three inches thick or so, cut off three yards, put the end in the fire, blew with might and main, and brought it out as white as paper. He and Colin then laid upon it till the end was flattened to an edge, which the smith turned up a little. He then handed the tool to the imp.

"Here, Gob," he said; "run with it, and the wedges will be ready by the time you come back."

Then to the wedges they set. And Colin worked like three. He never knew how he could work before. Not a moment's pause, except when the smith was at the forge for another glowing mass! And yet to Colin's amazement the more he worked the stronger he seemed to grow. Instead of being worn out the moment he had got his breath he wanted to be at it again; and he felt as if he had grown twice the size since he took hammer in hand. And the goblins kept running in and out all the time, now for one thing, now for another. Colin thought if they made use of all the tools they fetched, they must be working very hard indeed: And the convulsions felt in the smithy bore witness to their exertions somewhere in the neighbourhood.

And the longer they worked together, the more friendly grew the smith. At length he said—his words always adding energy to his blows: "What does the old woman want to improve Stonestarvit Moss for?"

"I didn't know she did want to improve it," returned Colin.

"Why, anybody may see that. First, she wants Cumberbone Crag a yard higher—just enough to send the north-east blast over the Moss without touching it. Then she wants a hot flue passed under it. Plain as a forehammer! What did you ask her to do for you? She's always doing things for people and making my bones ache."

"You don't seem to mind it much, though, sir," said Colin.

"No more I do," answered the smith, with a blow that drove the anvil halfway into the earth, from which it took him some trouble to drag it out again. "But I want to know what she is after now."

So Colin told him all he knew about it, which was merely his own story.

"I see, I see," said the smith. "It's all moonshine; but we must do as she says notwithstanding. And now it is my turn to give you a lift, for you have worked well. As soon as you leave the smithy, go straight to Stonestarvit Moss. Get on the highest part of it; make a circle three yards across, and dig a trench round it. I will give you a spade. At the end of the first day you will see a vine break the earth. By the end of the second, it will be creeping all over the circle. And by the end of the third day, the grapes will be ripe. Squeeze them one by one into a bottle—I will give you a bottle—till it is full.

Cork it up tight, and by the time the queen comes for it, it will be Carasoyn."

"Oh, thank you, thank you," cried Colin. "When am I to go?"

"As soon as the boys have lifted Cumberbone Crag, and bored the flue under the Moss. It is of no use till then."

"Well, I'll go on with my work," said Colin, and struck away at the anvil.

In a minute or two in came the same goblin whose head his father had hammered, and said, respectfully, "It's all right, sir. The boys are gathering their tools, and will be home to supper directly."

"Are you sure you have lifted the Crag a yard?" said the smith.

"Slumkin says it's a half-inch over the yard. Grungle says it's three-quarters. But that won't matter—will it?"

"No. I dare say not. But it is much better to be accurate. Is the flue done?"

"Yes, we managed that partly in lifting the crag."

"Very well. How's your head?"

"It rings a little."

"Let it ring you a lesson, then, Slobberkin, in future."

"Yes, sir."

"Now, master, you may go when you like," said the smith to Colin. "We've nothing here you can eat, I am sorry to say."

"Oh, I don't mind that. I'm not very hungry. But the old woman with the spindle said I was to work three days without dreaming."

"Well, you haven't been dreaming—have you?"

And the smith looked quite furious as he put the question, lifting his forehammer as if he would serve Colin like Slobberkin.

"No, that I haven't," answered Colin. "You took good care of that, sir."

The smith actually smiled.

"Then go along," he said. "It is all right."

"But I've only worked—"

"Three whole days and nights," interrupted the smith. "Get along with you. The boys will bother you if you don't. Here's your spade and here's your bottle."

V. THE MOSS VINEYARD

COLIN did not need a hint more, but was out of the smithy in a moment. He turned, however, to ask the way: there was nothing in sight but a great heap of peats which had been dug out of the moss, and was standing there to dry. Could he be on Stonestarvit Moss already? The sun was just setting. He would look out for the highest point at once. So he kept climbing, and at last reached a spot whence he could see all round him for a long way. Surely that must be Cumberbone Crag looking down on him! And there at his feet lay one of Jenny's eggs, as bright as silver. And there was a little path trodden and scratched by Jenny's feet, inclosing a circle just the size the smith told him to make. He set to work at once, ate Jenny's egg, and then dug the trench.

Those three days were the happiest he had ever known. For he understood everything he did himself, and all that everything was doing round about him. He saw what the rushes were, and why the blossom came out at the side, and why it was russet-coloured, and why the pitch was white, and the skin green. And he said to himself, "If I were a rush now, that's just how I should make a point of growing." And he knew how the heather felt with its cold roots, and its head of purple bells; and the wise-looking cotton-grass, which the old woman called her sheep, and the white beard of which she spun into thread. And he knew what she spun it for: namely, to weave it into lovely white cloth of which to make nightgowns for all the good people that were like to die; for one with one of these nightgowns upon him never died, but was laid in a beautiful white bed, and the door was closed upon him, and no noise came near him, and he lay there, dreaming lovely cool dreams, till the world had turned round, and was ready for him to get up again and do something.

He felt the wind playing with every blade of grass in his charmed circle. He felt the rays of heat shooting up from the hot flue beneath the moss. He knew the moment when the vine was going to break from the earth, and he felt the juices gathering and flowing from the roots into the grapes. And all the time he seemed at home, tending the cow, or making his father's supper, or reading a fairy tale as he sat waiting for him to come home.

At length the evening of the third day arrived. Colin squeezed the rich red grapes into his bottle, corked it, shouldered his spade, and turned homewards, guided by a peak which he knew in the distance. After walking all night in the moonlight, he came at length upon a place which he recognized, and so down upon the brook, which he followed home.

He met his father going out with his sheep. Great was his delight to see Colin again, for he had been dreadfully anxious about him. Colin told him the whole story; and as at that time marvels were much easier to believe than they are now, Colin's father did not laugh at him, but went away to the hills thinking, while Colin went on to the cottage, where he found plenty to do, having been nine days gone. He laid the bottle carefully away with his Sunday clothes, and set about everything just as usual.

But though the fairy brook was running merrily as ever through the cottage, and although Colin watched late every night, and latest when the moon shone, no fairy fleet came glimmering and dancing in along the stream. Autumn was there at length, and cold fogs began to rise in the cottage, and so Colin turned the brook into its old course, and filled up the breaches in the walls and the channel along the floor, making all close against the blasts of winter. But he had never known such a weary winter before. He could not help constantly thinking how cold the little girl must be, and how she would be saying to herself, "I wish Colin hadn't been so silly and lost me."

VI. THE CONSEQUENCES

BUT at last the spring came, and after the spring the summer. And the very first warm day, Colin took his spade and pickaxe, and down rushed the stream once more, singing and bounding into the cottage. Colin was even more delighted than he had been the first time. And he watched late into the night, but there came neither moon nor fairy fleet. And more than a week passed thus.

At length, on the ninth night, Colin, who had just fallen asleep, opened his eyes with sudden wakefulness, and behold! The room was all in a glimmer with moonshine and fairy glitter. The boats were rocking on the water, and the queen and her court had landed, and were dancing merrily on the earthen floor. He lost no time.

"Queen! Queen!" he said, "I've got your bottle of Carasoyn."

The dance ceased in a moment and the queen bounded upon the edge of his bed.

"I can't bear the look of your great glaring, ugly eyes," she said. "I must make you less before I can talk to you."

So once more she laid her rush wand across his eyes, whereupon Colin saw them all six times the size they were before, and the queen went on:

"Where is the Carasoyn? Give it me."

"It is in my box under the bed. If your majesty will stand out of the way, I will get it for you."

The queen jumped on the floor, and Colin, leaning from the bed, pulled out his little box, and got out the bottle.

"There it is, your majesty," he said, but not offering it to her.

"Give it me directly," said the queen, holding out her hand.

"First give me my little girl," returned Colin, boldly.

"Do you dare to bargain with me?" said the queen, angrily.

"Your majesty deigned to bargain with me first," said Colin.

"But since then you tried to break all our necks. You made a wicked cataract out there on the other side of the garden. Our boats were all dashed to pieces, and we had to wait till our horses were fetched. If I had been killed, you couldn't have held me to my bargain, and I won't hold to it now."

"If you chose to go down my cataract—" began Colin.

"*Your* cataract!" cried the queen. "All the waters that run from Loch Lonely are mine, I can tell you—all the way to the sea."

"Except where they run through farm-yards, your majesty."

"I'll rout you out of the country," said the queen.

"Meantime I'll put the bottle in the chest again," returned Colin.

The queen bit her lips with vexation.

"Come here, Changeling," she cried at length, in a flattering tone.

And the little girl came slowly up to her, and stood staring at Colin, with the tears in her eyes.

"Give me your hand, little girl," said he, holding out his.

She did so. It was cold as ice.

"Let go her hand," said the queen.

"I won't," said Colin. "She's mine."

"Give me the bottle then," said the queen.

"Don't," said the child.

But it was too late. The queen had it.

"Keep your girl," she cried, with an ugly laugh.

"Yes, keep me," cried the child.

The cry ended in a hiss.

Colin felt something slimy wriggling in his grasp, and looking down, saw that instead of a little girl he was holding a great writhing worm. He had almost flung it from him, but recovering himself, he grasped it tighter.

"If it's a snake, I'll choke it," he said. "If it's a girl, I'll keep her."

The same instant it changed to a little white rabbit which looked him piteously in the face, and pulled to get its little forefoot out of his hand. But though he tried not to hurt it, Colin would not let it go. Then the rabbit changed to a great black cat with eyes that flashed green fire. She sputtered and spit and swelled her tail, but all to no purpose. Colin held fast. Then it was a wood pigeon, struggling and fluttering in terror to get its wing out of his hold. But Colin still held fast.

All this time the queen had been getting the cork out. The moment it yielded she gave a scream and dropped the bottle. The Carasoyn ran out, and a strange odour filled the cottage. The queen stood shivering and sobbing beside the bottle, and all her court came about her and shivered and sobbed too, and their faces grew ancient and wrinkled. Then the queen, bending and tottering like an old woman, led the way to the boats, and her courtiers followed her, limping and creeping and distorted. Colin stared in amazement. He saw them all go aboard, and he heard the sound of them like a far-off company of men and women crying bitterly. And away they floated down the stream, the rowers dipping no oar, but bending weeping over them, and letting the boats drift along the stream. They vanished from his sight and the rush of the cataract came up on the night-wind louder than he had ever heard it before. But alas! When he came to himself, he found his hand relaxed, and the dove flown. Once more there was nothing left but to cry himself asleep, as he well might.

In the morning he rose very wretched. But the moment he entered the cowhouse, there, beside the cow, on the milking stool, sat a lovely little girl, with just one white garment on her, crying bitterly.

"I am so cold," she said, sobbing.

He caught her up, ran with her into the house, put her into the bed, and ran back to the cow for a bowl of warm milk. This she drank eagerly, laid her head down, and fell fast asleep. Then Colin saw that though she must be eight years old by her own account, her face was scarcely older than that of a baby of as many months.

When his father came home you may be sure he stared to see the child in the bed. Colin told him what had happened. But his father said he had met a troop of gipsies on the hill that morning.

"And you were always a dreamer, Colin, even before you could speak."

"But don't you smell the Carasoyn still?" said Colin.

"I do smell something very pleasant, to be sure," returned his father; "but I think it is the wallflower on the top of the garden-wall. What a blossom there is of it this year! I am sure there is nothing sweeter in all Fairyland, Colin."

Colin allowed that.

The little girl slept for three whole days. And for three days more she never said another word than "I am so cold!" But after that she began to revive a little, and to take notice of things about her. For three weeks she would taste nothing but milk from the cow, and would not move from the chimney-corner. By degrees, however, she began to help Colin a little with his house-work, and as she did so, her face gathered more and more expression; and she made such progress, that by the end of three months she could do everything as well as Colin himself, and certainly more neatly. Whereupon he gave up his duties to her, and went out with his father to learn the calling of a shepherd.

Thus things went on for three years. And Fairy, as they called her, grew lovelier every day, and looked up to Colin more and more every day.

At the end of the three years, his father sent him to an old friend of his, a schoolmaster. Before he left, he made Fairy promise never to go near the brook after sundown. He had turned it into its old channel the very day she came to them. And he begged his father especially to look after her when the moon was high, for then she grew very restless and strange, and her eyes looked as if she saw things other people could not see.

When the end of the other three years had come, the schoolmaster would not let Colin go home, but insisted on sending him to college. And there he remained for three years more.

When he returned at the end of that time, he found Fairy so beautiful and so wise, that he fell dreadfully in love with her. And Fairy found out that she had been in love with him since ever so long—she did not know how long. And Colin's father agreed that they should be married as soon as Colin should have a house to take her to. So Colin went away to London, and worked very hard, till at last he managed to get a little cottage in Devonshire to live in. Then he went back to Scotland and married Fairy. And he was very glad to get her away from the neighbourhood of a queen who was not to be depended upon.

VII. THE BANISHED FAIRIES

THOSE fairies had for a long time been doing wicked things. They had played many ill-natured pranks upon the human mortals; had stolen children upon whom they had no claim; had refused to deliver them up when they were demanded of them; had even terrified infants in their cradles; and, final proof of moral declension in fairies, had attempted to get rid of the obligations of their word, by all kinds of trickery and false logic.

It was not till they had sunk thus low that their queen began to long for the Carasoyn. She, no more than if she had been a daughter of Adam, could be happy while going on in that way; and, therefore, having heard of its marvellous virtues, and thinking it would stop her growing misery, she tried hard to procure it. For a hundred years she had tried in vain. Not till Colin arose did she succeed. But the Carasoyn was only for really good people, and therefore when the iron bottle which contained it was uncorked, she, and all her attendants, were, by the vapours thereof, suddenly changed into old men and women fairies. They crowded away weeping and lamenting, and Colin had as yet seen them no more.

For when the wickedness of any fairy tribe reaches its climax, the punishment that falls upon them is that they are compelled to leave that part of the country where they and their ancestors have lived for more years than they can count, and wander away, driven by an inward restlessness, ever longing after the country they have left, but never able to turn round and go back to it, always thinking they will do so tomorrow, but when tomorrow comes, saying *tomorrow* again, till at last they find, not their old home, but the place of their doom—that is, a place where their restlessness leaves them, and they find they can remain. This partial repose, however, springs from no satisfaction with the place; it is only that their inward doom ceases to drive them further. They sit down to weep, and to long after the country they have left.

This is not because the country to which they have been driven is ugly and inclement—it may or may not be such: it is simply because it is not *their* country. If it would be, and it must be, torture to the fairy of a harebell to go and live in a hyacinth—a torture quite analogous to which many human beings undergo from their birth to their death, and some of them longer, for anything I can tell—think what it must be for a tribe of fairies to have to go and live in a country quite different from that in and for which they were born. To the whole tribe the country is what the flower is to the individual; and when a fairy is born to whom the whole country is what the individual flower is to the individual fairy, then the fairy is king or queen of the fairies, and always makes a new nursery rhyme for the young fairies, which is never forgotten. When, therefore, a tribe is banished, it is long before they can settle themselves into their new quarters. Their clothes do not fit them, as it were. They are constantly wriggling themselves into harmony with their new circumstances—which is only another word for clothes—and never quite succeeding. It is their punishment—and something more. Consequently their temper is not always of the evenest; indeed, and in a word, they are as like human mortals as may well be, considering the differences between them.

In the present case, you would say it was surely no great hardship to be banished from the heathy hills, the bare rocks, the wee trotting burnies of Scotland, to the rich valleys, the wooded shores, the great rivers, the grand ocean of the south of Devon. You may say they could not have been very wicked when this was all their punishment. If you do, you must have studied the human mortals to no great purpose. You do not believe that a man may be punished by being made very rich? I do. Anyhow, these fairies were not of your opinion, *for they were in it.* In the splendour of their Devon banishment they sighed for their bare Scotland. Under the leafy foliage of the Devonshire valleys, with the purple and green ocean before them, that had seen ships of a thousand builds, or on the shore rich with shells and many-coloured creatures, they longed for the clear, cold, pensive, open sides of the far-stretching heathy sweeps, to which a gray, wild, torn sea, with memories only of Norsemen, whales, and mermaids, cried aloud. For the big rivers, on which reposed great old hulks scarred with battle, they longed after the rocks and stones and rowan and birch trees of the solitary burns.

The country they had left might be an ill-favoured thing, but it was their own.

Now that which happens to the aspect of a country when the fairies leave it, is that a kind of deadness falls over the landscape. The traveller feels the wind as before, but it does not seem to refresh him. The child sighs over his daisy chain, and cannot find a red-tipped one amongst all that he has gathered. The cowslips have not half the honey in them. The wasps outnumber the bees. The horses come from the plough more tired at night, hanging their heads to their very hoofs as they plod homewards. The youth and the maiden, though perfectly happy when they meet, find the road to and from the trysting-place unaccountably long and dreary. The hawthorn-blossom is neither so white nor so red as it used to be, and the dark rough bark looks through and makes it ragged. The day is neither so warm nor the night so friendly as before. In a word, that something which no one can describe or be content to go without is missing. Everything is common-place. Everything falls short of one's expectations.

But it does not follow that the country to which the fairies are banished is so much richer and more beautiful for their presence. If that country has its own fairies, it needs no more, and Devon in especial has been rich in fairies from the time of the Phoenicians, and ever so long before that. But supposing there were no aborigines left to quarrel with, it takes centuries before the new immigration can fit itself into its new home. Until this comes about the queerest things are constantly happening. For however could a convolvulus grow right with the soul of a Canterbury-bell inside it for instance? The banished fairies are forced to do the best they can, and take the flowers the nearest they can find.

VIII. THEIR REVENGE

WHEN Colin and his wife settled then in their farm-house, the same tribe of fairies was already in the neighbourhood, and was not long in discovering who had come after them. An assembly was immediately called. Something must be done; but what, was disputed. Most of them thought only of revenge—to be taken upon the children. But the queen hesitated. Perhaps her sufferings had done her good. She suggested that before coming to any conclusion they should wait and watch the household.

In consequence of this resolution they began to frequent the house constantly, and sometimes in great numbers. But for a long time they could do the children no mischief. Whatever they tried turned out to their amusement. They were three, two girls and a boy; the girls nine and eight and the boy three years old.

When they succeeded in enticing them beyond the home-boundaries, they would at one time be seized with an unaccountable panic, and turn and scurry home without knowing why; at another, a great butterfly or dragonfly, or some other winged and lovely creature, would dart past them, and away towards the house, and they after it, scampering; or the voice of their mother would be heard calling from the door. But at last their opportunity arrived.

One day the children were having such a game! The sisters had blindfolded their little brother, and were carrying him now on their backs, now in their arms, all about the place; now up stairs, talking about the rugged mountain paths they were climbing; now down again, filling him with the fancy that they were descending into a narrow valley; then they would set the tap of a rain-water barrel running, and represent that they were travelling along the bank of a rivulet. Now they were threading the depths of a great forest: and when the low of a cow reached them from a nigh field, that was the roaring of a lion or a tiger. At length they reached a lake into which the rivulet ran, and then it was necessary to take off his shoes and socks, that he might skim over the water on his bare feet, which they dipped and dabbled now in this tub, now in that, standing for farm and household purposes by the water-butt. The sisters kept their own imaginations alive by carrying him through all the strange places inside and outside of the house. When they told him they were ascending a precipice, they were, in fact, climbing a rather difficult ladder up to the door of the hayloft; when they told him they were traversing a pathless desert, they were, in fact, in a vast, empty place, a wide floor, used sometimes as a granary, with the rafters of the roof coming down to it on both sides, a place abundantly potent in their feelings to the generation of the desert in his; when they were wandering through a trackless forest, they were, in fact, winding about amongst the trees of a large orchard, which, in the moonlight, was vast enough for the fancy of any child. Had they uncovered his eyes at any moment, he would only have been seized with a wonder and awe of another sort, more overwhelming because more real, and more strange because not even in part bodied forth from his own brain.

In the course of the story, and while they bore the bare-footed child through the orchard, telling him they saw the fairies gliding about everywhere through the trees, not thinking that he believed every word they told him, they set him down, and the child suddenly opened his eyes. His sisters were gone. The moon was staring at him out of the sky, through the mossy branches of the apple trees, which he thought looked like old women all about him, they were so thin and bony.

When the sisters, who had only for a moment run behind some of the trees, that they might cause him additional amazement, returned, he was gone. There was terrible lamentation in the house; but his father and mother, who were experienced in such matters, knew that the fairies must be in it, and cherished a hope that their son would yet be restored to them, though all their endeavours to find him were unavailing.

IX. THE FAIRY FIDDLER

THE father thought over many plans, but never came upon the right one. He did not know that they were the same tribe which had before carried away his wife when she was an infant. If he had, they might have done something sooner.

At length, one night towards the close of seven years, about twelve o'clock, Colin suddenly opened his eyes, for he had been fast asleep and dreaming, and saw a few grotesque figures which he thought he must have seen before, dancing on the floor between him and the nearly extinguished fire. One of them had a violin, but when Colin first saw him he was not playing. Another of them was singing, and thus keeping the dance in time. This was what he sang, evidently addressed to the fiddler, who stood in the centre of the dance:

"Peterkin, Peterkin, tall and thin,
What have you done with his cheek and his chin?
What have you done with his ear and his eye?
Hearken, hearken, and hear him cry."

Here Peterkin put his fiddle to his neck, and drew from it a wail just like the cry of a child, at which the dancers danced more furiously. Then he went on playing the tune the other had just sung, in accompaniment to his own reply:

"Silversnout, Silversnout, short and stout,
I have cut them off and plucked them out,

> *And salted them down in the Kelpie's Pool,*
> *Because papa Colin is such a fool."*

Then the fiddle cried like a child again, and they danced more wildly than ever.

Colin, filled with horror, although he did not more than half believe what they were saying, sat up in bed and stared at them with fierce eyes, waiting to hear what they would say next. Silversnout now resumed his part:

> *"Ho, ho! Ho! Ho! And if he don't know,*
> *And fish them out of the pool, so—so,"*

here they all pretended to be hauling in a net as they danced.

> *"Before the end of the seven long years,*
> *Sweet babe will be left without eyes or ears."*

Then Peterkin replied:

> *"Sweet babe will be left without cheek or chin,*
> *Only a hole to put porridge in,*
> *Porridge and milk, and haggis, and cakes:*
> *Sweet babe will gobble till his stomach aches."*

From this last verse, Colin knew that they must be Scotch fairies, and all at once recollected their figures as belonging to the multitude he had once seen frolicking in his father's cottage. It was now Silversnout's turn. He began:

> *"But never more shall Colin see*

Sweet babe again upon his knee,
With or without his cheek or chin,
Except—"

Here Silversnout caught sight of Colin's face staring at him from the bed, and with a shriek of laughter they all vanished, the tones of Peterkin's fiddle trailing after them through the darkness like the train of a shooting star.

X. THE OLD WOMAN AND HER HEN

NOW Colin had got the better of these fairies once, not by his own skill, but by the help of that other powers had afforded him. What were those powers? First the old woman on the heath. Indeed, he might attribute it all to her. He would go back to Scotland and look for her and find her. But the old woman was never found except by the seeker losing himself. It could not be done otherwise. She would cease to be the old woman, and become her own hen, if ever the moment arrived when anyone found her without losing himself. And Colin since that time had wandered so much all over the moor, wide as it was, that lay above his father's cottage, that he did not believe he was able to lose himself there anymore. He had yet to learn that it did not so much matter where he lost himself, provided only he was lost.

Just at this time Colin's purse was nearly empty, and he set out to borrow the money of a friend who lived on the other side of Dartmoor. When he got there, he found that he had gone from home. Unable to rest, he set out again to return.

It was almost night when he started, and before he had got many miles into the moor, it was dark, for here was no moon, and it was so cloudy that he could not see the stars. He thought he knew the way quite well, but as the track even in daylight was in certain places very indistinct, it was no wonder that he strayed from it, and found that he had lost himself. The same moment that he became aware of this, he saw a light away to the left. He turned towards it and found it proceeded from a little hive-like hut, the door of which stood open. When he was within a yard or two of it, he heard a voice say: "Come in, Colin; I'm waiting for you."

Colin obeyed at once, and found the old woman seated with her spindle and distaff, just as he had seen her when he was a boy on the moor above his father's cottage.

"How do you do, mother?" he said.

"I am always quite well. Never ask me that question."

"Well, then I won't anymore," returned Colin. "But I thought you lived in Scotland?"

"I don't live anywhere; but those that will do as I tell them, will always find me when they want me."

"Do you see yet, mother?"

"See! I always see so well that it is not worth while to burn eye-light. So I let them go out. They were expensive."

Where her eyes should have been, there was nothing but wrinkles.

"What do you want?" she resumed.

"I want my child. The fairies have got him."

"I know that."

"And they have taken out his eyes."

"I can make him see without them."

"And they've cut off his ears," said Colin.

"He can hear without them."

"And they've salted down his cheek and his chin."

"Now I don't believe that," said the old woman.

"I heard them say so myself," returned Colin.

"Those fairies are worse liars than any I know. But something must be done. Sit down and I'll tell you a story."

"There's only nine days of the seven years left," said Colin, in a tone of expostulation.

"I know that as well as you," answered the old woman. "Therefore, I say, there is not time to be lost. Sit down and listen to my story. Here, Jenny."

The hen came pacing solemnly out from under the bed.

"Off to the sheep-shearing, Jenny, and make haste, for I must spin faster than usual. There are but nine days left."

Jenny ran out at the door with her head on a level with her tail, as if the kite had been after her. In a few moments she returned with a bunch of wool, as they called it, though it was only cotton from the cotton-grass that grew all about the cottage, nearly as big as herself, in her bill, and then darted away for more. The old woman fastened it on her distaff, drew out a thread to her spindle, and then began to spin. And as she spun she told her story—fast, fast; and Jenny kept scampering out and in; and by the time Colin thought it must be midnight the story was told, and seven of the nine days were over.

"Colin," said the old woman, "now that you know all about it, you must set off at once."

"I am ready," answered Colin, rising.

"Keep on the road Jenny will show you till you come to the cobbler's. Tell him the old woman with the distaff requests him to give you a lump of his wax."

"And what am I to do with it?"

"The cobbler always knows what his wax is for."

And with this answer, the old woman turned her face towards the fire, for, although it was summer, it was cold at night on the moor. Colin, moved by sudden curiosity, instead of walking out of the hut after Jenny, as he ought to have done, crept round by the wall, and peeped in the old woman's face. There, instead of wrinkled blindness, he saw a pair of flashing orbs of light, which were rather reflected on the fire than had the fire reflected in them. But the same instant the hut and all that was in it vanished, he felt the cold fog of the moor blowing upon him, and fell heavily to the earth.

XI. THE GOBLIN COBBLER

WHEN he came to himself he lay on the moor still. He got up and gazed around. The moon was up, but there was no hut to be seen. He was sorry enough now that he had been so foolish. He called, "Jenny, Jenny," but in vain. What was he to do? Tomorrow was the eighth of the nine days left, and if before twelve at night the following day he had not rescued his boy, nothing could be done, at least for seven years more. True, the year was not quite out till about seven the following evening, but the fairies, instead of giving days of grace, always take them. He could do nothing but begin to walk, simply because that gave him a shadow more of a chance of finding the cobbler's than if he sat still, but there was no possibility of choosing one direction rather than another.

He wandered the rest of that night and the next day. He could not go home before the hour when the cobbler could no longer help him. Such was his anxiety, that although he neither ate nor drank, he never thought of the cause of his gathering weakness.

As it grew dark, however, he became painfully aware of it, and was just on the point of sitting down exhausted upon a great white stone that looked inviting, when he saw a faint glimmering in front of him. He was erect in a moment, and making towards the place. As he drew near he became aware of a noise made up of many smaller noises, such as might have proceeded from some kind of factory. Not till he was close to the place could he see that it was a long low hut, with one door, and no windows. The light shone from the door, which stood wide open. He approached, and peeped in. There sat a multitude of cobblers, each on his stool, with his candle stuck in the hole in the seat, cobbling away. They looked rather little men, though not at all of fairy-size. The most remarkable thing about them was that at any given moment they were all doing precisely the same thing, as if they had been a piece of machinery. When one drew the threads in stitching, they all did the same. If Colin saw one wax his thread, and looked up, he saw that they were all waxing their thread. If one took to hammering on his lapstone, they did not follow his example, but all together with him they caught up their lapstones and fell to hammering away, as if nothing but hammering could ever be demanded of them. And when he came to look at them more closely, he saw that everyone was blind of an eye, and had a nose turned up like an awl. Every one of them, however, looked different from the rest, notwithstanding a very close resemblance in their features.

The moment they caught sight of him, they rose as one man, pointed their awls at him, and advanced towards him like a closing bush of aloes, glittering with spikes.

"Fine upper-leathers," said one and all, with a variety of accordant grimaces.

"Top of his head—good paste-bowl," was the next general remark.

"Coarse hair—good ends," followed.

"Sinews—good thread."

"Bones and blood—good paste for seven-leaguers."

"Ears—good loops to pull 'em on with. Pair short now."

"Soles—same for queen's slippers."

And so on they went, portioning out his body in the most irreverent fashion for the uses of their trade, till having come to his teeth, and said, "Teeth—good brads," they all gave a shriek like the whisk of the waxed threads through the leather, and sprung upon him with their awls drawn back like daggers. There was no time to lose.

"The old woman with the spindle—" said Colin.

"Don't know her," shrieked the cobblers.

"The old woman with the distaff," said Colin, and they all scurried back to their seats and fell to hammering vigorously.

"She desired me," continued Colin, "to ask the cobbler for a lump of his wax."

Every one of them caught up his lump of wrought rosin, and held it out to Colin. He took the one offered by the nearest, and found that all their lumps were gone; after which they sat motionless and stared at him.

"But what am I to do with it?" asked Colin.

"I will walk a little way with you," said the one nearest, "and tell you all about it. The old woman is my grandmother, and a very worthy old soul she is."

Colin stepped out at the door of the workshop, and the cobbler followed him. Looking round, Colin saw all the stools vacant and the place as still as an old churchyard. The cobbler, who now in his talk, gestures, and general demeanour appeared a very respectable, not to say conventional, little man, proceeded to give him all the information he required, accompanying it with the present of one of his favourite awls.

They walked a long way, till Colin was amazed to find that his strength stood out so well. But at length the cobbler said: "I see, sir, that the sun is at hand. I must return to my vocation. When the sun is once up, you will know where you are."

He turned aside a few yards from the path, and entered the open door of a cottage. In a moment the place resounded with the soft hammering of three hundred and thirteen cobblers, each with his candle stuck in a hole in the stool on which he sat. While Colin stood gazing in wonderment, the rim of the sun crept up above the horizon; and there the cottage stood, white and sleeping, while the cobblers, their lights, their stools, and their tools had all vanished. Only there was still the sound of the hammers ringing in his head, where it seemed to shape itself into words something like these: a good deal had to give way to the rhyme, for they were more particular about their rhymes than their etymology:

"*Dub-a-dub, dub-a-dub,*
Cobbler's man
Hammer it, stitch it,
As fast as you can.
The week-day ogre
Is wanting his boots.
The trip-a-trap fairy
Is going bare-foots.
Dream-daughter has worn out
Her heels and her toeses,
For want of cork slippers
To walk over noses.
Spark-eye, the smith,
May shoe the nightmare,
The kelpie and pookie,
The nine-footed bear:
We shoe the mermaids—
The tips of their tails—
Stitching the leather
Onto their scales.
We shoe the brownie,
Clumsy and toeless,

*And then he goes quiet
As a mole or a moless.
There is but one creature
That we cannot shoe,
And that is the Boneless,
All made of glue."*

A great deal of nonsense of this sort went through Colin's head before the sounds died away. Then he found himself standing in the field outside his own orchard.

XII. THE WAX AND THE AWL

THE evening arrived. The sun was going down over the sea, cloudless, casting gold from him lavishly, when Colin arrived on the shore at some distance from his home. The tide was falling, and a good space of sand was uncovered, and lay glittering in the setting sun. This sand lay between some rocks and the sea; and from the rocks innumerable runnels of water that had been left behind in their hollows were hurrying back to their mother. These occasionally spread into little shallow lakes, resting in hollows in the sand. These lakes were in a constant ripple from the flow of the little streams through them; and the sun shining on these multitudinous ripples, the sand at the bottom shone like brown silk watered with gold, only that the golden lines were flitting about like living things, never for a moment in one place.

Now Colin had no need of fairy ointment to anoint his eyes and make him able to see fairies. Most people need this; but Colin was naturally gifted. Therefore, as he drew near a certain high rock, which he knew very well, and from which many streams were flowing back into the sea, he saw that the little lakes about it were crowded with fairies, playing all kinds of pranks in the water. It was a lovely sight to see them thus frolicking in the light of the setting sun, in their gay dresses, sparkling with jewels, or what looked like jewels, flashing all colours as they moved. But Colin had not much time to see them; for the moment they saw him, knowing that this was the man whom they had wronged by stealing his child, and knowing too that he saw them, they fled at once up the high rock and vanished. This was just what Colin wanted. He went all round and round the rock, looked in every direction in which there might be a pool, found more fairies, here and there, who fled like the first up the rock and disappeared. When he had thus driven them all from the sands, he approached the rock, taking the lump of cobbler's wax from his pocket as he went. He scrambled up the rock, and, without showing his face, put his hand on the uppermost edge of it and began drawing a line with the wax all along. He went creeping round the rock, still drawing the wax along the edge, till he had completed the circuit. Then he peeped over.

Now in the heart of this rock, which was nearly covered at highwater, there was a big basin, known as the Kelpie's Pool, filled with sea-water and the loveliest seaweed and many little sea-animals; and this was a favourite resort of the fairies. It was now, of course, crowded. When they saw his big head come peeping over, they burst into a loud fit of laughter, and began mocking him and making game of him in a hundred ways. Some made the ugliest faces they could, some queer gestures of contempt; others sung bits of songs, and so on; while the queen sat by herself on a projecting corner of the rock, with her feet in the water, and looked at him sulkily. Many of them kept on plunging and swimming and diving and floating, while they mocked him; and Colin would have enjoyed the sight much if they had not spoiled their beauty and their motions by their grimaces and their gestures.

"I want my child," said Colin.

"Give him his child," cried one.

Thereupon a dozen of them dived, and brought up a huge sea-slug—a horrid creature, like a lump of blubber—and held it up to him, saying: "There he is; come down and fetch him."

Others offered him a blue lobster, struggling in their grasp; others, a spider-crab; others, a whelk; while some of them sung mocking verses, each capping the line the other gave. At length they lifted a dreadful object from the bottom. It was like a baby with his face half eaten away by the fishes, only that he had a huge nose, like the big toe of a lobster. But Colin was not to be taken in.

"Very well, good people," he said, "I will try something else."

He crept down the rock again, took out the little cobbler's awl, and began boring a hole. It went through the rock as if it had been butter, and as he drew it out the water followed in a far-reaching spout. He bored another, and went on boring till there were three hundred and thirteen spouts gushing from the rock, and running away in a strong little stream towards the sea. He then sat down on a ledge at the foot of the rock and waited.

By-and-by he heard a clamour of little voices from the basin. They had found that the water was getting very low. But when they discovered the holes by which it was escaping, "He's got Dottlecob's awl! He's got Dottlecob's awl!" they cried with one voice of horror. When he heard this, Colin climbed the rock again to enjoy their confusion. But here I must explain a little.

In the former part of this history I showed how fond these fairies were of water. But the fact was they were far too fond of it. It had grown a thorough dissipation with them. Their business had been chiefly to tend and help the flowers in which they lived, and to do good offices for everything that had any kind of life about them. Hence their name of Good People. But from finding the good the water did to the flowers, and from sharing in the refreshment it brought them, flowing up to them in tiny runnels through the veins of the plants, they had fallen in love with the water itself, for its own sake, or rather for the pleasure it gave to them, irrespective of the good it was to the flowers which lived upon it. So they neglected their business, and took to sailing on the streams, and plunging into every pool they could find. Hence the rapidity of their decline and fall.

Again, on coming to the sea-coast, they had found that the salt water did much to restore the beauty they had lost by partaking of the Carasoyn. Therefore they were constantly on the shore, bathing forever in the water, especially that left in this pool by the ebbing tide, which was particularly to their taste; till at last they had grown entirely dependent for comfort on the sea-water, and, they thought, entirely dependent on it for existence also, at least such existence as was in the least worth possessing.

Therefore, when they saw the big face of Colin peering once more over the ledge, they rushed at him in a rage, scrambling up the side of the rock like so many mad beetles. Colin drew back and let them come on. The moment the foremost put his foot on the line that Colin had drawn around the rock, he slipped and tumbled backwards head over heels into the pool, shrieking: "He's got Dottlecob's wax!"

"He's got Dottlecob's wax!" screamed the next, as he fell backwards after his companion, and this took place till no one would approach the line. In fact no fairy could keep his footing on the wax, and the line was so broad—for as Colin rubbed it, it had melted and spread—that not one of them could spring over it. The queen now rose.

"What do you want, Colin?" she said.

"I want my child, as you know very well," answered Colin.

"Come and take him," returned the queen, and sat down again, not now with her feet in the water, for it was much too low for that.

But Colin knew better. He sat down on the edge of the basin. Unfortunately, the tail of his coat crossed the line. In a moment half-a-dozen of the fairies were out of the circle. Colin rose instantly, and there was not much harm done, for the multitude was still in prison. The water was nearly gone, beginning to leave the very roots of the long tangles uncovered. At length the queen could bear it no longer.

"Look here, Colin," she said; "I wish you well."

And as she spoke she rose and descended the side of the rock towards the water now far below her. She had to be very cautious too, the stones were so slippery, though there was none of Dottlecob's wax there. About halfway below where the surface of the pool had been, she stopped, and pushed a stone aside. Colin saw what seemed the entrance to a cave inside the rock. The queen went in. A few moments after she came out wringing her hands.

"Oh dear! Oh dear! What shall I do?" she cried, "You horrid thick people will grow so. He's grown to such a size that I *can't* get him out."

"Will you let him go if I get him out?" asked Colin.

"I will, I will. We shall all be starved to death for want of sea-water if I don't," she answered.

"Swear by the cobbler's awl and the cobbler's wax," said Colin.

"I swear," said the queen.

"By the cobbler's awl and the cobbler's wax," insisted Colin.

"I swear by the cobbler's awl and the cobbler's wax," returned the queen.

"In the name of your people?"

"In the name of my people," said the queen, "that none of us here present will ever annoy you or your family hereafter."

"Then I'll come down," said Colin, and jumped into the basin. With the cobbler's awl he soon cleared a big opening into the rock, for it bored and cut it like butter. Then out crept a beautiful boy of about ten years old, into his father's arms, with eyes, and ears, and chin, and cheek all safe and sound. And he carried him home to his mother.

It was a disappointment to find him so much of a baby at his age; but that fault soon began to mend. And the house was full of jubilation. And little Colin told them the whole story of his sojourn among the fairies. And it did not take so long as you would think, for he fancied he had been there only about a week.

LITTLE DAYLIGHT

* * *

No house of any pretension to be called a palace is in the least worthy of the name, except it has a wood near it—very near it—and the nearer the better. Not all round it—I don't mean that, for a palace ought to be open to the sun and wind, and stand high and brave, with weathercocks glittering and flags flying; but on one side of every palace there must be a wood. And there was a very grand wood indeed beside the palace of the king who was going to be Daylight's father, such a grand wood, that nobody yet had ever got to the other end of it. Near the house it was kept very trim and nice, and it was free of brush-wood for a long way in; but by degrees it got wild, and it grew wilder, and wilder, and wilder, until some said wild beasts at last did what they liked in it. The king and his courtiers often hunted, however, and this kept the wild beasts far away from the palace.

One glorious summer morning, when the wind and sun were out together, when the vanes were flashing and the flags frolicking against the blue sky, little Daylight made her appearance from somewhere—nobody could tell where—a beautiful baby, with such bright eyes that she might have come from the sun, only by-and-by she showed such lively ways that she might equally well have come out of the wind. There was great jubilation in the palace, for this was the first baby the queen had had, and there is as much happiness over a new baby in a palace as in a cottage.

But there is one disadvantage of living near a wood: you do not know quite who your neighbours may be. Everybody knew there were in it several fairies, living within a few miles of the palace, who always had had something to do with each new baby that came; for fairies live so much longer than we, that they can have business with a good many generations of human mortals. The curious houses they lived in were well known also, one, a hollow oak; another, a birch tree, though nobody could ever find how that fairy made a house of it; another, a hut of growing trees intertwined, and patched up with turf and moss. But there was another fairy who had lately come to the place, and nobody even knew she was a fairy except the other fairies. A wicked old thing she was, always concealing her power, and being as disagreeable as she could, in order to tempt people to give her offence, that she might have the pleasure of taking vengeance upon them. The people about thought she was a witch, and those who knew her by sight were careful to avoid offending her. She lived in a mud house, in a swampy part of the forest.

In all history we find that fairies give their remarkable gifts to prince or princess, or any child of sufficient importance in their eyes, always at the christening. Now this we can understand, because it is an ancient custom amongst human beings as well; and it is not hard to explain why wicked fairies should choose the same time to do unkind things; but it is difficult to understand how they should be able to do them, for you would fancy all wicked creatures would be powerless on such an occasion. But I never knew of any interference on the part of a wicked fairy that did not turn out a good thing in the end. What a good thing, for instance, it was that one princess should sleep for a hundred years! Was she not saved from all the plague of young men who were not worthy of her? And did she not come awake exactly at the right moment when the right prince kissed her? For my part, I cannot help wishing a good many girls would sleep till just the same fate overtook them. It would be happier for them, and more agreeable to their friends.

Of course all the known fairies were invited to the christening. But the king and queen never thought of inviting an old witch. For the power of the fairies they have by nature; whereas a witch gets her power by wickedness. The other fairies, however, knowing the danger thus run, provided as well as they could against accidents from her quarter. But they could neither render her powerless, nor could they arrange their gifts in reference to hers beforehand, for they could not tell what those might be.

Of course the old hag was there without being asked. Not to be asked was just what she wanted, that she might have a sort of a reason for doing what she wished to do. For somehow even the wickedest of creatures likes a pretext for doing the wrong thing.

Five fairies had one after the other given the child such gifts as each counted best, and the fifth had just stepped back to her place in the surrounding splendour of ladies and gentlemen, when, mumbling a laugh between her toothless gums, the wicked fairy hobbled out into the middle of the circle, and at the moment when the archbishop was handing the baby to the lady at the head of the nursery department of state affairs, addressed him thus, giving a bite or two to every word before she could part with it:

"Please your Grace, I'm very deaf: would your Grace mind repeating the princess's name?"

"With pleasure, my good woman," said the archbishop, stooping to shout in her ear: "the infant's name is little Daylight."

"And little daylight it shall be," cried the fairy, in the tone of a dry axle, "and little good shall any of her gifts do her. For I bestow upon her the gift of sleeping all day long, whether she will or not. Ha, ha! He, he! Hi, hi!"

Then out started the sixth fairy, who, of course, the others had arranged should come after the wicked one, in order to undo as much as she might.

"If she sleep all day," she said mournfully, "she shall, at least, wake all night."

"A nice prospect for her mother and me!" thought the poor king; for they loved her far too much to give her up to nurses, especially at night as most kings and queens do—and are sorry for it afterwards.

"You spoke before I had done," said the wicked fairy. "That's against the law. It gives me another chance."

"I beg your pardon," said the other fairies, all together.

"She did. I hadn't done laughing," said the crone. "I had only got to Hi, hi! and I had to go through Ho, ho! and Hu, hu! So I decree that if she wakes all night she shall wax and wane with its mistress the moon. And what that may mean I hope her royal parents will live to see. Ho, ho! Hu, hu!"

But out stepped another fairy, for they had been wise enough to keep two in reserve, because every fairy knew the trick of one.

"Until," said the seventh fairy, "a prince comes who shall kiss her without knowing it."

The wicked fairy made a horrid noise like an angry cat, and hobbled away. She could not pretend that she had not finished her speech this time, for she had laughed Ho, ho! and Hu, hu!

"I don't know what that means," said the poor king to the seventh fairy.

"Don't be afraid. The meaning will come with the thing itself," said she.

The assembly broke up, miserable enough—the queen, at least prepared for a good many sleepless nights, and the lady at the head of the nursery department anything but comfortable in the prospect before her, for of course the queen could not do it all. As for the king, he made up his mind, with what courage he could summon, to meet the demands of the case, but wondered whether he could with any propriety require the First Lord of the Treasury to take a share in the burden laid upon him.

I will not attempt to describe what they had to go through for some time. But at last the household settled into a regular system—a very irregular one in some respects. For at certain seasons the palace rang all night with bursts of laughter from little Daylight, whose heart the old fairy's curse could not reach; she was Daylight still, only a little in the wrong place, for she always dropped asleep at the first hint of dawn in the east. But her merriment was of short duration. When the moon was at the full, she was in glorious spirits, and as beautiful as it was possible for a child of her age to be. But as the moon waned, she faded, until at last she was wan and withered like the poorest sickliest child you might come upon in the streets of a great city in the arms of a homeless mother. Then the night was quiet as the day, for the little creature lay in her gorgeous cradle night and day with hardly a motion, and indeed at last without even a moan, like one dead. At first they often thought she was dead, but at last they got used to it, and only consulted the almanac to find the moment when she would begin to revive, which, of course, was with the first appearance of the silver thread of the crescent moon. Then she would move her lips, and they would give her a little nourishment; and she would grow better and better and better, until for a few days she was splendidly well. When well, she was always merriest out in the moonlight; but even when near her worst, she seemed better when, in warm summer nights, they carried her cradle out into the light of the waning moon. Then in her sleep she would smile the faintest, most pitiful smile.

For a long time very few people ever saw her awake. As she grew older she became such a favourite, however, that about the palace there were always some who would contrive to keep awake at night, in order to be near her. But she soon began to take every chance of getting away from her nurses and enjoying her moonlight alone. And thus things went on until she was nearly seventeen years of age. Her father and mother had by that time got so used to the odd state of things that they had ceased to wonder at them. All their arrangements had reference to the state of the Princess Daylight, and it is amazing how things contrive to accommodate themselves. But how any prince was ever to find and deliver her, appeared inconceivable.

As she grew older she had grown more and more beautiful, with the sunniest hair and the loveliest eyes of heavenly blue, brilliant and profound as the sky of a June day. But so much more painful and sad was the change as her bad time came on. The more beautiful she was in the full moon, the more withered and worn did she become as the moon waned. At the time at which my story has now arrived, she looked, when the moon was small or gone, like an old woman exhausted with suffering. This was the more painful that her appearance was unnatural; for her hair and eyes did not change. Her wan face was both drawn and wrinkled, and had an eager hungry look. Her skinny hands moved as if wishing, but unable, to lay hold of something. Her shoulders were bent forward, her chest went in, and she stooped as if she were eighty years old. At last she had to be put to bed, and there await the flow of the tide of life. But she grew to dislike being seen, still more being touched by any hands, during this season. One lovely summer evening, when the moon lay all but gone upon the verge of the horizon, she vanished from her attendants, and it was only after searching for her a long time in great terror, that they found her fast asleep in the forest, at the foot of a silver birch, and carried her home.

A little way from the palace there was a great open glade, covered with the greenest and softest grass. This was her favourite haunt; for here the full moon shone free and glorious, while through a vista in the trees she could generally see more or less of the dying moon as it crossed the opening. Here she had a little rustic house built for her, and here she mostly resided. None of the court might go there without leave, and her own attendants had learned by this time not to be officious in waiting upon her, so that she was very much at liberty. Whether the good fairies had anything to do with it or not I cannot tell, but at last she got into the way of retreating further into the wood every night as the moon waned, so that sometimes they had great trouble in finding her; but as she was always very angry if she discovered they were watching her, they scarcely dared to do so. At length one night they thought they had lost her altogether. It was morning before they found her. Feeble as she was, she had wandered into a thicket a long way from the glade, and there she lay—fast asleep, of course.

Although the fame of her beauty and sweetness had gone abroad, yet as everybody knew she was under a bad spell, no king in the neighbourhood had any desire to have her for a daughter-in-law. There were serious objections to such a relation.

About this time in a neighbouring kingdom, in consequence of the wickedness of the nobles, an insurrection took place upon the death of the old king, the greater part of the nobility was massacred, and the young prince was compelled to flee for his life, disguised like a peasant. For some time, until he got out of the country, he suffered much from hunger and fatigue; but when he got into that ruled by the princess's father, and had no longer any fear of being recognized, he fared better, for the people were kind. He did not abandon his disguise, however. One tolerable reason was that he had no other clothes to put on, and another that he had very little money, and did not know where to get anymore. There was no good in telling everybody he met that he was a prince, for he felt that a prince ought to be able to get on like other people, else his rank only made a fool of him. He had read of princes setting out upon adventure; and here he was out in similar case, only without having had a choice in the matter. He would go on, and see what would come of it.

For a day or two he had been walking through the palace-wood, and had had next to nothing to eat, when he came upon the strangest little house, inhabited by a very nice tidy motherly old woman. This was one of the good fairies. The moment she saw him she knew quite well who he was and what was going to come of it; but she was not at liberty to interfere with the orderly march of events. She received him with the kindness she would have shown to any other traveller, and gave him bread and milk, which he thought the most delicious food he had ever tasted, wondering that they did not have it for dinner at the palace sometimes. The old woman pressed him to stay all night. When he awoke he was amazed to find how well and strong he felt. She would not take any of the money he offered, but begged him, if he found occasion of continuing in the neighbourhood, to return and occupy the same quarters.

"Thank you much, good mother," answered the prince; "but there is little chance of that. The sooner I get out of this wood the better."

"I don't know that," said the fairy.

"What do you mean?" asked the prince.

"Why how *should* I know?" returned she.

"I can't tell," said the prince.

"Very well," said the fairy.

"How strangely you talk!" said the prince.

"Do I?" said the fairy.

"Yes, you do," said the prince.

"Very well," said the fairy.

The prince was not used to being spoken to in this fashion, so he felt a little angry and turned and walked away. But this did not offend the fairy. She stood at the door of her little house looking after him till the trees hid him quite. Then she said "At last!" and went in.

The prince wandered and wandered, and got nowhere. The sun sank and sank and went out of sight, and he seemed no nearer the end of the wood than ever. He sat down on a fallen tree, ate a bit of bread the old woman had given him, and waited for the moon; for, although he was not much of an astronomer, he knew the moon would rise some time, because she had risen the night before. Up she came, slow and slow, but of a good size, pretty nearly round indeed; whereupon, greatly refreshed with his piece of bread, he got up and went—he knew not whither.

After walking a considerable distance, he thought he was coming to the outside of the forest; but when he reached what he thought the last of it, he found himself only upon the edge of a great open space in it, covered with grass. The moon shone very bright, and he thought he had never seen a more lovely spot. Still it looked dreary because of its loneliness, for he could not see the house at the other side. He sat down weary again, and gazed into the glade. He had not seen so much room for several days.

All at once he espied something in the middle of the grass. What could it be? It moved; it came nearer. Was it a human creature, gliding across—a girl dressed in white, gleaming in the moonshine? She came nearer and nearer. He crept behind a tree and watched, wondering. It must be some strange being of the wood—a nymph whom the moonlight and the warm dusky air had enticed from her tree. But when she came close to where he stood, he no longer doubted she was human—for he had caught sight of her sunny hair, and her clear blue eyes, and the loveliest face and form that he had ever seen. All at once she began singing like a nightingale, and dancing to her own music, with her eyes ever turned towards the moon. She passed close to where he stood, dancing on by the edge of the trees and away in a great circle towards the other side, until he could see but a spot of white in the yellowish green of the moonlit grass. But when he feared it would vanish quite, the spot grew, and became a figure once more. She approached him again, singing and dancing and waving her arms over her head, until she had completed the circle. Just opposite his tree she stood, ceased her song, dropped her arms, and broke out into a long clear laugh, musical as a brook. Then, as if tired, she threw herself on the grass, and lay gazing at the moon. The prince was almost afraid to breathe lest he should startle her, and she should vanish from his sight. As to venturing near her, that never came into his head.

She had lain for a long hour or longer, when the prince began again to doubt concerning her. Perhaps she was but a vision of his own fancy. Or was she a spirit of the wood, after all? If so, he too would haunt the wood, glad to have lost kingdom and everything for the hope of being near her. He would build him a hut in the forest, and there he would live for the pure chance of seeing her again. Upon nights like this at least she would come out and bask in the moonlight, and make his soul blessed. But while he thus dreamed she sprang to her feet, turned her face full to the moon, and began singing as if she would draw her down from the sky by the power of her entrancing voice. She looked more beautiful than ever. Again she began dancing to her own music, and danced away into the distance. Once more she returned in a similar manner; but although he was watching as eagerly as before, what with fatigue and what with gazing, he fell fast asleep before she came near him. When he awoke it was broad daylight, and the princess was nowhere.

He could not leave the place. What if she should come the next night! He would gladly endure a day's hunger to see her yet again: he would buckle his belt quite tight. He walked round the glade to see if he could discover any prints of her feet. But the grass was so short, and her steps had been so light that she had not left a single trace behind her.

He walked halfway round the wood without seeing anything to account for her presence. Then he spied a lovely little house, with thatched roof and low eaves, surrounded by an exquisite garden, with doves and peacocks walking in it. Of course this must be where the gracious lady who loved the moonlight lived. Forgetting his appearance, he walked towards the door, determined to make inquiries, but as he passed a little pond full of gold and silver fishes, he caught sight of himself, and turned to find the door to the kitchen. There he knocked, and asked for a piece of bread. The good-natured cook brought him in, and gave him an excellent breakfast which the prince found nothing the worse for being served in the kitchen. While he ate, he talked with his entertainer, and learned that this was the favourite retreat of the Princess Daylight. But he learned nothing more, both because he was afraid of seeming inquisitive, and because the cook did not choose to be heard talking about her mistress to a peasant lad who had begged for his breakfast.

As he rose to take his leave, it occurred to him that he might not be so far from the old woman's cottage as he had thought, and he asked the cook whether she knew anything of such a place, describing it as well as he could. She said she knew it well enough, adding with a smile: "It's there you're going, is it?"

"Yes, if it's not far off."

"It's not more than three miles. But mind what you are about, you know."

"Why do you say that?"

"If you're after any mischief, she'll make you repent it."

"The best thing that could happen under the circumstances," remarked the prince.

"What do you mean by that?" asked the cook

"Why, it stands to reason," answered the prince, "that if you wish to do anything wrong, the best thing for you is to be made to repent of it."

"I see," said the cook. "Well, I think you may venture. She's a good old soul."

"Which way does it lie from here?" asked the prince.

She gave him full instructions; and he left her with many thanks.

Being now refreshed, however, the prince did not go back to the cottage that day: he remained in the forest amusing himself as best he could, but awaiting anxiously for the night in the hope that the princess would again appear. Nor was he disappointed, for, directly the moon rose, he spied a glimmering shape far across the glade. As it drew nearer, he saw it was she indeed—not dressed in white as before: in a pale blue like the sky, she looked lovelier still. He thought it was that the blue suited her yet better than the white; he did not know that she was really more beautiful because the moon was nearer the full. In fact the next night was full moon, and the princess would then be at the zenith of her loveliness.

The prince feared for some time that she was not coming near his hiding-place that night; but the circles in her dance ever widened as the moon rose, until at last they embraced the whole glade, and she came still closer to the trees where he was hiding than she had come the night before. He was entranced with her loveliness, for it was indeed a marvellous thing. All night long he watched her, but dared not go near her. He would have been ashamed of watching her too, had he not become almost incapable of thinking of anything but how beautiful she was. He watched the whole night long, and saw that as the moon went down she retreated in smaller and smaller circles, until at last he could see her no more.

Weary as he was, he set out for the old woman's cottage, where he arrived just in time for her breakfast, which she shared with him. He then went to bed, and slept for many hours. When he awoke, the sun was down, and he departed in great anxiety lest he should lose a glimpse of the lovely vision. But, whether it was by the machinations of the swamp-fairy, or merely that it is one thing to go and another to return by the same road, he lost his way. I shall not attempt to describe his misery when the moon rose, and he saw nothing but trees, trees, trees. She was high in the heavens before he reached the glade. Then indeed his troubles vanished, for there was the princess coming dancing towards him, in a dress that shone like gold, and with shoes that glimmered through the grass like fire-flies. She was of course still more beautiful than before. Like an embodied sunbeam she passed him, and danced away into the distance.

Before she returned in her circle, clouds had begun to gather about the moon. The wind rose, the trees moaned, and their lighter branches leaned all one way before it. The prince feared that the princess would go in, and he should see her no more that night. But she came dancing on more jubilant than ever, her golden dress and her sunny hair streaming out upon the blast, waving her arms towards the moon, and in the exuberance of her delight ordering the clouds away from off her face. The prince could hardly believe she was not a creature of the elements, after all.

By the time she had completed another circle, the clouds had gathered deep, and there were growlings of distant thunder. Just as she passed the tree where he stood, a flash of lightning blinded him for a moment, and when he saw again, to his horror, the princess lay on the ground. He darted to her, thinking she had been struck; but when she heard him coming, she was on her feet in a moment.

"What do you want?" she asked.

"I beg your pardon. I thought—the lightning—" said the prince, hesitating.

"There is nothing the matter," said the princess, waving him off rather haughtily.

The poor prince turned and walked towards the wood.

"Come back," said Daylight; "I like you. You do what you are told. Are you good?"

"Not so good as I should like to be," said the prince.

"Then go and grow better," said the princess.

Again the disappointed prince turned and went.

"Come back," said the princess.

He obeyed, and stood before her waiting.

"Can you tell me what the sun is like?" she asked.

"No," he answered. "But where's the good of asking what you know?"

"But I don't know," she rejoined.

"Why, everybody knows."

"That's the very thing: I'm not everybody. I've never seen the sun."

"Then you can't know what it's like till you do see it."

"I think you must be a prince," said the princess.

"Do I look like one?" said the prince.

"I can't quite say that."

"Then why do you think so?"

"Because you both do what you are told and speak the truth. Is the sun so very bright?"

"As bright as the lightning."

"But it doesn't go out like that, does it?"

"Oh no. It shines like the moon, rises and sets like the moon, is much the same shape as the moon, only so bright that you can't look at it for a moment."

"But I *would* look at it," said the princess.
"But you couldn't," said the prince.
"But I could," said the princess.
"Why don't you, then?"
"Because I can't."
"Why can't you?"
"Because I can't wake. And I never shall wake until—"

Here she hid her face in her hands, turned away, and walked in the slowest stateliest manner towards the house. The prince ventured to follow her at a little distance, but she turned and made a repellent gesture, which, like a true gentleman-prince, he obeyed at once. He waited a long time, but as she did not come near him again, and as the night had now cleared, he set off at last for the old woman's cottage.

It was long past midnight when he reached it, but, to his surprise, the old woman was paring potatoes at the door. Fairies are fond of doing odd things. Indeed, however they may dissemble, the night is always their day. And so it is with all who have fairy blood in them.

"Why, what are you doing there, this time of the night, mother?" said the prince; for that was the kind way in which any young man in his country would address a woman who was much older than himself.

"Getting your supper ready, my son," she answered.
"Oh! I don't want any supper," said the prince.
"Ah, you've seen Daylight!" said she.
"I've seen a princess who never saw it," said the prince.
"Do you like her?" asked the fairy.
"Oh! Don't I?" said the prince. "More than you would believe, mother."
"A fairy can believe anything that ever was or ever could be," said the old woman.

"Then are you a fairy?" asked the prince.

"Yes," said she.

"Then what do you do for things not to believe?" asked the prince.

"There's plenty of them—everything that never was nor ever could be."

"Plenty, I grant you," said the prince. "But do you believe there could be a princess who never saw the daylight? Do you believe that, now?"

This the prince said, not that he doubted the princess, but that he wanted the fairy to tell him more. She was too old a fairy, however, to be caught so easily.

"Of all people, fairies must not tell secrets. Besides, she's a princess."

"Well, I'll tell *you* a secret. I'm a prince."

"I know that."

"How do you know it?"

"By the curl of the third eyelash on your left eyelid."

"Which corner do you count from?"

"That's a secret."

"Another secret? Well, at least, if I am a prince, there can be no harm in telling me about a princess."

"It's just princes I can't tell."

"There ain't any more of them—are there?" said the prince.

"What! You don't think you're the only prince in the world, do you?"

"Oh, dear, no! Not at all. But I know there's one too many just at present, except the princess—"

"Yes, yes, that's it," said the fairy.

"What's it?" asked the prince.

But he could get nothing more out of the fairy, and had to go to bed unanswered, which was something of a trial.

Now wicked fairies will not be bound by the laws which the good fairies obey, and this always seems to give the bad the advantage over the good, for they use means to gain their ends which the others will not. But it is all of no consequence, for what they do never succeeds; nay, in the end it brings about the very thing they are trying to prevent. So you see that somehow, for all their cleverness, wicked fairies are dreadfully stupid, for, although from the beginning of the world they have really helped instead of thwarting the good fairies, not one of them is a bit the wiser for it. She will try the bad thing just as they all did before her; and succeed no better of course.

The prince had so far stolen a march upon the swamp-fairy that she did not know he was in the neighbourhood until after he had seen the princess those three times. When she knew it, she consoled herself by thinking that the princess must be far too proud and too modest for any young man to venture even to speak to her before he had seen her six times at least. But there was even less danger than the wicked fairy thought; for, however much the princess might desire to be set free, she was dreadfully afraid of the wrong prince. Now, however, the fairy was going to do all she could.

She so contrived it by her deceitful spells, that the next night the prince could not by any endeavour find his way to the glade. It would take me too long to tell her tricks. They would be amusing to us, who know that they could not do any harm, but they were something other than amusing to the poor prince. He wandered about the forest till daylight, and then fell fast asleep. The same thing occurred for seven following days, during which neither could he find the good fairy's cottage. After the third quarter of the moon, however, the bad fairy thought she might be at ease about the affair for a fortnight at least, for there was no chance of the prince wishing to kiss the princess during that period. So the first day of the fourth quarter he did find the cottage, and the next day he found the glade. For nearly another week he haunted it. But the princess never came. I have little doubt she was on the farther edge of it some part of every night but at this period she always wore black, and, there being little or no light the prince never saw her. Nor would he have known her if he had seen her. How could he have taken the worn, decrepit creature she was now, for the glorious Princess Daylight?

At last one night when there was no moon at all, he ventured near the house. There he heard voices talking, although it was past midnight; for her women were in considerable uneasiness, because the one whose turn it was to watch her had fallen asleep, and had not seen which way she went and this was a night when she would probably wander very far, describing a circle which did not touch the open glade at all, but stretched away from the back of the house, deep into that side of the forest—a part of which the prince knew nothing. When he understood from what they said that she had disappeared, and that she must have gone somewhere in the said direction, he plunged at once into the wood to see if he could find her. For hours he roamed with nothing to guide him but the vague notion of a circle which on one side bordered on the house, for so much had he picked up from the talk he had overheard.

It was getting towards the dawn, but as yet there was no streak of light in the sky, when he came to a great birch tree, and sat down weary at the foot of it. While he sat—very miserable, you may be sure—full of fear for the princess, and wondering how her attendants could take it so quietly, he bethought himself that it would not be a bad plan to light a fire, which, if she were anywhere near, would attract her. This he managed with a tinder-box, which the good fairy had given him. It was just beginning to blaze up, when he heard a moan, which seemed to come from the other side of the tree. He sprung to his feet, but his heart throbbed so that he had to lean for a moment against the tree before he could move. When he got round, there lay a human form in a little dark heap on the earth. There was light enough from his fire to show that it was not the princess. He lifted it in his arms, hardly heavier than a child, and carried it to the flame. The countenance was that of an old woman, but it had a fearfully strange look. A black hood concealed her hair, and her eyes were closed. He laid her down as comfortably as he could, chafed her hands, put a little cordial from a bottle, also the gift of the fairy, into her mouth; took off his coat and wrapped it about her, and in short did the best he could. In a little while she opened her eyes and looked at him—so pitifully! The tears rose and flowed down her gray wrinkled cheeks, but she said never a word. She closed her eyes again, but the tears kept on flowing, and her whole appearance was so utterly pitiful that the prince was very near crying too. He begged her to tell him what was the matter, promising to do all he could to help her; but still she did not speak. He thought she was dying, and took her in his arms again to carry her to the princess's house, where he thought the good-natured cook might be able to do something for her. When he lifted her, the tears flowed yet faster, and she gave such a sad moan that it went to his very heart.

"Mother, mother!" he said—"Poor mother!" and kissed her on the withered lips.

She started; and what eyes they were that opened upon him! But he did not see them, for it was still very dark, and he had enough to do to make his way through the trees towards the house.

Just as he approached the door, feeling more tired than he could have imagined possible—she was such a little thin old thing—she began to move, and became so restless that, unable to carry her a moment longer, he thought to lay her on the grass. But she stood upright on her feet. Her hood had dropped, and her hair fell about her. The first gleam of the morning was caught on her face: that face was bright as the never-ageing Dawn, and her eyes were lovely as the sky of darkest blue. The prince recoiled in over-mastering wonder. It was Daylight herself whom he had brought from the forest! He fell at her feet nor dared look up until she laid her hand upon his head. He rose then.

"You kissed me when I was an old woman: there! I kiss you when I am a young princess," murmured Daylight—"Is that the sun coming?"

CLUNY MEDIA

Designed by Fiona Cecile Clarke, the Cluny Media *logo depicts a monk at work in the scriptorium, with a cat sitting at his feet.*

The monk represents our mission to emulate the invaluable contributions of the monks of Cluny in preserving the libraries of the West, our strivings to know and love the truth.

The cat at the monk's feet is Pangur Bán, from the eponymous Irish poem of the 9th century. The anonymous poet compares his scholarly pursuit of truth with the cat's happy hunting of mice. The depiction of Pangur Bán is an homage to the work of the monks of Irish monasteries and a sign of the joy we at Cluny take in our trade.

"Messe ocus Pangur Bán,
cechtar nathar fria saindan:
bíth a menmasam fri seilgg,
mu memna céin im saincheirdd."

Made in the USA
Middletown, DE
01 November 2023